MEMBERS ONLY

For more information about the author and her books, visit her website-www.shanteltessier.com You can sign up for her newsletter on her website.

WARNING

Due to the mature content, this book may contain triggers for some.

Photographer: Michelle Lancaster
Model: Matt Orchard
Cover designer: Shanoff Designs
Editor: Amanda Rash
Formatter: Melissa Cunningham @booklovedesigns

PLAYLIST

"Legends" by Sam Tinnesz
"Crazy" by LOWBORN
"King of the World" by WAR*HALL
"Buttons" by The Pussycat Dolls
"Raging on a Sunday" by Bohnes
"New Kings" by Sleeping Wolf
"Play With Fire" by Sam Tinnesz, Yacht Money

PROLOGUE
CROSS

Thirteen years old . . .

"HAPPY BIRTHDAY, SON," my mother says softly to me while we stand at the entrance of Oak Grove, my father's church.

I hate being here after hours. It gives me the creeps. The walls creak, and the wind always makes the old, stained windows rattle. It gives me a feeling so deep down in my bones that I'm cold for hours after I leave. I can't explain it, but it feels like evil is inside these walls. Which is stupid since this is a place of worship where people come to heal—God's house. My father says it has power, but I have yet to see that. I have never witnessed a miracle that couldn't be explained by science.

I step back from her, forcing her hands off my shoulders, and take a quick look around the empty structure. "Why are we here?" I ask, my hands shaking nervously. It's past midnight and officially my thirteenth birthday. She woke me from my bed and said we had to go for a drive.

1

Lowering her eyes, she sighs deeply, forcing my heart rate to speed up. "Mom ...?"

"Son," my father's voice booms behind me, and I spin around to see him walking our way. He's dressed in his business attire—a black button-down shirt with black slacks and a matching suit jacket. His dark hair is slicked back, and his face is freshly shaved. You wouldn't know just by looking at him that he's worth billions of dollars.

He comes to a stop and removes his hands from his front pockets, crossing them in front of him. The black ring in the shape of a crown on his right ring finger tells the world that he's a member of the Three Wisemen. It's a reminder that my father may play the martyr, but he does the work of the devil.

He and his two best friends started Kingdom—the largest, most corrupt hotel and casino here in Sin City. They each play their part outside their gilded cage. The only difference is they asked for their prison sentence. My father likes to pretend he's a disciple of God. That he does his work of ridding the world of evil. When the truth is, he creates it. He takes whatever the sinners have to offer and promises redemption, but instead, he feeds it to the devil as an offering.

Their sins are his currency. Knowledge makes you rich and powerful.

I take a step back from him, needing the space, and bump into my mother. Sidestepping quickly, I move to where I can see them both at the same time, whipping my head back and forth. "I wanna go home," I manage to get out, trying to calm my nerves when I want to scream. Why am I here? My father makes me attend church on Sundays when the congregation is present. That way, he can show off his perfect family along with the other Three Wisemen and their families. Appearance is everything in this city. Without a kingdom, there is no need for a King to rule.

"It's time," he states, walking over to me.

"For what?" I ask. My voice squeaks, and I want to punch myself for acting like such a little bitch.

2

Placing his hand on my back, he ushers me through the double doors and down the aisle. "The Lord forgives all sins until we reach the age of thirteen."

I look over my shoulder to see if my mother has followed us, and she has. She stands at the back in front of the double doors, just staring at us. "Yes, Father." But I've been saved since I was three. He reminds me every day that I'm a son of the Lord.

He looks down at me, giving me a kind smile, but it doesn't ease my fear. His green eyes look even brighter from the candlelight. I got his eyes, and I hate it. I wonder what he sold in order to get a son—an heir to continue his legacy once he's passed. His death can't come soon enough if you ask me. "Today, you have reached that age—age of accountability."

I have done a little research on this, but as far as I can find, there is no such thing in the Bible that states we must be saved by the age of thirteen. But I will never tell him that. No one argues with my father. His word is as strong as God's. "Yes, Father," I agree once again.

"You must repent for your sins."

My body begins to tremble at his choice of words, and I pray that he doesn't notice. *Sins?* What have I done? He is the one who pretends. I hear the stories around town. The way kids look at me and my friends at school. Evil doesn't just walk among us. It also lives in our houses. It intertwines itself in our everyday life so you can't break free. We're being trained, conditioned to take it over one day. We don't have a choice. We will be the Kings. The question is, what will we do with it?

My eyes go back to the scene before us. I've seen it before. The first time I was nine. I shiver from the memory of that night and the scar that reminds me of it.

We come to a stop, and he reaches up, grabbing the chain around his neck and removes the silver cross that my mother got him when he became a priest as if that was supposed to mean something. It might have once, but it no longer does. Not to me. It's his weapon of choice.

He hasn't always been a religious man. He and my mother weren't this way when I was born. The Three Wisemen took an oath and must do whatever it takes to uphold it.

"You must allow the Heavenly Father into your soul, son."

"I have, Father." My voice shakes, and I cross my arms over my chest, trying to shield my body. Not again. Why tonight? Why this birthday?

He sighs heavily, clearly not happy with my answer. "Remove your shirt."

I swallow the lump that forms in my throat. "Dad ...?"

"Remove your shirt, son," he demands. The echo in his voice bounces off the walls and cathedral ceiling.

I grip the white fabric and slowly pull it over my head. He reaches out for one of the candles. "But why ...?"

"Shh." He shushes me. "I'm going to save you, my child."

He runs the candle along the back of the silver cross. The flame licks the precious metal. Without looking down at me, he speaks. "Down on your knees."

My heart pounds, and blood begins to rush in my ears. There's no stopping what's to come. Either I will willingly do as I'm told, or he will force me, which will just make it worse. With shaky knees, I slowly lower myself to the cold floor.

"Place your chest to your thighs and reach your hands out in front of you."

Tears begin to blur my vision, but I blink them away, refusing to cry or look weak. To him, weakness is a tool. Something useful. I heard him once say, "A man must willingly sacrifice himself with dignity."

I hear him set the candle back and my body shakes as he places his hand flat on my back, holding me down while kneeling beside me.

"Dad—" My voice breaks as I try to catch my breath.

He interrupts me. "Bless him, Father, for he does not know what he does." Then he places the burning metal against my back, and I bite down on my tongue, refusing to scream into the silent church.

The smell of burning flesh hits my nose while blood slips between my lips and onto the floor under me. Every muscle in my body is taut while I hold my breath. "But he will. Being a King has a price that very few are willing to pay."

Sucking in a breath through gritted teeth, he removes the hot cross, and I sag to the floor.

"You must learn to endure pain, son," my father says, pulling me to my feet.

I sniff and quickly rub the back of my hand under my nose to catch the snot. When I swallow, I taste the lingering blood.

"People don't understand what it takes to be us." He goes on, and I look at my shoes, unable to meet his eyes. The shame I feel right now is too much.

My back is on fire from the branding he just gave me. As if a fucking cross is going to guarantee me a trip to heaven.

"You will see, son." He taps my shoulder, and I pull away from him.

He turns and walks away, leaving me standing alone at the front of the church. Moments later, I hear my mother's heels clap on the floor as she makes her way to me.

"He is teaching you to be better," she states, coming to stand next to me.

Lifting my head, I glare up at her, hating her for marrying him and for having me. Why would anyone want this life? Why would anyone want to hurt the innocent?

"Happy Birthday," she says once again. Reaching into the pocket of her jacket, she pulls out a small rectangular box.

I just stare at it.

"Go ahead and open it." She holds it out to me.

I take it from her hand and gently unwrap the white paper and see it's a black Zippo. *A lighter?* My birthday present is a lighter?

"We all have a cross to bear," she reads what's engraved on the back. "Fire is a symbol of the Holy Spirit." She goes on to explain. "Fire can bring warmth, but it can also be uncontrollably dangerous."

I look up at her. "You've always been fascinated by fire, Cross. Just like your father." I flinch at that thought. I hate being like him. "This is your faith. Your redemption. A reminder that we must all do what needs to be done." With those words, she takes my hand and guides me back down the aisle of the church.

ONE
CROSS

Thirteen years later . . .

CLICK.

The sound of my Zippo in my right hand, flipping open and closed, fills the meat locker—a room at Kingdom where the Dark Kings and I handle our business. The kind that others can't know about. An underground concrete room where no one can hear the screams of whatever unlucky bastard we drag down here. It's nothing more than one chair and table in the middle of the room—screwed down, of course, so neither one can be used as a weapon against us. Four concrete walls and floor. One light in the center of the ceiling.

It's our hell. We drag the sinners down here to make them pay for their sins.

My three best friends and I grew up being exactly what the Three Wisemen—our fathers—hoped we would be. And I'm thankful that none of them are alive today to witness that. I'd hate for my father to feel any satisfaction in regard to what kind of man I've become. I know the other Dark Kings feel the same way.

Our fathers knew us as weak little boys. Now at twenty-six, the world knows us as Titan, Bones, Cross, and Grave. Each one of us earned our nickname at different times in our life for various reasons. None of them good. People bow to us because we fucking earned it, not because our fathers gave it to us. We're nothing like them. We're worse. We just choose not to hide who we are. No, we parade it around Las Vegas in broad daylight.

Our newest victim sitting in the chair glares up at me as I lean casually against the concrete wall across from him. His brown eyes fall to my Zippo.

Click.

I flip it open and closed again. I do it all the time. Doesn't matter if I'm stressed or relaxed. It's a reminder that I was born to burn in hell. And if I wanted to, I could take everyone with me. My mother didn't realize just how right she was when she gave me this on my birthday.

"I'm not telling you shit!" he snarls, slapping his hands on the table. His once white T-shirt is ripped and hanging off one shoulder. He's got a bruise under his left eye from where Titan knocked him out before we dragged his ass down here.

We've been waiting for thirty minutes for him to regain consciousness and join the party.

"That's what they all say," Bones states from my right.

Titan leans against the back wall with his arms crossed over his chest. Grave stands to my left, texting away on his cell. I'm guessing to his pregnant girlfriend. He must have a lot to say because he's been typing for a good minute.

"We'll give you a second to think it over," Bones tells him, being nicer than normal.

The guy throws his head back laughing, spit flying from his mouth at the action. "I don't need a goddamn second. My lips are sealed."

"Well ..." Bones looks over at me, arching a dark brow. "Then he's no use to us."

"I agree," I say, flipping the Zippo shut and pocketing it. "Titan?" I look over at him and nod, giving the signal. The guy had his chance, which is more than what we usually offer. We're all in a pretty good mood today, so it's his choice to die.

Titan steps up behind him and yanks him from the chair, shoving him facedown onto the table. The man tries to fight him, but he yanks his arms behind his back, keeping him pinned down. Bones steps forward toward them.

"They will kill you!" the man shouts. "All of you and everyone you love!"

That gets Grave's attention. He looks up at the man from his phone, his fingers pausing over it, but says nothing.

"Where are they?" Bones directs his question to Titan.

"Back pocket," Titan clips.

Making his way around the table, Bones yanks a bag of zip ties from Titan's pocket and removes two from the plastic before dropping the rest to the floor. "Ya know, Kenneth," he starts as he slides the end of one through the other, pulling on it to make sure it's secure at the length he wants. "I'm not in the mood to get bloody today."

"Fuck you, Kings!" The guy thrashes on the table under Titan's weight. "You can't touch me ..."

Titan yanks him from the table and spins around so Kenneth now faces Bones.

"No one is untouchable," Bones states, then quickly wraps the zip tie around the man's neck. Kenneth tries to fight, but Titan has a good hold on him, giving Bones easy access to thread the zip tie before yanking it tightly against his skin. The sound of the zipper seals Kenneth's fate.

Titan then shoves Kenneth to the right. The four of us watch him as he falls to his knees, panic on his face while his hands try to pry it off. As if he has a chance. Not going to happen. Death doesn't leave any room for dignity. Not when you know it's coming. Your fight or flight kicks in no matter how little of a chance you know you have.

He'll die of strangulation, and afterward, we'll bury his ass in the desert. It's what we've been doing for years now. What we were taught. What we know. And thankfully, Las Vegas has plenty of space for us to hide our secrets.

To anyone that is visiting out of town, they come to Kingdom— our hotel and casino—to try their luck. The lights and glamor catch their attention, and they think they can come in and hit the jackpot on one of our machines or win big at the tables. But for those people who know the Kings, they know what we're about and what we're willing to do to keep things in order.

Nothing and no one will stop us! We own this town. We dominate the Strip. Bones, Titan, and I are only twenty-six, Grave twenty-five, and no one can compete with us. Even though our dads were the Three Wiseman, we still had to prove ourselves. Had to show Las Vegas we deserved what we were given. No matter the price.

The guy falls face-first on the floor, no longer struggling.

Titan bends down and checks for a pulse. "He's gone."

"Take care of him," Bones orders and storms out, pissed we didn't get the information we were looking for.

People pay us a lot of money to take care of their problems. Usually, the motherfuckers sing, telling us everything we need to know in hopes we'll let them go. That's never the case. You can't afford to look weak.

"I'll take him," Titan offers, pulling out his cell from his back pocket. "Nigel is going to help me."

"You sure?" I ask.

He nods, and I turn to Grave. He's no longer texting on his cell. "I have to be at the Airport in twenty. I've got a fight tonight."

Ah, now I understand why he was on his phone for so long. "I'll drive you," I offer.

"You guys stay out of trouble," Titan warns. "I don't want to spend my entire night digging."

Titan tries to keep us all in line. It's worse now that he's married to Emilee. Bones lives and breathes Kingdom. I'm not sure when he last got drunk or even took a vacation, for that matter. He's all business, all the time. Grave is a recovering addict with a pregnant girl-friend. And me? Well, I'm still trying to figure out who I am. Grave was my go-to party buddy. I could work all day here at Kingdom, then party all night—alcohol or drugs—and show up to work the following day just fine. Now that Grave is in a serious relationship, I have no one to go out with. It sucks, but I understand why he's changing his life for the better.

"Let's go, man. I can't be late," Grave says before exiting the room as well.

I go to leave but look at Titan. He's now leaning back against the wall again, waiting on Nigel. "You sure you're okay?" I double-check.

He nods. "Yeah." His eyes go to the door and then back to me. "Keep an eye on him, will ya?"

"Of course." Then I, too, turn and leave the room, knowing I may not be able to keep that promise, and the sad part is that Titan thinks I can.

ALEXA

"Do you come here often?" I call out to my friend Jasmine as she drags me through a crowd of people.

"All the time!" She throws over her shoulder at me, her red hair slapping her face.

I look around nervously at the Airport. It's not like any airport I've ever been to. No airplanes, no people traveling with luggage. Instead, it looks like a breeding ground for STDs and those gruesome murder scenes that you see on an unsolved murder mystery docu-mentary.

You can tell that an airport once occupied this large facility, but it's long been deserted and turned into what I can only assume is a playground for the scum of Las Vegas.

The Airport sits out in the middle of the desert, twenty miles from the Strip, but I've stayed away. Somehow, I let her drag me out here tonight. I needed new scenery, but I'm probably going to need a penicillin shot once we leave here.

From what little I know, Trey, Turner, and Tanner Mason own it. The three brothers obviously don't give a shit about what goes on here. I've never met them, and I'm beginning to understand why. This just isn't my thing.

A man bumps into me so hard it rips my hand from Jasmine's. She spins around. "Hey, say excuse me, motherfucker!" she throws at the guy's back.

He keeps on, not even bothering to look back. Thank God.

"Jasmine," I hiss. I'm not one to back down, but I don't know these people here. I'm kinda out of my element. I've lived in Sin City all my life, and I've never stepped foot in the Airport. I own a bar, and you hear chatter all the time, but I just thought the customers were exaggerating.

I was wrong.

"You gotta stick up for yourself here, Lex," Jasmine goes on.

"Okay—" She turns and jerks me forward once again by my hand, cutting me off.

We make our way down a flight of escalators that don't work and to an open area. It looks like it was once the food court, maybe. But now, a large bar runs along the right wall. A makeshift ring is to the right of it. People crowd around it like they're waiting for something to happen.

"Legends Are Made," by Sam Tinnesz blares from speakers that hang from the ceiling, and with further observation, I see black domes —security cameras. Well, that makes me feel a little better, but for all I know, they could be fake. Jasmine pulls us over to the bar, shoving others out of our way like she owns the place.

"Two shots of Patrón and two Long Islands," she yells at one of the bartenders.

The guy with a ring in his nose nods at her and turns to start making our drinks.

"Why did you bring me here tonight?" I ask, placing my elbow on the bar top.

"Because you needed a night out," she says simply with a big smile on her porcelain face. "You deserve it for as much as you work."

I nod, unable to disagree with her. I've been trying to get a night off for weeks now. But when you own a business, you never stop. Not unless you want to lose money. And that is unacceptable if you ask me. If you want it, you have to fight for it. I've never had a problem with going after what I want. How will you ever know if you don't try?

"Plus, when was the last time you got laid?" she asks.

I mumble, "Too long." But I don't want to make that mistake again.

"Exactly." Bumping her hip into mine, she laughs. "Gotta get some D."

I'm not here to hook up with anyone. Pretty sure no one here is my type anyway.

The bartender comes back over to us. "Here you go, Jasmine." He calls her by name, and it just confirms that she comes here too often. He places our shot glasses in front of us.

She hands him her card. "Start a tab for me, please?"

"Got it, babe." And he's off again.

"I have cash ..."

"Nonsense." She waves me off before I can even finish what I was saying.

I sigh but don't argue with her. Jasmine is the type of woman who gets whatever she wants. And going to war with her over a few drinks just isn't worth it. I've known her for about a year now, and she's one of my closest friends other than April. I've been friends with April since we were kids, but ever since she got pregnant, she no longer goes out. Her baby daddy is Grave—a Dark King. And he takes up all of her time. As it should be. She's really happy, and that's all I've ever wanted for her.

Jasmine has introduced me to a couple of other girls, one who happens to be married to another King. But again, I don't get to hang out with them much. I like to keep my circle small. Plus, when you're always working, it doesn't leave much time for a social life.

"Cheer up." Jasmine turns to face me with a smile on her face. She's gorgeous in that "I don't have to try hard" way. She dyes her short hair red, and it really complements her bright blue eyes. "I promise nothing will happen to you here. I know the Mason brothers."

"How well?" I challenge.

The Mason brothers' reputation is about the same as the Dark Kings—you fuck with them, you're dead.

Her red-painted lips pull back, showing off her white pearly teeth. "One of them I know extremely well."

I laugh and clarify, "So, you slept with him?"

"Of course, I did. And if you saw him, you'd spread your legs too." She winks at me.

"What are you girls doing here?" a man demands from behind us, cutting off my laughter.

We spin around to see two faces I recognize. They stand out in any crowd they walk through. Grave and Cross, two of the Dark Kings. You can't miss them. All four Kings are over six feet tall and covered in ink. Not to mention their presence just screams get the fuck out of my way. If you caught yourself alone with them in a dark alley, you'd clutch your purse tighter while your pussy would do the same for its own reason. They're dark, deadly, and extremely fucking attractive in a way that begs drag me to hell and show me what it's like to burn.

If you knew my track record with men, you'd know that I can pick them. And a King would be at the top of the list.

My best friend April's baby daddy is Grave. I know him pretty well since he and April got together. Cross, not so much. I met him at Emilee and Titan's wedding but didn't really get the chance to speak with him. But they're all the same—men fear them, and women worship them. And that makes them even more interesting to me. I think every woman wants a bad boy in their life at least once. Some of us crave that toxicity. Without it, life would be boring.

"I could ask you that same question," Jasmine speaks before throwing back her shot.

"I'm fighting tonight," Grave answers, crossing his inked arms over his bare chest and looking down his nose at us. Like he's angry he caught us here. My eyes run over the picture of my best friend tattooed on his arm. It's insane how much detail was put into it. It literally looks like she's right in front of me staring at me. It's kinda creepy. From her dark purple hair to her ice-blue eyes and her diamond septum piercing—she looks absolutely gorgeous. She drew it, and Cross tattooed it onto Grave's arm. April has always been an amazing artist.

"Where's April?" I ask, looking around. I hadn't told her I was coming out tonight. The last time I spoke to her, she was closing up her flower shop and heading home to shower and go to bed. Being pregnant is really taking it out of her.

Cross snorts at my question. "The Airport is the last place for a pregnant woman."

I look at him, and he's also glaring down at me. His pretty green eyes narrowed, dark brows creased, and his lips thin. It's like these men were born pissed off at the world. Hating everyone. I wonder if he's always been this way? And if so, why?

"You ladies shouldn't be here either," he states.

Ladies? I almost laugh at that. "You're going to make us leave?" I ask, arching a dark brow. These Kings are used to getting their way, or so I've heard. I'm sure they do whatever is necessary to achieve that. And that thought just made this night so much more interesting.

He steps toward me, and I tilt my head back to look at his glare. "If I say yes?"

Grave reaches out, slapping his hand on Cross's chest, and pulls him back a step. "We don't have time to drag them out right now kicking and screaming."

I smirk as Jasmine hands me my shot. Throwing it back, I turn to the bar, signaling to the guy with the nose piercing that we want another round. I'm not leaving now. My earlier reservations about the Airport are long gone, so I might as well make it worth it. My cell vibrates in my pocket, and I pull it out to see it's a text.

> CUNT: Why haven't you been answering my
> calls?

I ignore it just like the rest. You would think he'd get the hint eventually.

"Who did you guys come with?" I hear Grave ask Jasmine over "Crazy," by LOWBORN.

"Just us," she tells him.

"Well, you need someone to stay with you. I'm fighting soon," he states with a huff.

"I'll stay with them," Cross offers, sounding less than thrilled to babysit two grown women.

I turn back to face them and let out a chuckle as Jasmine asks, "We need a babysitter?"

"Here you do," Grave snaps at her. "I've told you this before."

She shrugs carelessly, rolling her eyes. Obviously, she's not as concerned about our life as he is. I think they just want to control everything they see.

"You guys want a drink?" I ask.

"No," Grave growls.

Jasmine elbows me, and I flinch, forgetting that he's a recovering addict. I've only known the sober Grave, so I have to remind myself that there's things we do that he doesn't. Doesn't matter if it's alcohol or drugs, he no longer does any of that stuff. That I know of anyway. He got clean for April, and I'm proud of him for that. I know it wasn't easy for either of them.

"Sorry," I mutter.

"No thanks." Cross shakes his head but doesn't bother looking at me. His green eyes scan the crowd as if he's hired security at a boy-band concert, and a bunch of screaming teenagers and their mothers are about to tackle us to the ground.

"Looks like it's just you and me." I smile at Jasmine.

She throws an arm over my shoulders. "Well, now that we have a babysitter, let's get fucked."

TWO

CROSS

I WATCH THE girls throw back their fifth shot since Grave and I found them. They just keep lining them up, which doesn't surprise me. People don't come here just to hang out, if you know what I mean.

Grave leans into my ear. "I'm on in five. Stay with them."

I nod. "Will do." Growing up in Vegas taught me a lot of things. One being that the Airport is no place for a woman who is alone or here with a girlfriend. Women have been robbed, raped, and gone missing from here and never seen again. Hell, the same goes for grown men.

Let's just say the Mason brothers don't know everything that goes on inside this building. Or, if they do, they turn a blind eye.

Normally, it's not my problem, but I grew up with Jasmine. I wouldn't say she's my friend, but she's best friends with some of my close friends, so I'd protect her. I know nothing about the bleach blonde other than her name is Alexa. I remember meeting her at Titan and Emilee's wedding.

. . .

"HEY, WHO'S THE HOT BLONDE?" I ASK GRAVE WITH AN ELBOW TO his side as he stands next to me in the hallway of the chapel that Titan and Emilee have rented out for their wedding.

I haven't seen my best friend in weeks because he's been in rehab, but he got a day pass today to attend.

He turns around to look at who I'm talking about. She stands at the other end of the hall talking to his girlfriend, April. Both girls have their hands on April's growing stomach. He spots her, starts shaking his head, and spins back around. "Stay away, man," he warns with a laugh.

"Why?" I ask curiously. My eyes drop to her ass as she turns to talk to another one of our friends' wives, Haven, giving me a back view. Fuck, I like it better than the side view. The champagne-colored dress leaves nothing to the imagination. It shows off every curve, and I see no underwear line. Meaning I could just lift the dress up and fuck her in the back room. She has her bleach-blond hair already up in a tight bun for me, easy to grip while she's on her knees with my cock in her mouth. She throws her head back, her laughter carrying down the hallway to us, and I imagine stepping up behind her, having her lift her dress while my right hand wraps around her throat and squeezes as I fuck her from behind. She won't be able to laugh or breathe, for that matter.

Fuck, I'm hard as fuck now.

"That is April's best friend. You fuck her, and I'll have to hear about it forever." He shakes his head again. "I actually like Alexa and don't need any added problems with my girl. So, stay away. Promise me!"

I nod. "Got it. I promise." But as I say the words, she turns around, and a set of green eyes meet mine. I don't look away. No reason to pretend I wasn't just imagining fucking her in a church full of people.

The smile drops off her face, and she averts her eyes to her heels while pushing an imaginary piece of hair behind her ear. Then very slowly, she lifts her eyes to me once again to see if I'm still staring.

I see you, Alexa, and I want you.

"I have to go to the bathroom," Alexa calls out to Jasmine, interrupting that memory of her. I didn't act on it then. Too much was going on at the time. Now, she's right here. Like God himself dropped her in my lap. If you believe in that sort of thing. I might have been raised in a church, but I'm sure as shit not religious.

"Okay." Jasmine interlocks her arm with Alexa's and pulls her from the bar.

I follow them, placing my hands in the pockets of my jeans. We clear the crowd and head down a dimly lit, narrow hallway. My eyes instantly drop to Alexa's ass and the way it sways in her tight jeans. I can see the outline of her cell in her back pocket. She wears a black tank top that doesn't quite reach the top of her jeans, showing me just a sliver of her tan skin and the two dimples right above her ass. Her bleach-blond hair is up in a messy bun, showing me the back of her neck just like last time. I imagine letting it down and wrapping my hand around it while holding her facedown with that ass up in the air while I pound into her pussy.

I just fucked a bitch last night. I shouldn't be this worked up, but I am. My cock is hard, and my mind is in the gutter. I keep reminding myself she's off-limits, but my dick doesn't give a fuck.

The forbidden fruit sort of thing.

They both laugh as they stumble along and push the women's bathroom door open. I step in behind them.

"Cross, we can pee on our own." Jasmine's laughter grows when she spots me following them.

"I'm sure you can," I say just as I see a man standing in the corner. His eyes go straight to the girls, and I square my shoulders, ready to fuck him up if need be. I stalk to the last stall and open the door for them. "Go in together," I order.

They giggle, thinking I'm overreacting, but thankfully obey. I turn, pressing my back to the now closed door and just stand there, making sure no one fucks with them.

A few minutes later, they open it up, and after washing their hands, we exit. A man I know by the name of Mitch exits the men's restroom across the hallway from us at the same time we do. He comes to a stop, spotting us. "Alexa?"

She freezes, bringing Jasmine to a halt since they're holding hands, but says nothing.

"Hey, babe." He smiles at her.

Babe? I don't remember her having anyone with her at the wedding. And she's not wearing a ring because I looked. Hate to say that wouldn't stop me anyway.

"I've been calling you." He steps into her. "Just sent you a text."

She takes a step back, bumping into me. I place my hands on her shoulders and pull her to my side, throwing my arm over her.

His eyes go to mine, and the smile drops off his face. "Cross?" He looks back at her. "Are you dating him?"

"Mitch." I acknowledge him. I've known this piece of shit scumbag for several years. Now I'm interested in what kind of past they have and how long it was for. And just how much she knows about him.

She doesn't answer his question in any way. He keeps his attention on her, going on. "Is this why you've been ignoring me, babe …?"

"Take my silence as a hint, Mitch. It's over." She finally speaks, and I'm actually surprised how put together it sounded, considering how much she's had to drink. She's leaning into my side pretty hard right now, needing the help to stand.

"Because of him?" He points at me.

"No. Because of you," she says matter-of-factly. With a smile, I pull them away and back down the hall.

We make our way through the crowd and over to the ring when I spot Grave standing beside it. His hands are fisted in a guy's shirt. He's holding him to his chest and shouting in the man's face.

Fuck! "Stay here," I order the girls as I shove them into a corner before I head over to Grave. "What the fuck is going on?" I demand when I come up to them. A quick look over my shoulder shows the girls still leaning up against the wall in the corner.

"Go the fuck home, Ethan!" Grave shouts, shoving the kid back.

"Ethan?" I ask, looking him over. Why does that name sound familiar? He's got a busted lip. He tosses his dark shaggy hair back, and I can see a cut on his forehead at the motion. Blood slowly runs down the side of his face. One look at his eyes, and I can tell he's on something. Ecstasy maybe. He's sweating profusely, but it's hot in here. No amount of A/C can keep up with the large crowd that's here tonight. His knuckles are busted, so the kid was obviously just in a fight.

"Fuck you!" he shouts, pointing his finger at Grave's face.

Grave goes to step forward to knock his ass out, but I grab him and pull him back. "He's not worth it," I tell him.

The kid looks me up and down, then snorts. "You Kings think you fucking rule everyone." His eyes go back to Grave. "Just because you knocked up my sister doesn't mean you're my brother," he spits out, then turns and walks off into the crowd, shouldering his way through.

Grave shrugs me off, and I let him go, holding my hands up. "What the fuck was that?" I ask.

He runs a hand through his hair. "April's brother." I got that. "The boy is pissing me off."

My cell starts vibrating in my pocket, and I dig it out quickly to check to see who it is.

Titan: How's it going?

Of course, he's checking on us. Instead of answering, I pocket it and turn to go get the girls, and they're gone.

Motherfucker!

ALEXA

Mitch ruined my buzz. Or at least that's what it feels like. I hate when I'm drunk and get mad. I find myself walking faster toward the large bar by the ring.

Jasmine notices and laughs. "Slow down. The bar isn't going anywhere."

"I need a drink," I state, looking over my shoulder to see if I can spot Mitch anywhere. What is he doing here? We were together for two years, and he never brought me here. Didn't even speak of it. But that's what guys do, right? Change their life when they get out of a relationship? Find new friends to hang out with. A new crowd to meet new people so they can get away from everyone who knows the truth about why it didn't work.

I was the one who lost our mutual friends. All because I wouldn't take him back. Like I was supposed to roll over and take the manipulation. Cheating is not something that I was going to overlook. Forget the lies that were told in order to cover it up.

But then I went and fucked it all up. Literally.

A while back, I was drunk one night out with April, Jasmine, and Emilee, and he messaged me. That was when I had him in my phone under his name. He said all the right things, and in a moment of weakness, I let him in. The following morning, I woke up at his place and changed his contact from Mitch to CUNT and told myself never again! The alcohol had temporarily given me memory loss of why I left him in the first place.

I've done nothing but ignore every text and every call since then. Self-respect is more important than sex—especially when you don't even get off from it.

"You okay?" Jasmine asks, her blue eyes searching my face for any sign that I'm about to lose my shit.

It's not going to take much tonight. "Fine." I lie.

"We can go home if you want—"

"No. I want to stay," I interrupt her. I don't know if Mitch is watching me or not, but I sure as hell don't want him to see me leave now. Not after he spotted me. That would make him think I care he's here, and I don't. And he thought I was here with Cross. That makes me smile. They seemed to know one another and obviously don't like each other. Nice. I can use that.

"Jasmine?" We both look to our right to see a guy coming toward us. I've never seen him before, but I can tell she knows him when she rolls her eyes at the sight of him.

"Trenton? We're both having shit luck tonight," she mumbles, then turns to face him.

He smiles at her, his eyes dropping to her chest. "It's been too long. Last time I saw you, you were here. It must be a sign. Let me buy you a drink."

"I'm good." She gives him her back.

His face morphs from happy to pissy at her dismissal. And like any other man who has a hurt ego, he goes for insults. "You're such a slut."

Original.

"Excuse me?" She slowly turns to face him.

"You heard me." He huffs, and his eyes now look her over as if the sight of her alone disgusts him. Typical man. "That picture you posted on social media earlier tonight made you look like a slut."

"Don't believe everything you see on the internet, Trenton," she says sweetly. "You of all people should know that."

"What's that supposed to mean?" he demands.

"I saw a picture of you on the internet last week of you and your kids. And we both know that you're no father."

His mouth drops open, and she gives him her back, once again silently telling him to fuck off. He gets the hint and takes off, letting out an audible growl in the process.

"An ex?" I ask.

"Something like that," she grumbles.

"We need to go out of town to party next time," I suggest. Get the fuck away from Sin City. No matter how big some might think this city is, I promise you, it's not big enough.

"Yes!" Her eyes light up. "I've been wanting to go to Miami. I've got some friends there."

"I'm down for wherever." At this point, I'll go to another country.

"What the fuck?" a man snaps from behind us.

We both spin around. I expect it to be another stalker ex, but it's Cross, and he looks pissed.

"I told you to stay put." He glares down at us.

I look up at him. "I'm not a fucking dog."

"I don't mind walking around on all fours," Jasmine jokes, trying to lighten the mood.

I don't laugh. I'm just not in the mood at the moment. Not after Mitch. Cross says nothing to that, so I give him my back and get the bartender's attention. I came to drink, and that's exactly what I'm going to do.

GRAVE WON HIS FIGHT, BUT I DIDN'T HAVE ANY DOUBT THAT HE would. And to my surprise, he didn't make us leave afterward. He's hanging out with Cross while Jasmine and I drink the night away.

The guys stand to our left while we wait at the bar for new drinks. I've lost count of how many shots we've had, but I haven't seen fuck-face anymore. Thank God.

We throw back our new drink, and I don't even taste it. My lips are now numb, tastebuds gone, and my throat used to the burn.

My eyes go over to Cross while he looks to be having an intense conversation with Grave. He wears a pair of combat boots, jeans, and a plain black T-shirt. He's covered in ink, just like the rest of the Kings. You wouldn't know the guy is a billionaire by the looks of it. I don't know much about the Kings other than they own Kingdom—the biggest hotel and casino on the Strip. Reaching up, he runs his hand down over his face, looking stressed all of a sudden. The action has me realizing that he has shaved his beard since I saw him last at Titan and Emilee's wedding. Now it's just a five o'clock shadow. I like it. Shows off his defined jawline. He's got the top of his dark hair spiked. He's trimmed it, the sides now short. His green eyes meet mine for a brief second, then he looks away, only to come back to mine. I don't look away. The alcohol gives me that extra courage I need.

We already played this game at the wedding, but I was sober. Nervous about what his strong stare meant. But right now, I like it. He looks like the kind of guy you'd call up whenever you need a good time but would never introduce to your father. Good thing I don't have one. Jasmine places another shot in front of me, and I take it, not looking away.

His eyes drop to my chest, and my heart picks up when he licks his lips, informing me he's thinking the same thing I am. The last guy I slept with was Mitch, and I'm not going there tonight.

But Cross? I could do that. Or let him do me. Yeah, why not? I should get to have fun, right? I'm a single woman who knows what she wants, and he's staring at me like he wants me too. He can sit on his throne while I kneel for him.

Make me your queen for the night.

"I'm ready to go," I announce to no one in particular.

Jasmine laughs. "Yeah, I noticed that."

I look over at her, and she's giving me a lopsided smile. I don't say anything. I'm not hiding what I want. Why should I?

"Let's go." She slides her arm into the crook of mine, and we stumble over to the guys. "We're ready."

"About time," Grave says, checking his watch. "Did you two come together?"

"Yep." I nod, my eyes still on Cross. He's got to be around six-two by the way I'm looking up at him, even in my heels. Now that I'm close and paying attention, I see how broad his shoulders are. His tight shirt shows me every curve of muscle that it hides. His right hand holds a cup of water. His left has a Zippo in it, flipping it open and closed. The small movement is mesmerizing in his tatted fingers, momentarily stealing my attention. I keep expecting him to light it.

Jasmine elbows me, and I look up. "I rode ..." Hiccup. "With Jasmine."

Grave turns to Cross. "You drive Alexa home, and I'll take Jasmine."

Fuck yes! I want to jump up and down at that, but I'm afraid I'll fall over.

Cross agrees with a nod. "Need me to follow you and give you a ride home after you drop her off."

Grave shakes his head. "She's coming with me. She can drive herself home in the morning." He then grabs her arm and yanks her from us.

"Have fun!" Jasmine calls out, laughing while he drags her through the crowd.

THREE

CROSS

S HE'S DRUNK, BUT it's not like I didn't see this coming. I don't even know the woman, but I could tell she was on a mission to drown whatever memories she has with Mitch. Can't say I blame her. I've done it all my life. But it was because of my father, not some bitch I loved and lost.

Falling forward, she trips over her heels, and I reach out to grab her. "Whoa," I say, bringing her to a stop. "You okay?"

"Yeah." She nods, pushing pieces of her bleach-blond hair back from her face. Some strands have fallen free from her messy bun throughout the night. "I don't remember parking this far out."

That's because she came with Jasmine. I didn't park where they had. "Here," I say, stepping in front of her and bending my knees. "Jump on. I'll give you a lift."

She laughs, placing her hands on my shoulders, and then she jumps up onto my back. I wrap my fingers around the thighs of her jeans and hold her in place as her arms come around my neck. Her face is by my ear, and I can hear her breathing.

My cock instantly hardens at the sound and feel of her breath on me, and sweat beads on my forehead.

29

Should have said no, Cross!

I try to think of anything else and slow my breathing while walking faster. I just need to get her home and drop her off. Get as far away as I can from Alexa, but the way her breasts press into my back, have me thinking of ripping that shirt off her.

We enter the parking garage, and I see some guys crowded around my white Pininfarina Battista. I've got the only one in town. They see us coming toward them, and they take a step back. "Nice car, man," one says as I walk over to the passenger side door.

"Thanks," I say before letting go of Alexa's legs and tapping her thigh to release my waist from her grip. It physically pains me to do it. I want her legs wrapped around me once they're gone, but this time, I want her to be underneath me.

She slides in, and I make my way to the driver's side. Starting it up, I look over at her. "Where to?" I meant it more as a "where do you live?" but what I wanted to say and the words that actually came out were two very different things.

She looks over at me. "Wherever you want to go."

That's an open invitation if I've ever heard one. Obviously, she doesn't want me at her house, or she would have suggested that. "Kingdom?" I question, unable to keep my eyes from dropping to her legs as she runs her hands over her jeans. Her nails are kept short and painted black. She wears a silver banded ring on her right hand. It's plain yet dainty at the same time.

"I don't gamble," she states.

My eyes meet hers. "Neither do I." What I have planned for her is much more intimate. I mean, if she's into a crowd watching, then that's fine too. I'm not shy.

She laughs, leaning her head back against the headrest, and smiles softly at me. Her green eyes drop to my jeans, and I refrain from groaning at the thoughts that run through my mind. My hand in her hair while she's bent over the center console with her lips wrapped around my cock ... "Kingdom it is." Not wanting to waste another second, I take off, getting the hell out of here.

We don't say much during the twenty-minute drive back to the Strip. I keep checking on her to make sure she hasn't passed out, and every time, she's looking out the window.

I pull up around the back of tower one, where the Kings and I have a private entrance. Parking the car, I help her out and up the fifteen stairs that lead to a set of black doors.

Her drunk eyes take in the white marble floor and black circle with the gold K in the middle when we enter the building. Lifting her head, she notices the mirrored ceiling and chandelier hanging in the entrance.

Nigel stands behind his black marble desk in the corner. Nigel is our right-hand man. He's more of a father to us than our actual fathers ever were. Guess it didn't take him and Titan very long to bury Kenneth. He looks up and smiles at us. "Good evening, Cross. Alexa. It's good to see you again." I'm not sure how he knows her other than maybe he met her at Titan's wedding.

"You too, Nigel," she tells him as I scan my key card for our private elevator. Only a King has access to it. Other than him, of course. It opens immediately, and we step inside. I have to refrain from ripping her clothes off right here and now. Just a few more minutes and she's all mine.

It comes to a stop on the Royal level to the suite that the Kings share. But no one will be here tonight. Titan hasn't stayed one night here since he married Emilee. Grave stays at his house with April, and Bones rarely sleeps. I'm sure he's at Glass—one of the many businesses he owns that we all pretend we don't know about.

Stepping into our suite, I turn to face her. "Would you like a drink?"

She places her hands on my chest, gripping my shirt. "I think I've had enough."

My hands go to her hips, and I yank her to me. The thought crosses my mind that this is a mistake. That she's off-limits to me. I try to think of my best friend and how it would affect him. "I made a promise not to touch you," I rush out, hoping she pushes me away.

She surprises me by smiling, and it's anything but innocent. Her pretty green eyes drop to my lips before returning to mine. "I can keep a secret." Then her lips are on mine.

ALEXA

His hands go from my hips to my thighs, and he lifts me off my feet like I weigh nothing. My legs wrap around his waist, and my fingers grip his spiked hair as I part my lips for him, silently begging him to kiss me deeper.

I moan into his mouth when he understands that I need more. His tongue touches mine, and he tastes like cinnamon. Mine has to taste like alcohol, but that doesn't seem to bother him.

He starts walking, and then he's fumbling to open a door. We enter a room, and he slams the door shut with his foot. It's pitch-black in here. And I groan that I won't be able to see all of his tattoos. I'm not one of those women who are self-conscious about my body. Either you find it sexy or you don't, so sex with the lights on has never bothered me.

We fall onto what I'm guessing is a bed, and all the air rushes out of my lungs when he pulls his lips from mine. I reach out aimlessly in the dark, grabbing at anything I can find. I feel his shirt, and I yank on it. He helps himself out of it, and then I hear a belt being undone followed by a zipper.

Fuck, yeah!

I rush to undo my pants and curse myself for wearing skinny jeans—they're too tight and a pain to get off. My drunk ass limbs can't move fast enough. But then I feel his hands on me, pushing, pulling, and then he's on top of me. And he's naked. My hands run over his large biceps and to his back, my fingertips running over waves of muscles as he flexes.

My pussy throbs in anticipation.

He slides a hand between my legs, and I arch my back. "Oh, God

..." I trail off as he thrusts a finger into me, quickly followed by another. He doesn't have to do much to get me ready, and I'm not in the mood for foreplay. I want to be fucked—held down, hair pulled, slap my ass and call me your good little slut, fucked!

I reach down between us and find his dick. My hand wraps around the base, and my fingers don't even touch. My breathing comes faster as I run up his shaft. Holy shit! He's packing. I could cry right now because this is what I needed. I have no doubt he knows how to use it.

He lowers his head to my chest, and I feel his breath on my neck when I start to stroke him. My mouth salivates at his thickness and length.

He lets out a moan, and I pause. Slowly, I run my thumb over the head, and I feel ... is that metal? He's pierced?

I practically whimper. A Prince Albert.

I start to play with the barbell, but he rips my hand away with a grunt, and then he's no longer on top of me. I'm about to protest when he grips my hips and flips me over onto my stomach.

"Yes!" I pant, past caring how desperate I sound. A woman should never be ashamed of what she wants.

I can't get up on my knees fast enough for him. He's yanking my ass up in the air, and then he's pressing against my pussy. I lower my face to his bed, inhaling the scent of fresh linen. It doesn't ease the throbbing between my legs. Before I can take in another breath, he pushes into me.

I cry out into the dark room as he stretches me to accommodate his size. I'm gasping for a breath and reach my hands out in front of me, looking for anything to push against. Finding a headboard, I flatten out my hands as he moves.

I close my eyes, and he pins me down with his front to my back, making it hard to breathe. Then he readjusts himself, ripping my hands from his headboard and brings them behind my back, holding them with his hand. The room spins as he fucks me into his mattress.

I hear him talking but can't understand what he's saying over my heavy breathing and moans. His free hand slaps my ass, and I dig my face into his bed, not afraid of asphyxiation at the moment. I want to tell him that he feels amazing, but I can't speak. Not right now. I can barely breathe. The room continues to spin, the alcohol clearly altering my perception of things.

But it doesn't take me more than a few minutes before I'm crying out his name while coming all over his dick. He isn't far behind me.

Once he's done, he falls off next to me, and we both lie side by side, breathing heavily and covered in sweat. I can't even find the willpower to roll over at this point.

"You didn't use a condom." It's the first thing I say, and I'm thankful it's dark because he'd be able to see how red my face is that I said that out loud.

"Nope," he replies breathlessly.

I laugh at that and try to move my heavy limbs but still get nothing. I'll have to crawl out of here. "Not worried about knocking me up?" He doesn't know I'm on birth control.

"If it bothers you so much, I'll wear one next time," he says, starting to get his breathing back under control while I'm over here flopping around like a fish out of water. Legs shaking, heart still pounding, and sucking in breath after breath.

Round two? Yes, please. "Next time? Boy, aren't you cocky?" I sure as hell won't be playing hard to get.

I feel the bed shift, then his hand on my lower back. It travels down over my ass and my still parted legs, and he lazily runs two fingers over my soaked pussy. "You saying you don't want that again?" He thrusts a finger in me.

I lift my ass, my hands digging into his comforter. A whimper escapes my parted lips. My pussy's still throbbing from coming so hard. "Cross ..."

"Yeah, baby?" he asks huskily before I feel his lips on my shoulder. He trails kisses across my back and up to my neck before a second finger enters me, and I'm rocking my hips with each thrust.

"Fuck," I moan, closing my eyes. Or maybe they've rolled back into my head. At this point, I can't tell.

"Yeah," he whispers before his thumb starts playing with my swollen clit. "That's what I'm going to do to you. All night long." Then his teeth sink into my neck.

FOUR

CROSS

FUCK, SHE'S A drug. That hit I haven't had in weeks. That one taste of freedom that I've been craving.

I get fucked up to forget my past. Only I don't crave it to feel in control of my life; it just helps dull the memories of how I got here. I didn't pick Kingdom. It didn't matter that none of us Kings wanted the responsibility. Or to be killers. It started out as playing a role we weren't able to escape. Now we revel in it.

When my time is up, I won't even get a chance to atone for my sins. No, I'll go straight to hell and burn for eternity. Which is fair. I didn't expect it to be any other way. When you're raised to fear the light, you seek out the darkness.

"Yes," she cries out as my fingers fuck her sweet, wet cunt in my bed. I could go again and again with her. And that's exactly what I plan on doing.

Removing my hand, I grab her hips and flip her onto her back. I get up and move to sit between her shaking legs. I kept the lights off for a reason. It's killing me right now not to see her body, but I don't want her seeing mine. Too many questions will surface that I'm not in the mood to answer. She isn't some woman I'm going to fuck tonight and then kick out afterward. No, I'll see her tomorrow and the next day. Not only because she's April's best friend but also because I already can't get enough.

I don't care what any man tells you. We know pretty quickly if we're going to let you go or want you to stick around.

Throwing her left leg over my shoulder, I grip the base of my already hard cock and guide it into her pussy, forcing a whimper out of her. I go slow this time, gently pressing into her until my balls hit her ass. Then I lean forward, my chest pressed to hers. We're sweaty and both panting. My hands find her messy bun, and I grip her hair, pulling it loose. My lips find her neck, and I start to kiss her slick skin until I find her ear.

Her hands run down my back until she finds my ass. She digs her nails into it while trying to lift her hips, begging me to move. To fuck her.

"I'm going to take my time this round," I whisper into her ear, nibbling on it.

She groans, irritated at that confession. "Please?" she breathes.

My lips trail down the side of her neck, and I smile against the skin while I lift my hips just a bit, allowing my cock to slide out. Teasing her.

"Cross," she growls. Letting go of my ass, she brings her hands to my hair, and she pulls on it aggressively. My cock throbs as I push into her just as slowly as when I pulled out. It's driving me just as crazy as it is her. "I don't want slow," she admits shamelessly.

I smile. "How do you want it?"

"Fuck me." She lifts her hips. "Please. I need it."

Her voice sounds as desperate as her body feels. She's trembling, breathing heavily, and I can feel her heart pound in her chest with mine pressed against it. As much as I want to drag this out, I want what she wants.

"Okay," I whisper, softly kissing the corner of her lips. "But only because that's what I want." She needs to understand that I control her. Not the other way around.

I let go of her hair and sit up. Grabbing the back of her knees, I press them forward, shoving them into her chest. Her ankles cross, and I hold them in place as I start to move. My hips slam forward, my cock fucking her cum-soaked pussy. My mouth waters, wanting to lick it clean while she cries into the dark room.

I give her what she wants. What I've craved since I saw her at the wedding. She's my dirty little secret. Mine to do with as I please. I'm going to fucking make it worth it because when I'm done with her, she'll come crawling back.

It feels like hours later, but I know it can't be much longer before I'm coming inside her again. The sound of her getting off did me in. I lie down beside her, listening to her panting from her second orgasm.

I smile to myself in the darkness with one hand behind my head and the other on my bare chest.

"You said you made someone a promise ..." She pauses to catch her breath. "Who and what did you promise exactly?'

"I promised Grave that I wouldn't touch you," I say honestly. Why lie about it? We're both adults, and we made the decision to have sex.

"Why?" she asks, sounding confused.

I chuckle. "You expected me to turn you down?"

"No." I hear her shift, and then her hand is on my chest. I tense at the sudden contact, and I can tell she notices. She goes to pull her hand away, but I reach out and hold it in place. "Why did he ask you that?"

"Because he was afraid it would get between you and April's friendship. And then that would interfere with his relationship with her." I spell it out for her. Plain and simple.

She laughs. "She's my best friend. I'd never allow a fuck to get between us."

I don't have anything to say about that.

After a few seconds, she speaks again. "Wait ... when did he have you promise this to him? Tonight?"

I'm really surprised he had me drive her home, considering I had already asked about her before. I think his mind was elsewhere after his encounter with Ethan. "No. At Titan and Emilee's wedding."

"You wanted to sleep with me then?" she asks, and I hear her yawn. The alcohol and two orgasms were getting the best of her. I was going to wait twenty minutes and go again, but I guess that'll have to wait for another night.

"Of course. Why do you sound surprised?"

"Because we hadn't even met," she whispers, her body fading fast.

"So?" I run my hand through her matted hair. "I saw you. That was enough."

Men aren't as complicated as women seem to think. If we want you, you'll know. Even the ones who try to act all hard are easy to catch.

She doesn't respond to that. Within a few seconds, I hear her breathing even out, letting me know she's asleep.

I close my eyes and let out a long breath, fully satisfied and tired as fuck.

ALEXA

I WAKE UP to find myself alone in a king-sized bed. Sitting up, I allow the covers to fall to my waist. I look around the room to see a wall made of windows to my right. The black curtains have been pulled back to allow the sunlight to enter the room. It's large with a single dresser to the left, and a TV hangs on the wall across from me. The floor is white marble with a black diamond design. It's all very classy, but it's what I expected from a King.

Pushing the black covers off me, I stand, the room swaying a little from all the alcohol I consumed last night. I should have stopped long before we left. I spot my cell phone on the floor by my bra and underwear. Picking it up, I see I have two messages. The first one is from Mitch.

CUNT: It was nice seeing you last night.
Let's have dinner this week.

I know I had a lot to drink, but does he not remember what happened? That he thought I was there with Cross? I hope the motherfucker saw me leave with him. But I can't get that lucky.

Ignoring it, I open the second one. It's from Jasmine.

Jasmine: Meeting the girls for breakfast.
Seven o'clock at Empire in Kingdom.

Looking at the clock, I see it's six thirty. God, why the fuck am I up so early? I wanted to sleep in ...

A door to the right opens, and I jump back, placing my hands over my tits and pussy to try to shield what little I can. Cross stands there in the doorway dressed in a plain, long-sleeved white T-shirt and blue jeans with combat boots. He's got his dark hair spiked and the sleeves rolled up, exposing his tatted arms.

My thighs tighten as I stand here butt fucking naked in the middle of his room. "I, uh ..." I stop talking when he pushes off the doorway and starts walking to me.

He comes to a stop before me, his green eyes sweep over my very exposed body, and a rush of guilt runs through me from last night. He said he had promised Grave that he wouldn't sleep with me. I practically jumped him.

"Good morning," he says roughly, making goose bumps cover my exposed skin, and my nipples instantly harden.

"Morning," I whisper, lowering my eyes to the floor.

He places his finger under my chin and lifts it to where I have to look up at him. "I have to get to work, but stay as long as you want." Then he leans forward and gently kisses my lips.

I keep them closed, not kissing him back. I haven't had the chance to brush my teeth like him. I can taste the lingering alcohol on my own breath, and that alone makes me want to vomit.

He pulls away and lets go of my chin, slowly running his

knuckles down my neck and over my chest bone. My breathing picks up. His eyes follow his touch and then lift to meet mine. "I put my number in your phone. Text me later." With that, he pulls back and exits the room, leaving me alone to catch my breath.

I rush to his bathroom and find a toothbrush on his counter, not even bothering to wonder why he has an extra one still in the package. Total playboy move, but whatever. At least he's considerate of his one-night stands.

Once done, I bend over, throw my hair up into a messy ponytail and then use the restroom before getting dressed in the clothes I wore last night. I don't even have time for a whore's bath. This'll have to do until I can get home and soak in the tub.

Making my way to the twentieth floor, I enter Empire at a quarter till seven to see April and Jasmine already seated. "Hey, ladies." I scoot into the booth with a smile. They both sit across from me. April looks like her glowing self. She has her dark purple hair down and her makeup done. Her lips match her hair, and her winged black eyeliner is on thick.

Jasmine looks rough. "Have you been home?" I ask.

Jasmine has her face covered with a big pair of white Versace sunglasses, and her red hair is up in a messy bun. Well, kind of. It's so short that a lot of pieces have fallen to frame her face. Pretty sure she still has her makeup on from last night just like me.

"No." She sighs. "I left the moment I got to their house last night." She points at April sitting next to her.

"I was wondering where you were this morning," April says. "I went into the room, and there was a piece of paper on the bed, but nothing had been written on it."

"Shit. I could have sworn I left you a note." Jasmine shrugs. "Must have imagined it."

"Where did you go?" I wonder.

"I climbed out the window and had someone pick me up," Jasmine answers vaguely.

"You what?" April laughs. "You climbed out the window? Why didn't you just use the front door?"

"It was fine. Felt like I was fifteen again." Jasmine sips her coffee.

"How do you feel?" I ask, looking her over.

She pushes her glasses to the top of her head, and sure enough, her once flawless makeup is smeared under her eyes. It looks like she has been crying, but that could just be the result of a good fucking. "Like I'm seventy and just had back surgery," she says matter-of-factly. "My pussy is still feeling the aftershocks of the 9.5 dick that pounded it last night."

We both laugh. "Hey, before Emilee and Haven get here, I need to tell you guys something, but you have to keep it a secret." My eyes dart around the restaurant to make sure the girls haven't arrived yet.

"With my life." Jasmine pretends to slit her throat, showing her commitment to keeping my secrets.

April chuckles at her but nods. "Of course."

I can trust both of them. I'm not so sure about Haven and Emilee, though. They're both married, and I'm not sure how much they tell their husbands. "I slept with Cross last night."

"What?" April gasps, her ice blue eyes wide.

"I knew that was going to happen." Jasmine waves it off. "I wouldn't be surprised if you guys did it in his car before you even left."

"I waited until we got back here." I laugh.

"Why is that a secret?" April asks, looking confused all of a sudden.

"I guess Grave told him I was off-limits." I shrug, having problems remembering everything that was said last night. At one point, I was hammered. The other part, I was exhausted. "Not sure why or what that meant. But he made Cross promise not to touch me at Titan and Emilee's wedding."

April frowns, tilting her head.

I can't keep secrets from her. I understand that I told Cross I can, but I didn't know it was going to involve April. I'm not sure what I was thinking about who he wanted to keep it from, but I have to tell her.

"But why?" she asks again. "That doesn't make sense."

"Because you and I are friends," I answer.

She sighs, running a hand through her hair. "Grave has been ... fragile ever since he got out of rehab."

"What do you mean by fragile?" Jasmine asks before shoving a piece of toast into her mouth.

"Just overprotective, I guess is the right word."

"Well, you're pregnant with his child. What do you expect?" Jasmine adds.

"Please don't tell him," I add quickly. "I don't want it to put a strain on his relationship with Cross." I don't know Grave well enough to know how he would react to this news. And it's not like I plan on doing it again. It was just a one-night stand—multiple times. They, however, see each other every day. They're not only best friends but also business partners.

"Of course not." She shakes her head. "Your secret is safe with me."

"You know my lips are sealed." Jasmine nods. "Unless it's for a dick. Then they're pretty open."

We both laugh at her.

"So how was it?" April asks, wiggling her dark eyebrows.

"Let's just say I was extremely drunk, but it was very memorable."

"Plan on making it a casual thing?" she digs.

"No." I throw up both of my hands. "It was a one-time thing."

"Sure, it was." Jasmine nods her head once. "I bet you let him hit it again tonight."

I snort, but the truth is I wouldn't turn him down if he called. Good dick is hard to find these days.

A cell rings, and April pulls hers out of her purse. Looking at it, she sighs. "I need to take this. It's my brother."

Jasmine stands to let April out and sits back down when she

walks out of the restaurant. Sitting back down, she lifts her empty cup of coffee, begging anyone to come by and refill it. "I need a truck full of this shit today."

"That bad, huh?"

"I haven't even been to bed yet." She covers her mouth to yawn. "And I'm pretty sure I'm still drunk."

"Well, at least it was worth it."

She winks at me. "He always is."

I don't ask who she's talking about because she keeps who she hooks up with pretty secretive. It's none of my business. As long as she's getting what she wants, that's all that matters.

"Sorry, ladies." April returns to her seat.

"Everything okay?" I ask.

"Yeah ..." She doesn't sound so sure. "Ethan is just acting weird."

"How so?" I ask, curious about Ethan.

April and I haven't gotten to spend much time together lately. She supplied the flowers for Titan and Emilee's wedding, and when the happy couple did an article in the paper, they name-dropped Roses. April's shop blew up. She's been slammed with order after order ever since then.

Her brother was in trouble a while back, and Grave had to dig him out of it. I don't know the extent of it, but it cost Grave quite a bit of money.

"He seemed to have been doing better, but we're not as close as we once were. And we no longer live together since I moved in with Grave, so all I can do is guess." She shrugs.

"Well, I'm sure if he was in trouble, he would come to you or Grave," I say, and Jasmine looks away as if to check out of the conversation, not wanting to stick her nose into anything. Makes me wonder if she knows something.

"Yeah," April agrees but doesn't seem convinced.

I look up to see Titan enter the restaurant with his wife in hand, followed by one of the King's best friends, Luca Bianchi, and his wife as well. Titan stands out just like the rest of the Kings with all of his ink. But Luca looks more business type. He wears the expensive three-piece suit, whereas Titan is dressed casually.

"Can't find the place on your own?" Jasmine asks Emilee.

She ignores her and turns to kiss Titan before plopping down next to me. Emilee has her dark hair up in a bun and no makeup on her face. Her blue eyes meet mine. "Why are we here so early? What happened to our lunch dates? I wanted to sleep in."

"April picked the time." Jasmine calls her out.

"Hey!" April shoves her shoulder. "Some of us have jobs to do."

"You have fun with that. I'm going to drink two more cups of coffee, then go home and sleep the day away," Jasmine states.

Haven sits down next to Jasmine, making them scoot in more to give her room as her husband and Titan leave the restaurant.

I like her, but I haven't spent any time with her husband. No reason to. We've been around each other here and there but never spoke to one another directly. Her husband, Luca, seems ... different. He's best friends with the Kings, but I can't find the connection. He doesn't work for Kingdom that I know of, and she doesn't work at all. From what I know, the girls all grew up together.

"Where's your babysitter?" April asks Haven.

"Nite? He had to go upstairs with the guys. I guess they're having an important meeting." She shrugs. "I don't ever ask. Sometimes, it's better off not knowing."

"You know there is a law—spousal immunity—where the spouse can't testify against their significant other," Jasmine offers her. "So even if you did know where he buried the bodies, you don't have to say."

The girls laugh it off like it's a joke, but a part of me knows they're being serious, and that makes me even more interested in Cross. I know it's wrong. That comment from Jasmine alone should make me delete his number from my phone and run, but it does the opposite. Ever heard of curiosity killed the cat? Well, call me a dead pussy.

FIVE

CROSS

I SIT AT our conference table on the thirteenth floor in tower one as Nite, Luca, and Titan enter. Grave sits across from me, icing his right hand. He got in some good hits last night at the Airport. Bones already sits at the head of the table.

Nite takes the seat to my left, and Luca sits next to Grave. He places his cell on the table, and I flip my Zippo open and closed as I stare at it.

The conference room has jammers all over it, so we conduct our business here. Secretive meetings where we talk about shit that cannot be repeated. No cell phones or electrical devices will work in this room, just in case someone tries to record anything. The Kings cover our asses.

"What's the issue?" Bones asks Luca.

He undoes his suit jacket before answering. "Well, the fact that Kenneth didn't give you anything to go on doesn't look good."

"The guy wasn't going to talk," Grave states, leaning back in his seat and getting comfortable.

"He was dead. Doesn't matter who did it. The guy was on borrowed time," Bones agrees with his brother.

47

"Maybe, but we needed to know when that shipment was going to arrive," Luca says.

"There's got to be someone else who knows something." Titan is the one who speaks.

"The Mason brothers," Grave offers.

"No." Bones shakes his head.

"Just because you don't like them doesn't mean they can't be helpful," Grave snaps at him.

"I don't want them involved," Bones goes on.

"And I don't want people I love killed." Grave stands, throwing his ice pack into the center of the custom black table where a skull is carved out. "Some of us actually have something to lose here, Bones."

His brother sighs, looking up at him, but he doesn't argue. I can understand Grave's frustration. Titan and Bones have nothing to do with the Mason brothers, but I don't mind them.

"I can go speak to them. Dig around a little," I offer. "If I don't think they can help, then I won't give anything away."

The room falls silent, and Luca looks at Nite. "You can go with him."

Nite nods as if it was a question. Nite is our secret weapon per se. The guy doesn't speak. He's been a mute since college.

"Then it's decided," Grave states before turning and exiting the room, shoving the double doors open.

Bones bows his head, running his hand through his hair, obviously not pleased. But what can he do at this point? He may be Grave's older brother, but Grave has always done what he wants to do. The kid wasn't nicknamed Grave for nothing. He's always had a death wish.

"We'll go tonight," I say, and once again, Nite nods, letting me know that's fine. I have no doubt that Grave will go with me as well.

"Don't leave him there with them alone." Bones finally speaks, thinking the same as me before he too gets up and leaves the room.

I exit the conference room and get to my office. I pull out my cell and see if anything comes through now that I have service. Nothing.

I pull up Alexa's number on my cell. I had put mine in her phone and then called myself. I told her to text me later, but I wasn't going to rely on her to take that step. If need be, I'll take it myself.

I write her out a text but then delete it and decide to just go see her tonight after I'm done at the Airport. It'll be harder for her to reject me in person.

———

Grave and I get out of my car at the Airport. Nite pulls up beside us and gets out of his. We make our way into the building and to the Mason brothers' office. Grave hasn't said two words to me since we left Kingdom, but I'm not taking it personally. He's been in a pissy mood since we were here last night.

We enter the office, and Turner Mason—the middle brother—sits at the table. A duffel bag sits open in the center with money falling out of it onto the surface. He wears his shoulder holster with a Desert Eagle on each side. The Mason brothers shoot first and never ask questions.

Trey Mason—the baby—sits on his brother's right. He spots us first. Pushing his chair back, he balances it on the back two legs and places his black boots up on the table. He locks his fingers behind his head, wearing a fucking smirk on his face.

I don't see the eldest brother, Tanner, but the guy to Turner's left quickly gets my attention. Because I just saw him last night. Mitch stands there with his back toward us, his hands on a woman's ass and his tongue down her throat. And it must be my lucky day because I also know the woman he's giving mouth to mouth to.

"Look, it's two Kings and a Nite," Trey announces to the room, alerting everyone of our presence.

Mitch shoves the woman away and spins around. His wide eyes meet mine. "Cross ..."

The woman gasps and quickly shoves her skirt down back into

place as if I've never seen her pussy before. I've made it very clear that we're not exclusive, and she can fuck whoever she wants.

"I'm, uh ..." Rachel rushes out, shoving her way through Grave and me and exiting the office.

"You can leave too." I direct my attention to Mitch.

He squares his shoulders, about to tell me to fuck off when Turner snaps his fingers. "Out."

Mitch doesn't argue with him. No one ever wins with the Mason brothers or the Kings, for that matter. He exits much less dramatically than the girl.

"To what do we owe the honor?" Trey asks, that stupid smirk still on his face. I want to push him backward so he'll fall out of his chair.

I don't mind the Mason brothers even though I really don't want to work with them. But Grave was right. If anyone knows what we need, it'll be them. I direct my attention to Turner. "We need to speak to you privately."

"Get the fuck out, Trey!" he orders his baby brother without a thought.

Turner Mason is all business, all the time. He reminds me of Bones.

Trey rights his chair and stands, giving his brother a go to hell look as he exits, knowing better than to argue with him. The Mason brothers aren't afraid to fight, and that includes each other.

"What do you guys need?" Turner asks.

"Have you had any problems with your shipments lately?" Grave gets to the point.

Turner tilts his head and frowns slightly. "No." He answers slowly. Not as if he had to think about it, more as if whether he should divulge that information to us or not.

The Mason brothers are like the Kings—they each have their own role in their business. Turner Mason is a contract killer; he is also in very tight with the Mexican Cartel. He makes monthly trips down to Arizona to exchange *cargo,* if you know what I mean. Hence the bag that sits on the table overflowing with cash and the guns strapped to his sides.

"Why do you ask?" He places his hands on the table.

Grave runs a hand through his hair, frustrated that this is going to be another dead end. "We had a client come to us, wanting us to take care of a problem. We found a guy ... and let's just say he's now buried in the desert because he refused to talk."

"What was the shipment?" Turner asks.

"Diamonds," I answer. He has to know what he's looking for. Otherwise, this visit was pointless. People will sell and trade anything.

Turner nods his head once. "I will keep an eye out and let you know if I hear anything that sounds off."

"Thanks," I say and turn to leave, ready to get the fuck out of here, but Turner stops me when he speaks to Grave.

"But I do have some information that you may want to know."

Grave steps forward, getting closer to the table where Turner's still casually sitting. "What is it?"

"Your boy? He's ten grand deep."

"Son of a bitch." Grave growls, shoving the door open and stepping into the hallway outside of the Mason brother's office.

"Who is he talking about?" I ask, following him. Nite is on my ass as well.

"Fucking Ethan," he snaps over his shoulder before coming to a stop and turning to face Nite and me. "Can I ride with you?" he asks Nite. "I need to run by somewhere."

Nite nods once and pulls his keys out of his pocket.

"I can take you," I offer.

Grave waves me off, and I look at Nite. "Text me if you need me."

Nite walks off, trying to keep up with Grave when I hang back and pull out my cell to check it. Still nothing from Alexa. Deciding I'll make my move, I pocket my phone and head toward the parking garage. I'm almost to my car when I hear my name being called out behind me.

"Cross?"

I turn around and let out a sigh when I see Rachel running after me. Giving her my back, I say, "I have somewhere to be."

"Hey?" She grabs my shoulder and spins me around to face her. "That was nothing. He's nothing," she rushes out, licking her lips. Her once dark red lipstick now rubbed off due to her kissing Mitch back in Mason's office.

I'm not sure why she cares what I saw. It doesn't change anything between us. "It's fine. You can fuck whoever you want."

She flinches and lets out a deep breath from running to catch up with me. "I just wanted you to know that ... he ..."

"Mitch." I say his name, and her light brown eyes widen as if I wouldn't know him. A part of being a King is knowing everyone.

She crosses her arms over her small chest. "I just want you to know that this won't affect my ability at the shop."

I nod. Ah, I get it. She doesn't want to get fired. Rachel here works for me at my tattoo shop inside of Kingdom. I started fucking her not long after I hired her. "You're fine." I dismiss her and get into my car, having somewhere to be too.

ALEXA

A LITTLE AFTER one a.m., I'm standing behind the register, closing out a tab, when I look up to see Cross sitting at the bar.

"Hey. What are you doing here?" I ask, looking around to see if he's alone, which he is. No other King in sight.

"Came to see you." His green eyes drop to my chest, and he licks his lips.

My thighs tighten, and my heart instantly picks up. I look away from him, biting my lip. "And why would you do that?" I haven't messaged him today because I didn't want him to think that I thought last night was more than it was. I'm a big girl and understand what a one-night stand is. Last night wasn't my first rodeo in that depart-ment. I'm twenty-two, not sixteen.

"I think you can guess why," he replies.

My eyes snap back to his, and he leans forward. Placing his tatted forearms on the bar top, I remind him, "We said one night." I lie because I'm not really sure what all was said last night, but it's worth a try.

He slowly shakes his head, the corner of his lips turning up into a soft yet very heart-stopping smile. "I don't remember making that promise."

My wet pussy reminds me that it wants a replay while my mind says back the fuck up and say hell no. A King is the last thing I need to get addicted to. Especially one who promised his best friend he wouldn't. "Well, we did." I close the register and walk over to the other end, placing Jake's change in front of him. "Do you need me to call you an Uber?" I ask the old man.

Lucky's isn't a hip bar, if you know what I mean. I took it over last year. Lucky was a friend of my mother's, and when he passed, he left it to me. He had no kids and no siblings. I had my first job here when I was sixteen. It was just my brother and me with my mother, and we fell on hard times. He hired me and paid me cash under the table—because of my age—to pick up after everyone. I had dreams to go to college and do something else with my life, but that doesn't mean I don't love what I do now.

"No, I'm good," he answers through a cough. "My friend is coming to get me."

I smile at him. "Okay. I'll see you tomorrow."

Then I lift the bar at the end and walk down the hallway to my office. I instantly spin around when I hear someone enter behind me. Cross is shutting the door. "What are you doing?"

"You," he says matter-of-factly.

"I'm working," I answer, trying to ignore the butterflies in my stomach and give him my back. I don't have time to become Cross's little fuck toy, no matter how much I want that. This is the very reason I avoided messaging him today. What was I going to say? Hey, let's fuck? Or hey, thanks for last night? It was going to be awkward no matter what I chose to say. So, I just didn't. I never thought he'd show up here.

Grabbing my arm, he spins me around, and before I can protest, his hands cup my face, and his lips are on mine. He kisses me deeply, passionately. Like I'm dying, and he's trying to give me his air.

My arms go around his neck without thought, and I lean into him, pressing my body into his, and I feel his hard dick push against my lower stomach. I moan at the feel of it, the memory of last night. The King knew what he was doing. Not like I'm surprised. Guys like him are usually the best fucks and toxic as hell.

I suck in a deep breath when he pulls away.

"I've got work to do," I protest one last time, trying to make my body understand what my head is screaming.

You're sober now, Alexa. Just say no.

He spins me around and picks me up, dropping me onto the old brown leather couch. His hands quickly go to my jeans, and I don't stop him. Instead, I tell my mind to shut the fuck up and push my hair back from my face. Lifting my hips, I give him better access to remove them. Then he drops to his knees beside the couch and throws my legs over his broad shoulders.

My breath picks up as I look down at him kneeling between my wide-open legs, totally exposed to him, wishing I could see his body in the light like he can see mine. "Just relax, babe," he says as his eyes slowly devour me.

I arch my back and reach out, grabbing his spiked hair when he lowers his head between my legs and licks my pussy.

"Yes ..." I trail off, bucking my hips while he fucks my cunt with his tongue.

My eyes are closed, my head tilted back, and I swear I'm drunk all over again. His arms are wrapped around my hips, holding them down while I try to buck my hips with each thrust of his tongue. He plays with my clit at the same time, and I'm unable to keep still.

My body breaks out in a cold sweat, and I'm gasping to breathe.

My back arches painfully off the leather couch, and I bite into my tongue to keep from yelling while I come.

I'm lying here spent, shaking like a leaf on a tree when he stands to his full height. I reach out aimlessly, grabbing his shirt and yanking him toward me. His right hand goes to the back of the couch to catch himself so he doesn't fall on top of me.

My hand snakes around his neck, and I pull his face down to mine. Sticking my tongue out, I lick along his cum-stained lips.

He lets out a growl from deep in his chest, rumbling against mine. My hands go to the hem of his shirt, and I start yanking it up. I want him inside me. I know I just got off, but I'm going to be greedy. He was the one who came here wanting me. Why can't I use him?

He pulls away and leans his head down, allowing me to yank his shirt up and over his head.

I pause, my hand on his left pec as my eyes travel over his ink. This is the first time I've seen him shirtless in the light.

He's got a skull wearing a tilted crown on his right pec with cross-bones underneath it, and the silver cross dangling from around his neck catches my attention. I've never noticed it before. He must keep it tucked inside his shirt.

When I reach out and grab it, his hand immediately wraps around my throat. He stretches his arm out, holding my head down to the couch.

I look up at him, and his emerald eyes are glowing. There's a story there—with the cross. One that he doesn't want to share.

I hold my hands out to my side and adjust my back on the couch, silently letting him know that we don't have to get personal if he doesn't want to. It's just a hookup. Another one.

Letting go of my neck, I go to speak, but he yanks me up by my wrists. He plops down onto the couch and jerks me down onto his lap where I straddle him. My hands go to his belt while his find my hair. Then he's pulling me in for a deep kiss.

I STAND AND BUTTON MY JEANS WHILE HE ZIPS HIS. "THIS CAN'T happen again," I say.

He smirks, pulling his shirt up and over his head. Once again, I didn't get to explore his body. He held me tightly to his body the whole time. I'm pretty sure he did that on purpose. I think the fact that I touched the cross around his neck put him on alert. "That's cute."

I roll my eyes. "I'm serious, Cross." *No, I'm not.*

He walks over to me. "Why is that? We're both adults having fun, right?"

"Yeah, but ..."

"Then why would you turn down sex when you can have it whenever you want?" He arches a brow.

When I don't argue, he knows he's won. I'm pretty sure he already knew it, but I was trying to play hard to get.

The corner of his lips turn up into a sexy smirk, and I push past him. Turning the knob, I open the door and go to storm out but come to a stop when I see my brother standing on the other side. His hand is out as if he was about to open the door and enter. Thank God Cross and I are done and dressed because the door wasn't locked.

"What the ...?" He trails off as his eyes run over my knotted hair and flushed cheeks.

I quickly look down to make sure my shirt is covering my breasts and right side out. *All good.* "Can I help you?" I ask, pushing my right hip out while hanging on to the door for balance. My legs are still shaking.

Cross comes up behind me, wrapping his arms around me from behind like he's pissing on his territory. He has no clue who this is. As far as he knows, this is just another Mitch. I have to refrain from smiling. Is he jealous?

My brother looks up at him, and his dark eyes narrow. He knows exactly who he is. My brother hates the Kings. He's got all these conspiracy theories about them and talks about how evil they are. That's the appeal.

"Cross, this is my brother. Derek, this is Cross." I'm not going to pretend Derek is someone he's not.

Neither one of them says anything to one another. Just an awkward silence follows. I push off the door and turn in Cross's arms. "I need to close up." It's too late to deal with them right now.

He cups my face and leans his head down. "I'll see you tomorrow, gorgeous." Then he kisses my lips. It's a slow and sensual kiss. I can still taste myself, and it makes me moan. When he's done, he pulls away and slaps me on the ass before leaving the room, shouldering past my brother.

"What in the fuck are you doing, Alexa?" Derek doesn't waste a second.

I exit the office as well and walk down the hallway back to the bar. Giving a quick look around, I see it's empty, and he's already started clearing off the tables.

"Who I fuck is none of your business," I say and start picking up the empty glasses on the bar top.

"Are you fucking kidding me?" he snaps. "Your best friend fucks a King, so you have to as well?"

I spin around on him. "Don't talk about April like that." My brother used to have a thing for her. Hell, he probably still does. He's a sore fucking loser that she didn't pick him.

"You have no idea what kind of person he is." He points at the front door.

"It's just sex." I shrug. "Like you've known every girl you've fucked."

"I ..." He lifts his arms, running both hands through his dark hair, giving a rough laugh. "I can't believe I'm hearing this." They drop to his sides. "He is evil. They are evil. The Kings ..."

"You're not a saint, Derek, so quit pretending you're better than them," I snap, getting extremely pissy. Why does he care who I hook up with? Or what they've done? As far as I know, they've never hurt him. Cross didn't act like he knew him. He definitely didn't know he was my brother; he thought he was a threat to his newest fuck buddy.

57

"I am better than them!" he shouts.

"Get the fuck out of my bar!" I scream at him.

Silence fills the empty space before he lets out a long breath. "So that's how it is?" he asks, surprised.

"Yes!" I hiss. I'm not in the mood right now. I'm exhausted, and my body feels hungover. Is that a thing? Orgasm to the point you need to recover. I still have at least an hour here cleaning up the place.

"Fine!" He laughs like I'm stupid. Then he turns around and storms out the back, leaving me pissy.

SIX
CROSS

CLICK

I flip my Zippo open as Titan glares at me from across the conference table.

We always start our day off with a meeting, even if we don't have anything to go over. We shoot the shit for a couple of minutes, then go on with our day, but I know what Bones will want to talk about today. He currently sits at the head of the table, staring down at his watch.

"Sorry I'm late." Grave comes rushing in the double doors with a water in one hand and a KitKat in the other.

Bones sighs but sits up straighter, ready to get down to business. "Were you guys able to find out anything last night at the Airport?"

"No," I answer. "But we spoke to Turner, and he's got his eyes and ears open. If he sees or hears anything, he'll let us know."

"You believe that?" Bones asks.

Grave nods. "Yeah," he says through a bite of his KitKat—breakfast of champions. "He has no reason to lie to us."

"Except for the fact that he's a Mason," Bones argues.

Grave rolls his eyes but doesn't comment. Instead, he continues to shove chocolate into his mouth like he hasn't eaten in days.

"Well, then I guess that's all we can hope for." Bones slams his palms down on the table and stands, exiting. Obviously pissed off. That's pretty much how Bones is most of the time.

"I rushed into work for that?" Grave snorts. "I could have slept in another hour."

"Welcome to being a responsible adult," Titan says, slapping Grave on the shoulder and getting up before leaving.

I close my Zippo and put it in my pocket before I stand. I would usually ask him if he wanted to go to Glass—the strip club to blow off some steam, get fucked up, and fuck strippers—but Grave doesn't do that now, and for once, I'm not in the mood to go.

I wasn't surprised to see Derek at Lucky's last night. I knew who he was the moment I saw him. I've done my homework on Alexa. Father left when they were younger. Mother's dead. Derek is all she has. And he hates me, as he should. I'm not good for her, but it doesn't mean I'll stop seeing her.

"How did things go last night with Ethan?" I ask Grave, trying to get her off my mind for now. I know that's where he had Nite take him. He wanted to keep me out of it for a reason. Maybe so Bones won't find out. We all know Nite doesn't talk, but he knows all of our secrets.

He shrugs. "Same ole shit, just a different day."

I'm not sure what that means exactly, but I don't dig. If Grave has a problem that needs to be fixed, he'll come to me.

I make my way down to the casino floor and over to my tattoo shop. I opened up Tit for Tat about two years ago, and it's my baby, other than Kingdom. The guys and I share the hotel and casino, but we each have something that is just ours.

Titan has the Queens. They are our ladies of the night. Our very discreet escort service we supply for the elites around the world. Men fly in from all over to be with one of our girls.

Grave has the nightclub—Crown.

I have the tattoo shop.

And Bones ... well, he buries himself in Kingdom. His other businesses are outside of these walls.

I push open the glass door for Tit for Tat and see the brunette's head snap up from behind the front desk.

"Cross ..." She rushes out from behind it. "About last night ..."

"Don't care," I tell her, walking through the lobby and to the hallway. I've been fucking my assistant ever since I hired her. Not my best idea, but we were both very open about it not being serious. She needed this job because she slept with her fiancé's brother, and he called off the wedding. So, it wasn't like I expected her to belong to me. I know men get shit for this, but not all girls are for you. Some are just to use. And women see men the same way.

"It's not what it seemed." She goes on, trying to explain herself.

"I don't care," I say honestly. Why she thinks I care who she fucks is beyond me.

"Cross ..."

I come to a stop and spin around, her body running into mine. I reach out and place my hands on her shoulders. "It's fine, Rachel. You are free to fuck whoever you want." I'm not going to tell Alexa what I saw at the Airport. I highly doubt she'd care what Mitch is up to. She has definitely moved on from him no matter what their past is. They weren't married—I checked—and they don't have kids together. So she is free of his ass.

"But ..."

"Now, I have an appointment in twenty minutes, and I need to get set up." I push off her and turn, giving her my back and entering one of my many rooms, ready to start my day with a gorgeous bleach blonde with green eyes still heavy on my mind.

ALEXA

I SIT IN my car outside of Kingdom, my fingers hovering over the text that I got from Cross earlier today.

Cross: Good morning, gorgeous. See you
tonight?

Gorgeous? Why do I smile like an idiot every time I read that? I'm not the type of woman who cares about pet names. Or so I wasn't. And the see you tonight part? I'm glad he's keeping it sexual and not trying to take me to dinner. I can buy myself dinner.

Placing my cell in my purse, I exit my car just as a guy walks up to me dressed in a three-piece black suit.

"Good afternoon, miss. Are you checking into the hotel?"

"No. Just here to try my luck," I say, handing over my keys. Half true. I'm not here to gamble, but I'm not sure how well Cross will take to me just dropping by to say hi. Casual sex and clingy woman can look the same to a man.

I make my way up the stairs and step into the casino. Machine's ding, and people are hollering at the tables. I've never been much of a gambler and haven't stepped foot in a casino as much as I have in this week at Kingdom.

I'm not sure where to find him exactly. I know that tower one is for the Kings only and where their suite is, but it's midday. I know he's not in bed. I pull my cell out of my purse and call Jasmine.

"Hello?" she answers, sounding half asleep.

"Quick question. If I was at Kingdom looking for Cross, where would he be?" It's a long shot, but the best one I've gotten at the moment.

"Tit for Tat," she answers through a yawn.

"And what is that exactly?"

"It's his tattoo shop. If he's not there, then he's on the thirteenth floor of tower one. That's where their offices are."

"Okay. Thank you. Go back to bed now." I laugh.

"No. No. I need to get my ass up. In fact, I need some food. You're at Kingdom now?" she inquires.

"Yeah," I say, looking around to see where the hell Tit for Tat is.

"Lunch at Empire? Give me an hour?" I hear her shower come on.

"Yep. Meet you at the restaurant." I hang up and see that I had a new text message come through while I was on it.

CUNT: Please call me. I need to talk to you.

Ignore.

A cocktail waitress dressed in a black halter top with black booty shorts walks by, carrying a tray of drinks. I step out and stop her. "Excuse me? Where's Tit for Tat?"

"Walk past the poker tables and take a right. You can't miss it," she says, nodding toward the tables to my left.

I thank her and adjust my purse on my shoulder. My heels dig into the soft black carpet covered in what looks like gold confetti. This place is a dream—literally. People come here hoping to win big and return home a completely different person—a wealthy one.

I pay attention to the gold chandeliers hanging from the ceiling to avoid the fact that I woke up this morning and shaved my entire body after reading his text. Even though he's already seen it, I wanted it to be as smooth as possible and smell amazing. I even did a conditioning treatment. Like hello? What the fuck am I doing? This is not how a woman acts over a fuck boy. But then I remind myself nothing is wrong with self-care, and my mind was back on track. Hygiene is important.

Passing the end of the poker tables, I turn right and see the red neon sign that reads Tit for Tat above the black tinted windows.

Bingo!

Reaching up, I fix my hair to frame my face and take in a deep breath, smoothing my shirt down. Then I walk over to the door. Opening it up, I have a smile on my face, but it drops off the moment I step inside and see the woman standing behind the desk.

"Alexa!" She swallows nervously.

What in the actual fuck? Rachel Myers stands before me in the flesh. The same girl I caught Mitch cheating on me with. She works for Cross? I knew this was too good to be true. Can't a girl just find a good fuck without any drama?

She has a spike between her eyes and a hoop hanging from her nose. Her jet-black hair is up in a high ponytail, and she's got several tattoos all over. I always wondered what he saw in her. I mean, I'm not saying she's not pretty, but I'm just curious how he could want both me and her? We're so different. "Uh ..." She averts her eyes to the notebook in front of her. "Do you have an appointment?" she asks, flipping through the pages quickly.

"No. I'm here to see ..."

"Alexa," Cross says, coming from around the corner with a smile on his face. "What are you doing here?"

My eyes drop to his black combat boots. They run up his ripped jeans and black Kingdom T-shirt. He's got the sleeves rolled up, showing off his tatted forearms.

"She doesn't have an appointment," Rachel growls, still looking for my name in the book.

"I thought that text this morning was an invitation," I answer his previous question, ignoring hers. I said all I needed to say to her when I found her naked in my bed with Mitch.

Reaching up, he rubs his stubble and smiles at me. "It was." Taking my hand, he pulls me down the hallway, both of us ignoring the bitch at the front desk.

I've got so many questions right now, but I shove them down for two reasons. One, they're none of my business. And two, like Haven once said, I'm probably better off not knowing.

He opens a door at the end of the hall and pulls me inside. It only takes a second for us to get undressed before he's fucking me on a tattoo chair.

HE'S ZIPPING UP HIS JEANS WHILE I LIE HERE, CUM DRIPPING out of my cunt with my legs wide open, my skirt pulled up to my waist. I knew I wore this outfit for a reason. This is the kind of stuff you don't learn about sex. When your body is spent and you're so high from your orgasm—if you're lucky—that you just don't give a fuck what you look like.

Reaching over, he hands me a few tissues to clean myself. Once done, I sit up and drape my legs over the side of the chair.

"If a text gets me this kind of treatment, what will a morning phone call get me?" he asks, coming to stand between my legs. He places his hands on my bare thighs, and I know he can feel them still shake. "I could get used to this." He leans forward, nuzzling my neck and kissing my skin.

I throw my head back and take in a deep breath. "Keep doing that." My hands run up and down his back. "And you can have it every day."

A knock on the door has him pulling away, but he stays between my legs, covering my exposed pussy in case whoever it is decides to barge in.

"What?" he demands, making me jump.

"Your next appointment is here," Rachel growls.

"I'll go. I've taken up enough of your time," I say, pushing him away. He takes a few steps back to allow me to get off the chair. I pick up my thong off the floor and then yank down my skirt.

"Dinner tonight?" he asks, pushing my matted hair from my face.

"That sounds like a date." I arch a brow.

"If you consider me eating your pussy while lying naked in my bed, then yes, it's a date," he says, running his tongue across his pretty teeth. God, the guy has a billion-dollar smile. My pussy tightens just thinking about that.

"It's a date," I say, gently kissing his lips, then walking out of the room. As I pass by the front desk, I see Rachel standing there out of the corner of my eye. My skin burns from her glare. "You can write me down for an appointment every day," I throw over my shoulder on my way out.

I make my way up to Empire and see Jasmine already seated. I sit down, and she smiles at me. "You just got fucked, lucky bitch."

I run a hand through my hair to make sure there are no knots. "Maybe. You?" I ask, looking over her perfectly fixed hair and makeup.

She rolls her eyes. "I need twenty chicken nuggets and a Bible."

"Why?" I wonder through a laugh at that combination. "Need to bless some chickens?"

"No. I'm starving and need to repent," she answers, scanning the menu in her hands.

"I didn't take you to be a religious person." I chuckle.

"Well, when I'm on my knees, I'm not praying. If that's what you mean."

The woman sitting in the booth to our left raises her brows, listening to our conversation. "Just what did you do?" I ask.

"What haven't I done is more appropriate," she mumbles, closing the menu and placing it on the table. "Anyway, enough about me. You're obviously still seeing Cross."

I nod. "Seems so."

Jasmine snorts at my vague response. "Well, when a King decides he wants something, there's no escape."

I go to ask what she means by that, but my cell beeps. I pull it out of my purse to see it's another text.

CUNT: Alexa?! Call me ASAP!

I lock my cell and toss it onto the table. Placing my elbows on the edge, I run my hands through my hair in frustration. "I think I need to change my number."

"Fuckface still won't leave you alone?"

"Nope." I sit up straighter. "It wasn't this bad until he saw us with Cross at the Airport."

"You know what we should do?"

I tilt my head to the side. "No. What?" You never really know what will come out of her mouth, so I have no clue what she's thinking about.

"We should design an app called Rate the Dick. Where we upload past sexual encounters and others can leave reviews so women can know what kind of guy they are."

I laugh and nod. "That's a great idea."

"For instance, I got a text from a guy last night that I haven't fucked in over a year. He sent me a picture of his dick." She rolls her eyes. "It was just the picture, then he immediately sent another message saying *sorry, wrong bitch.*"

"Did you respond?" I wonder.

"Of course. I said *still disappointing women, I see.*"

I chuckle, taking a drink of the water that she already had waiting for me.

"He then called me a slut." She shrugs. "Like that was an insult. Please, he was so small I felt like I was scissoring a woman."

I spit that water out all over the table, covering my phone, and the woman next to us chokes on her eggs.

"Like I'd miss that." Jasmine snorts.

I sit back in my seat, cleaning off my cell with my napkin. "I feel the same way about Mitch. I'm not Jesus, nor do I have Alzheimer's. I don't forgive, and I don't forget." All of a sudden, he just expects me to come crawling back to him. It's not going to happen.

"Men. I wish we could kill them after we're done with them," she says with a sigh. "At least that would give us something to look forward to."

"Amen, sister," I agree.

"Anyway, I know the bar keeps you busy. How is the studio doing?"

"I sold it."

"What when?" she asks surprised.

"Last month." I shrug, no biggie. "The people who own the coffee shop beside me wanted to expand and made me an offer I couldn't refuse." My mom had bought a small studio back when she was in college. It was a run-down hole-in-the-wall that her friend's dad was selling. He sold T-shirts out of it. She bought it and turned it into a dance studio. She left it to my brother and me when she passed. Derek wanted nothing to do with it, and I was tired of having to keep up with it. I'd much rather have that money to put into Lucky's someday.

SEVEN
CROSS

I PULL MY black leather jacket on, then glance down at my Rolex. "Fuck! Fuck!"

"What?" Alexa asks. She's hopping around my tattoo shop, trying to get dressed.

We've been meeting up for a couple of weeks now. And when I say hooking up, I mean fucking every damn chance we get. Which is twice today so far. "We're going to be late," I tell her just as I feel my cell vibrate in my back pocket. I pull it out to see it's Titan. "Hey, I'm on my way—"

"You're late," he interrupts me. Titan has this thing about punctuality.

"I know."

"And so is Alexa," he adds. "But you wouldn't know anything about that, would you?"

I roll my eyes. "Nope."

He chuckles softly. "I knew you wouldn't. Anyway, get your ass over here."

"I'm coming ..."

"I'm sure you were." *Click.*

"Fuck," I hiss.

"What now?" she asks, pulling on her white T-shirt before moving on to her black heels. She then goes back to her jeans, zipping them up, and I wish I could remove them again. "I think Titan knows about us."

Her wide green eyes meet mine, and she sucks in a breath. "What? How? Did you say something?"

"Of course not." But honestly, I haven't been all that secretive. At first, I was, but I've been pretty careless. The guys know I've been up to something or someone, but I thought they all had their own shit going on and wouldn't notice my absence. I was wrong. Well, Titan and Bones are always watching. Grave doesn't give a fuck what anyone does. He couldn't care less. But if he knew I was fucking Alexa? He'd care. He'll know I broke my promise. He's been busy with his own shit the past couple of weeks. He hasn't come to me, but I think it's April's brother. Grave's been going to the Airport a lot.

"Then how would he know?"

"Doesn't matter." I grab her hand and yank her out of Tit for Tat.

I lock up the doors to the shop and take her hand once again, turning to the floor. Slot machines are lined up row after row, going off.

"Cross, this isn't good!" she shouts as I drag her across the floor to the elevators.

I rush into one that is open. I'm about to tell her it's okay, but a girl who doesn't look a day over twenty enters behind us with a man who could be her dad. By the way his hand grips her ass, though, I'm guessing that's not the case.

I lean up against the mirrored wall and pull the Zippo out of my pocket with my free hand. I start flipping it open and closed.

Feeling eyes on me, I raise mine to see the girl staring at me. She lets her eyes run down over my Kingdom shirt and to my ripped jeans. Then she looks at Alexa and frowns. Like she's not good enough for me. It's the other way around. I'm not good enough for her. I'm just a plaything. A guaranteed fuck. She'll get tired of me and move on, but until then, I'm going to take advantage of it for now. Men like me don't settle down. We've got too much to prove to the world. Too many wrongs to right. There's no time in our life for women. Not the good kind anyway.

The man's hand slides down her ass and between her legs. She closes her eyes as he leans down and whispers in her ear. The elevator dings, interrupting them, and they walk off.

"Well, that was interesting," Alexa mumbles.

I snort. That's an understatement.

She turns to me, and I do the same. I can't help it. Letting go of her hand, I cup her face with it. Her green eyes search my face. She looks terrified, her white teeth nibbling on her bottom lip. I pull it free with my thumb.

"I told April and Jasmine," she rushes out.

"Okay."

"No, Cross." She steps into me. "I told them about us."

I nod once. "I understood what you meant." *I just don't give a fuck.*

"I mean, it was right after the first night. But only Jasmine knows we've been hooking up for a few weeks now." She pulls away from me to pace the small space. "I couldn't keep it a secret from April. She's my best friend. They both promised me they wouldn't tell anyone. And I believe them. But if Titan knows ..."

"Hey." I grip her arm, yanking her to a stop. "It's okay."

"But—"

"It wasn't April or Jasmine. It was me," I interrupt her, but she goes on.

"We said that no one was to know." She looks on the verge of tears, and I wonder why she's so upset. We're allowed to do whatever we want to do.

"Alexa ..."

She pulls away from me, and I let her go. "Grave cannot know what we're doing. You said so yourself. You promised him." She runs a hand nervously through her bleach-blond hair. "April thinks Grave is fragile right now." I frown at that because he seems fine to me. A little preoccupied, but definitely okay. I haven't seen him this determined to be his best self ... since ever. "And if he found out you've been lying to him ..."

"Alexa, calm down." I bring her to a stop once again. "I'll tell him tonight, okay? Does that make you feel better?"

She averts her eyes to her heels and nods her head once.

"Come here." I pull her into my chest and hug her tightly, kissing her forehead. "You're getting all worked up over nothing."

"I just ..." She sighs heavily, wrapping her arms around my chest. "I just worry about April and Grave, you know? I want them to be happy. They deserve that."

"Hey." I pull back just enough to cup her chin and force her to look up at me. "They are happy. And you and me having sex isn't going to ruin that."

The elevator comes to a stop once again. "Come on." I grab her hand and pull her off at our stop. A man who I know as Mack stands by the outside of the elevator. "Hey, Cross." He nods at us, and I don't like the way his eyes linger on her chest. I hold her hand a little tighter.

I nod back and walk down the long hallway. Taking a right at the end, I come to a door that reads **_Grave_** across it.

"Maybe we should go in separately," Alexa offers, pulling me to a stop.

I think about that for a second. Titan is the one who guessed it, but that doesn't mean he's told the others. "Sure." I nod. Alexa is already upset about the situation, and I don't want to make it worse. "You go in first. I'll come in after."

Letting go of my hand, she enters, and I wait a beat before doing so myself. I'm not going to stand out here forever. If they figure it out, then they figure it out.

Ten heads turn to look at me. "Made it!" I throw my hands up.

Bones stands, leaning up against the counter to the far right with his tatted arms crossed over his chest. Titan stands next to him, legs spread while Emilee stands between them with her back to his front. His arms around her shoulders. Grave sits on the black leather table, his legs dangling over the edge in nothing but a pair of black shorts that reads KINGDOM in gold letters on the waistband. April stands next to him. Alexa is beside her. She avoids looking at me directly while pretending to read something on her phone. A thought crosses my mind that it's that fucker, Mitch. I have yet to ask her about him. I'm afraid she'd take it the wrong way because women always over-think shit. And when you start asking about exes, they think you're considering a future with them. Case in point—what just happened on the elevator.

Jasmine sits on the counter next to Bones, and Nite stands leaning up against the far wall. Luca and his wife, Haven, stand to the left of him. All conversations come to an abrupt stop, making me feel like I interrupted something. I'll ask Alexa later if they did the same thing when she entered.

"About time," Titan announces.

"Yeah, well, I was a little busy."

Grave snorts. "I hope you weren't fucking that assistant of yours."

Alexa's head snaps up, and her eyes land on mine. I don't say anything to that, but I do see that Titan notices Alexa's gaze burning a hole in me, confirming what he was already guessing. We haven't had the Rachel speech. She's never asked, and I've never offered any information on her.

"Your assistant at Tit for Tat?" Emilee is the one who speaks. "She was very rude to me that one time I was looking for you." She crosses her arms over her chest at that memory when she was trying to find the Palace suite. "She acted like I was going to fuck you right then and there in your shop when I just needed help finding Titan."

I watch Jasmine tense. She and April both know about Alexa and me. So, they think I'm fucking both of them. Why do I want to correct them? Biting my tongue, I decide now is not the time. I need to tell Grave first and not in front of everyone. After his fight, I'll get him alone and fill him in.

Grave adds, "Yeah, Rachel's had a thing for him ever since Cross hired her." He shakes his head with a laugh. "I told him not to fuck her, but he couldn't resist."

Fuck!

Titan's eyes go back and forth between Alexa and me, but she's no longer looking at me. Her eyes are back down on her cell, and she's typing away. *It better not be to fucking Mitch.*

"Grave ..." April stands in front of him, patting his legs. "It's none of our business who Cross gets with."

He just laughs as she tries to divert the conversation.

"I'm not sleeping with her," I add quickly, watching to see how Alexa reacts. Nothing. Her eyes stayed glued to her phone.

"Maybe not right this very second." Grave snorts.

Emilee smiles. "I hope you fired her then."

Nope. But it's on my list of things to do now. She's been acting weird ever since I told her I didn't give a fuck who she slept with. And then add the fact that she saw me with Alexa. Rachel has left me alone, but she still seems to linger around the shop after her shift is over. The other day, I caught her standing behind me, silently reading my text over my shoulder. I think she thought she'd get a glimpse of a text between Alexa and me, but I was talking to Titan. Should have fired her right then and there, but I was in a hurry to get out of there to meet up with Alexa. I was running late.

The door behind me opens, and a man speaks. "You've got five minutes, Grave."

April pats his thigh. "We're going to go take our seats. Be careful, okay?"

He reaches out, sliding his hand into her purple hair, and leans forward, kissing her. "Always," he tells her when he pulls away.

ALEXA

I WALK OUT of the room with the girls while the guys stay behind to be with Grave before he fights. I try to smooth my hair without the girls noticing that Cross's hands were in it just minutes ago. My legs still shake, and my thong is now wet. I didn't get a chance to clean up, and I hate that. I'm going to have to sneak away to the restroom shortly.

My hand tightens on the railing as I try to walk down the stairs in my heels. The place is crawling with people. Kingdom has one of the largest convention centers in Las Vegas with over ten thousand seats, and it's a packed house tonight. They currently have the lights turned down low, making it already hard to see while "New Kings" by Sleeping Wolf blares through the speakers.

April is walking in front of me. She slows to meet my pace and whispers in my ear, "I'm sorry about that."

"It's fine." I dismiss her. Cross can sleep with whoever he wants. We never said it was exclusive. Hell, it was never supposed to be more than once. By the way that Rachel acted the first time I saw her at Tit for Tat, I knew they had something going on. Maybe not right then, but they definitely had a past.

"Hey." She brings me to a stop, and the rest of the girls keep walking. "I know you, and you don't do one-night stands. You don't do hookups."

I place my hands on her shoulders. "Thanks for worrying about me, April. But I'm fine. I promise. Cross and I are just hooking up. There is nothing else there." I shrug. "If he wants to fuck someone else, then I can too." I can't say I'm lying, but the thought of him also fucking Rachel makes me sick to my stomach. Just because of who she is.

She bites her purple-painted lip and then wraps her arms around my shoulder before we descend the rest of the stairs.

I didn't expect Cross to be a virgin, but I do expect honesty. So, maybe we just need to sit down and go over some guidelines. If we decide to continue this.

The girls and I make it down to our front row seats and sit right behind the ring card girls. The lights shut off completely, bathing us in darkness. So much for using the restroom. It'll just have to wait. The lights start blinking, making it hard to focus on anything. The crowd is whooping and hollering as "King of the World" by WAR HALL begins to play.

They announce Grave's opponent, and everyone boos him. When Grave starts coming down the aisle, the crowd's noise is so loud, you can't hear yourself think. I lift my hands, placing them over my ears. He enters the ring as the rest of the Kings stand next to it, watching and coaching him on.

The girls and I jump to our feet, watching intently. Jasmine stands to my right, her elbow linked through mine. I can feel pins and needles on my skin as I watch Grave block a hit and serve his own. I'm not sure why I'm so nervous. April stands to my left. I feel her hand curl around my forearm, and her nails dig into my skin.

"He's going to be okay!" I shout over the crowd, trying to calm her even though I know it won't do any good.

Grave gets hit and stumbles back a few feet. Her nails dig even deeper, and I hiss in a breath. "April, he's ..." I look over at her, and my breath catches. She's bent over. Her dark purple hair shielding her face from me, but I know something's wrong. "April?" I shout, bending over as well. The process pulls my arm free from Jasmine. "April? You okay?" I ask, pulling her hair away from her face.

Her eyes are tightly shut, her free hand rests on her stomach, and tears run down her face.

"What's wrong?" Jasmine calls out, also noticing.

"I don't know—"

"The baby," April interrupts me. "Something's ... wrong," she cries.

"Take her to the hospital," Jasmine orders Haven and me.

"Get Grave!" Emilee shouts as the crowd roars, letting me know that Grave is pulling ahead.

"No ..." April protests, shaking her head quickly.

As much as I hate to say it, it's too late. None of us can stop the fight. And I don't want Emilee trying to stop it just to cause a distraction and get Grave hurt.

"Take her to the hospital. Emilee and I will come with the guys as soon as Grave is done," Jasmine orders, bending down and handing me April's purse.

EIGHT

CROSS

THE THING YOU need to know about the Kings is that we are brothers—some by blood, others by choice—so when one of us is hurting, we are all hurting. And right now, we're all in hell—burning alive.

I sit at the conference table on the thirteenth floor of tower one at Kingdom. Titan sits across from me, silently staring at the skull carved out of the table that easily seats twenty people. Bones takes his seat at the head of the table. Silence fills the room. No one really knows what to say. We're not men who make small talk. And nothing any of us say could change what happened last night.

"Okay ..." Bones starts but is interrupted.

The door opens, and Grave enters. He looks like shit. His hair is standing straight up, going every direction. Eyes red and face splotchy. He holds a bottle of water in his hand, looking hungover. But I know that's not the case. Grave has come a long way in the past few months from who he once was before April entered his life.

"Kyle." Bones jumps to his feet, calling his brother by his real name with concern. "What are you doing here?"

Grave makes his way over to the table and falls down beside

Titan. "Where else would I be?" he asks, unable to meet his brother's eyes. His voice sounds as tired as he looks.

Bones runs a hand through his hair and lets out a long breath, softening his voice. "You should be at home. With April."

He doesn't say anything to that. Just sits there staring off into nothing. After he won his fight last night, we went back to the room to celebrate. Jasmine and Emilee had come running in to tell us that they didn't know what was going on, just that Haven and Alexa had taken April to the hospital.

Grave ran out of there so fast we couldn't keep up. Once we arrived at the hospital, we found out April had lost the baby. As much as my heart breaks for Grave and April, I'm also terrified that this will throw him over the edge. Grave is a recovering addict, and he's been doing so well. I couldn't be prouder of him, but this? How do you get through such a loss? Grave has always felt things more than anyone I've ever known. He would drown those feelings with booze, sex, drugs. Whatever he could get his hands on.

Bones walks around the table to stand behind his brother and places his hand on his shoulder. Grave jumps at the contact and pulls away. "Go home, Grave," Bones tells him with sad eyes. "Go home and be with April."

Grave's eyes drop to his hands resting on the table. "She doesn't want me there," he whispers. "She got up this morning and went to work."

I look at Titan, and he's frowning. I mean, I know everyone handles loss differently, but this? They lost their child. Why aren't they at home grieving together? How are they up and functioning? I've never wanted children, but that doesn't mean I can't sympathize with what they're going through.

Titan licks his lips. "Grave, it's okay to feel—"

"Don't tell me how to feel!" Grave explodes, knocking his fists on the table. "I'm here to fucking work. Let's work," he snarls.

Silence follows his outburst, and I sigh, fidgeting with my Zippo. Bones walks back over to his chair and nods once. "Okay.

Let's start the meeting. Have we heard anything about the shipments?"

"No," I answer.

Bones growls. Everyone is getting extremely irritated about these damn shipments. Someone somewhere has to know what's going on.

"Maybe we should just order a shipment of our own," Titan suggests.

"That'd be too suspicious." I shake my head.

"How so?" he asks.

"Because we don't buy diamonds," I answer with a growl. "I think it would look obvious that we killed one of Kale's men when we walk in and start purchasing shipments worth millions in diamonds from him."

Bones rubs his chin, thinking it over. Grave stays silent, staring off into nothing. Physically, he came into work today, but mentally he's in another universe.

"What if we partnered with the Masons?" Titan offers, sitting up straighter looking over at Bones. "They make the order, but Cross and I go with him to pick it up. They can say they've hired us for protection."

I give a rough laugh. "Everyone knows the Mason brothers are like us. They are their own protection."

"What do you suggest?" Titan snaps at me. "That we do nothing?"

"You know how I feel about the Masons," Bones adds, ignoring Titan's outburst.

"I'm not a fan of them either, but we need to get to the bottom of this before our client comes after us for not getting the information that we promised," Titan adds.

Bones lets out a frustrated sigh, and I know Titan has won. "Fine. But take Nite with you. Three is better than two." With that, he gets up leaving the room.

ALEXA

I'm behind the bar at Lucky's when my cell vibrates in my back pocket. I pull it out to see Cross is calling me. Although it's after closing hours, I make my way to the back office to take the call because I don't want my brother to hear my conversation. He hasn't said one word to me since he found out I was sleeping with Cross. Just shows up to work his shifts and then goes home. "Hello?"

"Hey," he says softly.

I drop my head and look down at my black boots. I haven't spoken to him since last night. Haven and I were with April when they informed her complications were causing her to miscarry the baby. Grave arrived shortly after. I wanted to stay for her, but I left with Jasmine, knowing that she and Grave wanted to be left alone.

"I would ask how your day went, but I bet it was about as good as mine was." He sighs.

"Grave ignoring you like April is ignoring me?" I ask. I've tried reaching out to her a hundred times today, and my calls have gone unanswered, my text unread.

"I wish that were the case. All of a sudden, the guy has fallen headfirst into Kingdom. He's been practically MIA for years, and now Bones can't get him to leave. You said April is ignoring you?"

I fall into the chair at the desk, making it squeak with my weight. "Yeah, I've been calling her, but it goes straight to voicemail. This afternoon, I found myself taking the long way to work and drove by Roses and saw her car. I went in, and she totally blew me off." She pretended to be busier than I know she was. I took the hint and left, not wanting to add more stress.

"I just hate it for them," he says softly.

"Me too," I say, placing my right elbow on the old wooden desk and my face in my hand. I've been friends with April since we were kids. We've been through a lot together, but she's never shut me out like this.

"Alexa." He sighs my name, and I close my eyes, expecting him to end this. Too much is going on. Grave needs him now more than ever. We can't continue sneaking around like this. He was going to come clean with Grave last night after his fight. He can't do that now. "About yesterday."

I open my eyes and frown as I stare at my messy desk. "What about it?"

"Before Grave went to fight. Him bringing up Rachel—"

"It's fine," I interrupt him. Another thing that seems small compared to everything else.

"No. It's not."

I sit back and run a hand down my face. I'm too exhausted to go into his line of women right now. "It is, Cross. We're not together. You can fuck whoever you want."

There's a long pause on his end. I pull it away from my ear to make sure he hasn't hung up on me. Instead, he changes the subject. "What are you doing once you're done at the bar?"

I look up at the clock on the wall. It's almost three a.m. We've been closed for half an hour. "Going home," I answer. It's been a long twenty-four hours, and I'm exhausted. I didn't get much sleep last night, and I doubt I will tonight either. April is heavy on my mind, and I feel like my hands are tied. I can't do anything to help her.

"Why don't you come up to Kingdom?" he offers.

I bite my lower lip. "For what exactly?"

"Stay the night with me," he answers as if I should have known that's what he meant.

I stand, needing the space. "Are you sure that's a good thing? I mean, although everyone suspects what we're doing, we haven't actually told them. And what if someone sees us? It's not the time—"

"No one is here tonight," he interrupts me. "Titan hasn't stayed here since he married Emilee. Bones is still working and will be doing it all night because that's just what he does. And Grave left hours ago to go home. I'm guessing to be with April. It'll just be you and me."

"Yeah," I say. Maybe a good night fuck is what I need to help me sleep. "I'll text you when I'm on my way." I hang up before he can say anything else.

I pocket my cell and exit the office just in time to see my brother grab his jacket. He doesn't even acknowledge me with a head nod. Just walks toward the exit. I hear the back door open and close, and I start to wipe down the bar. It's the last thing I have to do before I can get out of here. But the front door opens, getting my attention, and I frown when I realize that he didn't lock it before he left. We always exit out the back since that's where we park. The alley isn't the safest place this late at night. Hell, nowhere in this town is safe this time of night. Why chance it?

I'm thinking of ways I can beat his ass for his lack of responsibility when I look up to see a redhead enter the bar with a smile on her face and an oversized Louis Vuitton on her shoulder. She's harmless. "Hey, girl," Jasmine greets me.

"Hey." I smile at her, but it drops the second I catch sight of Bones entering behind her.

Cross and I don't typically talk or share life experiences when we're together. We definitely don't discuss the other Kings. My brother has said some stuff in the past regarding Bones—he runs with the Mafia or some shit like that. Honestly, I wouldn't be all that surprised if it was true. Cross had mentioned Bones was working at Kingdom tonight, so why is he here?

"What's up?" I ask as she plops down across from me at the bar. Bones takes the seat next to her, not saying a word. I look away from him and his blue eyes. The guy is as intimidating as he is rich.

"Remember the first time you met me?" she asks, avoiding my question.

"Yeah." I draw out the single word.

A YEAR AGO

I'M STANDING BEHIND THE BAR; IT'S A FRIDAY NIGHT AND PACKED. There's some convention in town, so the bar is busier than usual. I'm having problems keeping up with the large crowd. A man walks up and slaps down a twenty, rambling off what he wants.

"Excuse me?" I yell over the music and turn my face to give him my ear when my eyes land on a woman sitting at the end of the bar with a man. She's laughing at something he said while looking down at her full drink I had just served her. Reaching out, she places her hand on his shoulder and leans in, speaking into his ear. He nods a few times, and she gets up, heading to the bathroom.

"Did you get that?" the guy yells in my ear.

I pull away, holding up a finger to him when I see the guy now sitting alone, looking around nervously.

"Miss?" the guy calls out again, trying to get my attention, but I ignore him. My eyes remain focused on the other man. He reaches into his pocket, pulling out his fist. He takes another quick look around before dropping a pill into her drink. Picking up the glass, he swirls it around to dissolve the evidence and then quickly sets it back down.

I rush over to my brother, who stands a few feet from me. "Call the police," I say into his ear.

"What?" He turns to face me.

"Do it now. Tell them a guy just tried to drug a woman." Before he can respond, I run out from behind the bar and rush to the bathroom, shoving customers out of my way.

I enter the women's restroom and come to a stop when I see the woman standing at the sink fixing her lipstick. "I need to talk to you."

"You saved my life." Jasmine gives me a smile, interrupting the memory.

I shuffle from foot to foot uncomfortably, not wanting to rehash this conversation, especially in front of Bones. "I wouldn't go that far ..."

"I would. The cops arresting that guy led to them uncovering a sex trafficking ring. You saved me."

My face heats up, turning red. I don't do well with compliments.

"Anyway," she goes on. "I tried to repay you ..."

I snort at that statement. "The next day, you showed up with a two-hundred-thousand-dollar car." A woman I had only met the night before bought me a car. I thought she was out of her mind. I still think that.

"I told you I'd pay for the tag and insurance ..."

"I'm not accepting it," I remind her. She does this often. She still has it in her garage. As though I'm just going to call her up one day and say *hey, you know that Audi R8 Spyder you bought me? Yeah, I'll take that now.*

"This isn't about the car." She reaches into her Louis Vuitton bag and pulls out a large manila envelope. Setting it on the bar, she pushes it toward me.

"What's this?" I ask.

"This is me repaying you."

I look from her to Bones, but he still hasn't said one word. His blue eyes are on mine, and I look away. His stare is so intense it makes me nervous.

Opening up the envelope, I pull out a set of papers. **KINK** is written across the top of it in bold black letters. Never heard of it before. "What is this?"

"I want to go into business with you," she states.

I begin to laugh but immediately stop when neither one of them joins me. I clear my throat at the awkward silence that follows. "Business? What kind of business?" Is this like her Rate the Dick app idea?

"Kink is an elite BDSM club. I recently found out about it when I was in New York. It's a gold mine, Lex. We've spoken to the owner of the New York location, and he wants to meet with us this weekend."

I run a hand through my bleach-blond hair. "I ... uh, you want to own a sex club?" I didn't even know they existed. I mean, you hear about shit like this, but I've never been to one before.

"Yes." She clasps her hands.

I open my mouth, but nothing comes out, so I close it. Taking in a deep breath, I try again. "You want to turn my bar into a sex club?"

"No." She shakes her head quickly. "Just your basement. You own the bar. A hundred percent yours. I just want to go in on Kink with you. We renovate the basement that you don't use into the club, and I'll run it. You can be involved as much or little as you want, but we split the profit fifty-fifty."

I look at Bones. "What do you have to do with this?" I'm curious as to why he's here with her. What is his involvement?

He leans forward, placing his tatted forearms on the bar, and I find myself leaning back just a bit, hoping he doesn't notice. "Kink is an exclusive men's club, per se. They have twenty-five locations around the world. Not a single one is owned or run by a woman."

None of that sentence answered what I just asked. "Meaning?" I frown, needing further explanation. I'm fucking tired.

"Meaning that we need Bones as a partner," Jasmine answers.

"So, you will own a percentage of it?" I clarify. How would Jasmine and I be fifty-fifty if he owns a portion as well?

"Just on paper," he states.

"He's not taking anything from Kink. Bones is not investing any up-front costs or involvement whatsoever. Dillan Reed is just a name on a piece of paper."

I'm guessing Dillan Reed is his real name. Which, if you ask me, doesn't fit him at all. *Bones?* That makes more sense. The guy looks like he'd beat you to death with his fists. Or a hammer. Whatever is closest to him at the time.

I drop my eyes to read over the documents some more. I see two million, and my mouth drops. "Jasmine," My gaze shoots to hers. "I don't have this kind of money."

"You don't need it. I've got it covered," she rushes out.

Is she insane? Shaking my head, I shove the contract back over to them. "No."

"Alexa—"

"I'm not doing it." I turn, walking into the cooler just to get away from them.

The door opens behind me, and Jasmine enters. "Just hear me out," she says, placing her hands up defensively.

"The answer is no." I reach down and grab a case of Bud Light even though I'm not sure what the fuck I'm going to do with it.

"Lex." She places her hands on my shoulders and spins me around to face her. "I told you I would repay you for what you did. And this is my payment."

"Even if I agreed, I can't *repay* you." I have some money saved up after selling the studio, but not even close enough to cover my half. And I believe in paying your way. I'm not a leech.

"Your friendship is all the payment I need." She removes her hands from my shoulders and takes the beer from mine, setting it on the floor by my feet. "Look, Kink will be a success. You know how I know?" She doesn't let me answer. "Because I'm going to devote my life to it."

That's not what I'm concerned about. "It's not fair," I argue. "For you to put up all that money and me nothing."

"You saved me," she whispers, dropping her eyes to her red Louboutin heels. "No one has ever done that for me before."

My chest tightens for her. She may be a friend of mine, but Jasmine keeps a lot to herself. She hides her sadness and insecurities behind jokes and sarcasm. "Jasmine, that's what friends do. They look out for one another."

"But you weren't my friend at the time," she says, her green eyes meeting mine once again. "Come to New York with Bones and me. Visit Kink with us. If you're not one-hundred-and-fifty-percent sold after that, then we don't do it."

"Why my bar?" She has the money to buy any space on the Strip. I mean, sure it's not like real estate is available everywhere here, but she's got to find something better with all the connections she has in this city. *Why mine?*

She gives me a warm smile. "I already told you. This isn't about the space or the location. It's about you. This is about someone once helping me and me returning the favor." She steps into me. "Let me do this for you, Lex. For us."

With a sigh, my mind wanders to the possibility of us doing this. "I don't know anything about a sex club." That's my only argument.

She laughs softly. "You think I do?" Shaking her head, she adds, "But I do know that I won't let you down, Lex. I've got this. Please trust me."

"And Bones?" I ask, trying to think of any excuse to get out of it. I hate to admit that it sounds like a great opportunity, but things are never as they seem. "What if he fucks us?" If the man is in with the Mafia, then he has some serious fucking pull in this town.

"Bones is not that type of guy. I swear on it. He will not fuck us over in any way with this deal. He's a best friend, and he just wants to help us as much as I want to help us. I trust him."

I've always wanted something more for myself. What if this is it? I'm not a religious person, but what if this is my chance? God throwing me a bone, saying let this woman help you? I never thought it'd be a sex club, but prayers never come how you asked for them. "I'll go to New York," I say, letting out a breath. What could it hurt?

She squeals, jumps up and down, and then wraps her arms around me.

"But I can't promise anything," I add quickly.

"I understand." She takes a step back and nods once, a huge smile on her face. And I can't help but do the same.

NINE
CROSS

I OPEN THE door to our Royal suite to see Alexa standing at the door. She's got her purse in one hand and her cell in the other. "Come in."

She steps inside and looks around. The guys and I have lived here since we took over Kingdom four years ago. We have a family compound outside of the city but living here is just easier. A casino never sleeps, so neither do we. We're always on call and need to be here in case something happens. But Bones and I are the only ones left who ever stay here anymore.

"Would you like a drink?" I offer.

"Please. Vodka." She sits down at the bar and sighs heavily.

"Everything okay?" I ask, knowing April is heavy on her mind.

Running a hand through her blond hair, she answers, "Not really."

I set the drink down in front of her. "What happened?"

She picks it up and just holds it. "Jasmine and Bones showed up at the bar tonight after I spoke to you."

I frown. "Together?"

"Yeah. She ... well, they had a business opportunity for me."

"What kind?" I'm not really all that surprised. Bones owns multiple businesses. He tries to keep them under wraps, but we all pretend we don't know.

She sets the drink down and pulls out some papers, placing them on the bar. I pick them up and read over them. "So, she's doing it."

"You knew she wanted to do this?" she asks, arching a dark brow.

"Well, I've heard talk. Titan and Bones went to New York a while back with the girls. Jasmine was upset when she didn't get to go to Kink with them. What's so bad about this?"

"I've always wanted something more, but I feel like now is the worst time." She sighs.

"Why is that?"

She drops her eyes to the bar top. "April."

I let out a breath.

"She's going through so much right now. I shouldn't be going to New York and starting up a new business. I should be here for her."

I place the papers down and walk around the bar. Touching her face, I force her to look up at me. Her pretty green eyes look tired. "You can't make someone open up to you, Alexa. All you can do is tell them that you're there for them. It's up to them when they choose to do so."

"I know." She pulls away. "But what if she doesn't know I'm here for her?"

"She does." Just like Grave knows we're here for him as well. He's just choosing to push us all away. That's Grave. I'm not going to force him to talk to me, but he knows we're here when he's ready.

"I just hate it." She picks up the papers, and her eyes look them over. "The timing sucks, you know?"

"It usually does," I agree with her. "But what if this is your chance and you miss it? April wouldn't want you to pass on it because of her."

"I guess." She sets the papers back down and picks up the drink, taking a sip. Setting it back down on the bar, she keeps a hold of it, staring off into the kitchen.

I remove it from her hand, and her eyes meet mine. "Come on." I say, pulling her off the barstool and toward my bedroom. We enter, and I don't even bother turning the light on. I've got the curtains pulled shut like usual. I like my room pitch-black when I sleep. I see the lights of Sin City every day. When I'm here, I like to shut the world out.

I find her face and cup either side of it. My lips touch hers gently, and I kiss her, just feeling her out. I didn't call her to come over just to fuck her. If that was the case, I'd kick her out afterward. Every time she's come over, she's stayed until the next day. I like falling asleep with her next to me. If she's here with me, she's not somewhere else with Mitch.

Her hands grip my shirt, and she kisses me back, more aggressively than I had planned, but I take the invitation.

My hands drop to her shirt, and I rip it up and over her head, only parting our lips to do so. Then they're back on hers. I bend down, grab her thighs and lift her off her feet before both of us go falling onto my bed. She's moaning underneath me, and I continue to devour her mouth with mine. Lifting my hips, I slide my hand down her stomach and into her jeans. She spreads her legs for me the best she can while I find her pussy. I slide a finger in, immediately finger-fucking her wet cunt.

She pulls away and gasps for breath. I trail kisses down her chest to her breast, yanking her damn bra out of the way. I should have ripped her clothes off the moment she walked into the suite. Taking a nipple into my mouth, it hardens as I suck on it. My teeth gently nibble on it, and she cries out, arching her back. Removing my hand from her pants, I sit up and quickly undo them. She helps me get them off, then I'm undoing mine. I pull out my already hard dick and slide into her. No foreplay. No condom.

Fuck those. I've used them before, but I'm not going to with her. We haven't yet, so why start now?

I have the urge to go slow with her tonight and make love to her, which is fucking ridiculous. I don't do that shit. But I under-

93

stand the situation. She's exhausted, and I'm just a needy moth-erfucker.

Pulling out of her, I slowly enter her, and she tightens around my cock. I groan, "Fuck, baby."

"Cross." She sighs, her arms coming around my neck.

I grab her hands, intertwining our fingers together, and pin them down next to her head and start moving a little faster, but still going slow enough just to tease her.

Her heels dig into my ass, trying to get me to speed up, but I'm not going to budge. I know what I want and how I want it.

"Please ..."

I cover her mouth with mine and swallow her words as I continue teasing her while wondering if she did this with Mitch. Did he love her? Did he just fuck her? What happened between them that made them break up? If I'm being honest with myself, I'd say I'm sorry for the son of a bitch. Because I don't want to fuck this up.

ALEXA

SLIDING OUT OF Cross's bed, I grab my cell off the nightstand and tiptoe to his adjoining bathroom so I don't wake him. He just fell asleep a few minutes ago. Turning on the soft light, I look down at my cell. It's a little after five in the morning. He'll only get about a two-hour nap at this point.

I open my messages and go to April's.

> Me: If you need anything, just let me know. Even if it's just to talk. Or you need someone to listen. Please, know I'm here. Love you.

I send the message and close my eyes. I hate it for my best friend, for Grave, and for all the Kings. I know they all feel a loss.

My phone vibrates, signaling I have a message, and I open it up.

> April: I do need a favor. Can you cover
> Roses for me Friday morning for a few
> hours?

> Me: Yes. Everything okay?

After I send it, I roll my eyes and wish I could delete it. *Of course, she's not okay, Alexa!*

> April: Yes.

She's lying, but why? Why won't she just come out and talk to me? I don't know how to respond to that, so I take the fact that she even messaged me back as a good sign and leave it at that. At least she is asking for help, even if it's for something small.

Turning the light off, I make my way back through his pitch-black bedroom, hoping not to trip over the trail of clothes on the floor. I manage to get onto the bed and crawl in next to him.

He moves, and I stiffen, hoping I didn't wake him. I feel his body shift, and then he's pressed up against my back, wrapping an arm around my waist and pulling me into him. I relax and close my eyes.

I WAKE TO DARKNESS AND STRETCH OUT, BLINKING A FEW TIMES for my eyes to adjust but still nothing.

Reaching over, I run my hand over the nightstand and feel for my cell. I grab it and light up the screen, making me blink rapidly at the bright light. "Shit." I sigh, seeing that it's almost eleven o'clock. Rolling over onto my side, I pull up Cross's number and call him.

"There she is," he answers, sounding cheerful. "Good morning, gorgeous."

I groan but hate that I smile at the way he calls me gorgeous. "Why didn't you wake me when you left?"

"I wanted you to sleep. I kissed you goodbye, and you didn't even

95

move."

He kissed me goodbye? Why does that make my breath quicken? "Well, you should have tried harder." His head between my legs would have done the trick.

He chuckles. "I'll remember that next time."

"Seriously." I push my hair from my face and sit up, feeling his cool sheets on my naked body. If I was him, I'd never leave this bed. "I don't like being here without you."

There's a long silence on his end before he speaks. "Why?" he asks, sounding concerned all of a sudden.

"Because what if one of the Kings sees me here?" This is their suite. I'd hate for Bones to find me in the kitchen making coffee. I just feel like I'm not allowed here if Cross isn't here.

He sighs. "I hate to tell you, Alexa, but at this point, they know what we're doing."

"Not Grave." Cross had planned on telling him, but I know that conversation never took place. Not with everything else that has happened since then.

"You're right. But he won't be coming there anytime soon. Now, lie back down and get some more sleep," he offers.

I smile at his bossiness and lie back down. "It's almost noon. I've slept long enough." But as I say it, I yawn.

"See," he states, hearing me, and I laugh. "How about this? You go back to bed, and I'll take lunch in an hour."

"Meaning?" I arch a brow, staring up into the darkness of his bedroom.

"I promise I'll wake you up this time."

"How can a girl turn that down?" I joke, nibbling on the end of my nail.

"You don't get a choice. Now, get some rest. See you soon." He hangs up.

I drop the phone to my chest and smile to myself. As much as I want to go back to sleep, I don't. Instead, I get up and go into his bathroom. I need to prepare his lunch after all.

TEN

CROSS

I HANG UP and pocket my cell phone, ignoring the look Titan is giving me. I wasn't lying to her. At this point, everyone knows except for Grave.

"So—"

"None of your business," I interrupt Titan and he laughs. "Let's go."

Titan, Nite, and I enter the Airport through the double doors off the parking lot. We make our way over to the elevators and hit the button for the fifth floor. When the doors open, a man stands on either side with a machine gun in his hands.

They nod at us. "Kings, Nite. Mr. Mason is waiting on you."

"Thanks, Harry." Titan nods back at him. As much as shady shit goes on here, the Mason brothers have very tight security on this level. Their operation isn't anything like Kingdom. It's not legal. Everything they do is off the books. They have millions of dollars stashed all over the Airport. We may not be on the up and up, but Kingdom is a good front for other things. The Airport is not. They make very large payments to very important people in this state to keep their doors open. Everyone wants their cut.

We walk to the door at the end of the hall and step inside. The table that normally has people crowded around it is empty, which is surprising. People are always in here doing drugs off it or counting out cash. Turner must have cleared them out for us.

I walk to the closed door at the back of the room, knowing it's their office. I knock on it.

"Come in." I hear Turner call out.

We enter the room, and Turner Mason sits behind the desk on his cell phone. He holds up a finger for us to give him a second, and he stands, turning his back to us. "I said that wouldn't be acceptable," he snaps. "Get it fucking done!" He hangs up and turns back around. "To what do I owe this pleasure?" he asks, sitting back down in his seat and gesturing for us to do the same.

"We need you to set up a meeting with Kale," I say, getting to the point.

"Kale Freeman?" he asks, making sure he heard me right.

"Yes," Titan clips.

He leans back in his chair. "Interested in the diamond business, Kings? That's surprising." His eyes slide to Nite, who of course hasn't said a word. He never does. Sometimes I forget he's even in the room when I'm with him. Then he looks at Titan. "I'm guessing this has to do with your client and their shipment. I'm going to need a little more to go on if you want me to set up a friend of mine."

If it's smuggled into the country, Turner knows where from and by who. Working for the cartel has given him inside information about everything. He's also their personal hitman. He takes out their competition for them, keeping them on top.

Titan snorts. "Kale isn't friends with anyone. He's only looking out for himself."

"Funny, I've heard people say that about the Kings," Turner states.

Titan jumps up from his seat, and I grab his hand, standing myself. "Yes, this is about the shipment." Things have changed. We've gotten nowhere.

98

He brings his right hand up to his face, slowly running his finger over his lips. "What's in it for me?"

"Half the shipment," I state.

His eyes widen for a brief second, and he sits up straighter. "Let me get this straight. A buyer came to you and said that he's missing a shipment that he purchased from Kale?" I nod. "And that buyer is willing to give half of it away for a finder's fee?"

"Something like that," Titan growls.

Turner smirks, sitting back in his seat again. He places his right ankle up on his left knee. "What's in it for you?" He asks the billion-dollar question.

"Kale Freeman," I say simply.

"Ah, I see. They want you to retrieve the shipment and then kill him for his lack of business skills." He chuckles.

"That's what happens when you're not true to your word," Titan states. "Guys have been killed for less."

I sigh, not wanting this to turn into a pissing contest. "You set up the meeting for you. We just happen to tag along. You place an order, and we track it. See just how long the process takes and if you actually receive it."

"And what happens to me?" he asks, hands out wide. "When Kale is dead, and his men connect the dots?"

I smile. "We take over his business. His buyers will have no choice but to come to us. As partners."

He tilts his head to the side. "The Kings and the Masons in bed together."

Titan snorts, looking away from him with disgust.

"Well, Luca and Nite will be involved as well." It's a multibillion-dollar business. We can all split it and still see massive profits.

"How does Bones feel about this?" he asks. Grave and Trey Turner—the baby brother—used to be best friends. But things got heated, and they got in trouble. Tanner Mason—the eldest brother—went to jail for Trey. Bones has hated them ever since. None of us really know what happened or how it went down, but it's in the past.

Tanner is now free, but when he went into the slammer, Turner took over the business. He still handles most of it.

"We wouldn't be here if he didn't agree." I lie. He doesn't know the extent of our plan that Titan and I discussed on the way here. Nite agreed with head nods. But I'll fill Bones in when it all works out.

"Well, Kings ..." He stands, straightening his suit jacket and offering his right hand. "Let's get us a meeting."

Exiting his office, I quickly glance at my watch. I'm glad this didn't take long because I've got a gorgeous blonde sleeping in my bed who I need to wake up.

ALEXA

FRIDAY AFTERNOON, I'M at Roses—April's flower shop that her mother left her when she passed away—when Jasmine and Emilee walk in. "How's your day been?" Jasmine asks.

"Good," I answer, closing out my banking app on my phone. Ever since she came to me about Kink, I've had all kinds of ideas running through my mind for Lucky's. I hate it. The hopes. The dreams. Things I've wanted to do for years and now feel like this is my chance to make those changes. If not, when? I've been too afraid to make any changes to the bar in case I fail. But now, I have a reason. A chance to actually do better. To grow. But it's not going to come free.

Like Cross said, timing is rarely on our side.

"So, did April ever tell you why she wanted you to cover for her today?" Jasmine asks.

I shake my head as the door opens, making the bell ring, and April walks in. She has her dark purple hair up in a big messy bun and very little makeup on, but she looks well put together. It's unsettling how she's reacting to the loss of their baby. "Hey," I say, standing up straighter. "How are you doing?"

Jasmine glares at me like I'm an idiot for asking such a stupid

100

question, but I can't help it. I feel if I ask it enough, she'll eventually break down and talk to me.

April sets her purse on the counter and looks at us, ignoring my question. "Congratulations on the new business."

Did Cross talk to Grave? He's the only one I've spoken to about it. Maybe it was Jasmine. I exchange a look with her, and she slowly shakes her head. "How did you ...?"

"Emilee told me. That's great news," April throws over her shoulder as she walks toward her office.

Jasmine and I turn to Emilee.

"Sorry," she whispers quickly. "I went over to their place the other night to try to talk to her, and she wouldn't say anything about herself. She just sat there staring at the wall, and I started word vomiting." Her large blue eyes start to fill with tears, biting her lip. "I hope it wasn't a secret."

"Of course not," Jasmine assures her with a hand on her shoulder.

"I'm so sorry. I panicked," Emilee rambles. "I didn't know what else to say."

"It's okay. I promise. Don't worry about it."

"We should celebrate," April announces, walking back into the front of the shop from her office.

"Oh, no—" I start.

"That's not necessary," Jasmine interrupts me.

"Nonsense." April waves us off. "We're celebrating. Tomorrow night. At our house."

"Well, technically, it's not official yet," I state, trying to turn her down nicely.

April's face falls, and she looks down at her hands as a silence fills the shop. "I just ... I need something. To take my mind off ... you know? A distraction."

Jasmine, Emilee, and I rush over to her immediately, giving her a big hug. April can throw us whatever kind of celebration party she wants. If that is a step to help her grieve, then we'll let her do it. I did promise that I'd give her anything she needed.

"What should I bring?" I ask.

ELEVEN
CROSS

APRIL INSISTED THAT we have dinner at Grave's and her place to celebrate the girls buying into Kink. We've been here for two hours, and it's awkward as fuck. There's a big elephant in the room. No one has laughed or told any jokes, for that matter, like our usual Sunday morning breakfasts that we've been having ever since she moved in with him.

Bones has just openly stared at his brother. Grave has asked to talk to Titan privately in the other room twice now. And I have to pretend I haven't been fucking Alexa. I love my friends, but I'm so ready to go home.

We're all sitting at their formal dining table when April stands from her seat and excuses herself to use the restroom.

Chatter is at a minimum. What little there has been was April trying to get Jasmine and Alexa to talk about their future plans with Kink, but they honestly don't have any at the moment. Not until they are for sure going to buy in. They leave for New York tomorrow to tour the Kink club there.

We're silently eating when April re-enters the room. We all look up to just see her standing under the archway. Grave drops his fork to his plate and jumps to his feet. "April? Are you okay?" He looks her over for any obvious injuries, but she seems to be fine.

She has tears in her ice-blue eyes as she stares at him. I can feel the air shift in the room. A weight dropping on all of us. Her pain. Their pain. It's unimaginable.

The first tear falls, and he steps closer to her. "April ...?"

"Are you using again?" she asks him.

He comes to a stop. His lips curve down, and his brow creases. "No." He squares his shoulders, proud he can answer that question truthfully. I've been around him so many times in the past when Bones asked him that, and he lied. "Why would you—?"

"It's okay," she interrupts him again, licking her lips. "I mean ... it's not." She sighs, nervously running her hands through her hair. "But if you are, I'll help you."

"April, I'm clean," he tells her, stepping toward her, but he stops when she takes one back, matching it. His face falls at her retreat, looking like a wounded dog. Grave has always worn his emotions on his face. He doesn't understand how not to feel.

"So much has happened," she says and sniffs. "I understand if you have." Her hands go to her stomach. "The loss of the baby ..." She chokes on the word.

He steps into her, and this time, she doesn't pull away. He wraps his arms around her, bringing her to his chest, and she starts crying. He kisses her hair. "I'm clean. I made you a promise, and I'm not going to break it. Ever."

I glance down at Bones, who sits there watching his younger brother. He's probably racking his brain trying to think if there has been a time since Grave was released from rehab that he might have seemed high. I can't think of one. But I'm also not around him twenty-four seven anymore. Ever since then, he's been more dedicated at Kingdom and spends all his free time with her.

April gets my attention as she pushes herself away from Grave. She digs into the pocket of her jeans and yanks out a pill bottle. Grave takes a step back, running a hand down his clean-shaven face.

"I just found these in one of our guest bathrooms." She shakes it in front of him, the pills clanking together. "It has your name on it."

His hands drop to his sides as Bones gets to his feet. "Grave—?"

"I can explain," he interrupts Bones, but he keeps his eyes on April.

"I googled what it says on the bottle, and the pills inside don't look the same," she tells him.

"April ... I swear, I haven't ..."

"Don't!" she shouts, losing what little nerve she has, and her bottom lip begins to tremble. "Grave ... please tell me this isn't because of the baby? Because of me?" Fresh tears run down her cheeks.

"No. No. No." He rushes to her once again. "They're not mine."

"Then whose are they?" she demands, shoving him away. Her emotions are all over the place for more reasons than one. "Huh? Who else would be taking pain pills with your name on the bottle in our house?" She throws the bottle at him.

He lifts his tatted arm that showcases her face on it to shield himself from the bottle. They bounce off his forearm and hit the floor. The lid pops off, and the remainder of the pills scatter across their marble floor. I see Bones looking at the floor. I do the same and quickly count five.

Grave looks down at them, and I watch his shoulders drop in disappointment. That he let her down. Let himself down.

Once an addict, always an addict.

"Grave. Be honest with me." Her voice cracks again. "Are you using?"

He can't look her in the eyes. They stay on the floor, staring at the pills that used to give him an escape from this very feeling. Silence fills the large room, putting everyone on edge. While April waits for him to admit he relapsed and needs help. She places her hands over her mouth to quiet her sob, but it's too late. April spins around and runs out of the formal dining room. The girls all get up from the table and rush after her.

Grave jerks his jacket off the back of the chair he was seated at and starts to leave, but Bones grabs his shoulder, spinning him around. "Where do you think you're going?"

"Out!" he snaps.

"Grave, I don't think—"

"I don't give a fuck what you think!" he shouts and shoves him away. Seconds later, we hear the front door open and close.

Bones chases after him, yelling his name.

I lean back in my seat and run my hand down my face.

"He's not using," Titan speaks softly, breaking the silence.

"How do you know?" I ask, looking up at him across the table. He and Grave have become very close since he went off to rehab. Titan was the one who drove him there. And I'd be lying if I said I wasn't jealous of the relationship they now have.

"Because I'm the one he calls at all hours of the night when he wants a hit but chooses not to take one. Or when he wants to drink an entire bottle in hopes it'll help him sleep. Those may have had his name on them, but he's not taking them." Then he too gets up, following Grave and Bones out the front door and leaving Luca and me alone.

I sit back, remove my Zippo from my pocket, and start flipping it open and closed while I try to think of who could be using them. Here at their house of all places. Who would be over here that we know uses? I'm not at home very often, so I don't know who comes and goes here. April doesn't have a lot of girlfriends. Her circle is pretty tight. Jasmine and Emilee don't use. Neither does Haven. And I know that Alexa doesn't. Who the fuck ...?

My jaw tightens, slamming the lighter shut. I know exactly who it is and why Grave didn't give them up.

Motherfucker!

I rush out of the house just like the others and jump in my car that's parked in Grave's driveway. Squealing the tires, I pull out my cell, dialing a number that I never use, but I still have it. One of those things that's good to have for a rainy day.

"Cross. Well, this is a surprise," the man says, answering after the first ring. I can practically hear his smile through my car's speakers. "What is this three times in the same number of weeks?"

"I need a favor," I say through gritted teeth, hating that I even had to make this call in the first place. Everything has a price.

Turner Mason lets out a low whistle. "Well, you know those cost you, right?"

I refrain from growling. "Yeah."

"What may I do for you?" he asks happily.

"Ethan Davis. Know where I can find him?"

He gives a soft chuckle. "Well, Cross. It's your lucky day! He just so happens to be right here."

I let out a long breath. At least it'll be worth it. I'd do anything for my best friend and his girlfriend. Not like the Mason brothers can demand my soul. I sold that to the devil years ago. And if everything goes right with Kale, we'll be business partners.

ALEXA

JASMINE AND I sit on the end of Grave and April's bed with her. Jasmine holds her hand while I rub her back, and Emilee paces back and forth. Haven stands over by the window with her back to us as she stares out over the city. She hasn't said anything, which surprises me. She's usually the first one to have an opinion on something. Maybe she understands how fragile April is right now after losing the baby.

"This was my biggest fear," April cries softly.

"I don't think he'd lie to you." Jasmine jumps to Grave's defense.

"Me either. But ..." She shakes her head. "Who else could it be?"

"He's hiding something." Haven finally speaks, turning to face us.

"You don't know that," Jasmine snaps.

April sniffs. "I've shut him out to avoid this."

I sigh at her confession.

"I didn't want him to feel," she admits with a sob. Pulling her hand free from Jasmine's, she covers her face with her hands. "I didn't want him to turn to drugs. I can't lose him too." Turning, she buries her face into my shirt.

I hug her tightly and start to rock us back and forth gently.

Haven opens her mouth, but Jasmine snaps her fingers at her, shaking her head. Haven rolls her eyes and spins back around, giving us her back.

"He's not going anywhere," I tell her, my chest tightening. This is why she's kept everything in and why she refuses to open up to anyone. She was trying to take all the burden on herself to save Grave. "April ..."

The sound of a door banging open from downstairs cuts me off. "Cross ... what the fuck?" Luca, Haven's husband, yells from the first floor.

We all jump to our feet and rush out to see what's going on. Looking down over the banister, we see a guy lying on the floor in the middle of their foyer. Face bloody along with busted knuckles. His shirt is ripped, and his jeans are dirty. He looks up at April, making his way to a sitting position, and wipes the bloody drool off with the back of his hand.

We start our way down the stairs, not nearly as fast as we left the bedroom. Once we hit the landing, I look at Cross wide-eyed. It can't be ...

"Ethan." April steps toward him, but I pull her back. He looks like a feral cat ready to attack. She's been through enough shit already tonight. I feel the need to protect her from everyone at this point. "What the hell happened to you?"

"Tell her," Cross demands, kicking him with his shoe.

"Fuck you!" he spits out at Cross.

"Dude? What are you ...?" Luca starts, but Cross bends down, grips Ethan by his hair, and forces him to stand.

"Tell. Her," he growls.

"Cross. Don't." Grave shakes his head, coming to join the commotion. Titan and Bones are right behind him.

When did he come back? Last I had heard, he left. Bones must have brought him back.

"I'm not going to let it go down this way," Cross tells Grave. "Not to you. Not now."

"What is he talking about?" April asks Grave, turning to face him.

"Nothing," he dismisses her, unable to meet her eyes.

Cross gives an evil laugh, and it makes the hairs on the back of my neck stand up. I've never seen him like this—a Dark King. I've heard stories from the girls, and the town knows how Kingdom is run. But he seems different right now. Like he has nothing to lose.

"Don't do this," Cross says to Grave. He's pleading with his best friend. "Don't let her think you're still the same guy."

"This doesn't concern you!" Grave shouts, stepping up to them.

Cross shoves Ethan to the side, and he trips, falling to the floor once again. Cross bumps his chest to Grave. Bones goes to intervene, but Titan pulls him back. *What the fuck?* Why isn't anyone stopping this?

"It does!" Cross shouts. "You are my brother, and I won't let her think that you haven't changed."

"Fuck you!" Grave shoves him.

Cross grabs his shirt and yanks Grave into him. "I won't let her think any less of you."

Grave's bottom lip begins to tremble.

"Do you hear me? I know it. Titan and Bones know it. You are not the same man you once were. You've come too far for that, Kyle," Cross says, softening his voice at his best friend.

Grave sniffs but shakes his head, whispering, "I won't do it. I won't do that to her."

Silence covers the room. My hands are shaking, my heart pounding. What is going on? What does Cross know, and what has Grave done? What is he protecting April from?

Cross lets go of him and takes a step back, squaring his shoulders once again. "Fine, then I will."

"No—"

"April, your brother here stole Grave's pills from him months ago. He's the one who's using in your house," Cross announces, interrupting his best friend.

April's wide eyes go from Cross to Grave. He looks murderous as he stares at the back of Cross's head. His chest rises and falls fast with his heavy breathing. His hands are fisted down by his sides. I see Bones step closer to them, expecting Grave to pounce on Cross.

"What?" April blinks, and fresh tears run down her face. She looks at her younger brother, who's still on the floor but now sitting up. "Is this true? You've been using?"

He won't meet her eyes. Instead, he stares at the blood spots on the floor in front of him.

"But ..." She swallows. "You've been working. Doing better. Staying out of trouble. I've seen you—"

"Some addicts care what others think and hide it well," Cross says matter-of-factly, interrupting her.

Her watery ice-blue eyes go from Cross to Grave, and when he doesn't look at her, she looks at her brother once again. "Answer me!" she shouts, running to him. Grave grabs her but not before she gets a swing at his face, knocking him to his side on the floor. "How long?" she cries as her feet leave the ground from Grave's hold.

Ethan bites his lip and continues to ignore her, pushing himself back up to a sitting position.

"How fucking long?" she screams this time, trying to get out of Grave's hold.

"April?" Grave spins her around to face him. His hands cup her tear-streaked face. "April, look at me. Take a deep breath."

"Oh, my God," she cries, her body caving into his. "Grave ... I-I'm so sorry."

"Don't. Don't do that to yourself." He shakes his head at her, pulling her into his chest and hugging her tightly. Her hands dig into his shirt while he kisses her head. Her legs give out, and he picks her up, carrying her away from the foyer.

TWELVE

CROSS

I TURN TO look down at the jackass who almost ruined my best friend's life. I don't know much about the kid, but he can't even be twenty-one yet. He cost Grave fifty grand months back when the Mason brothers were after him. Grave paid them off, and he was to pay Grave back. I'm not sure how that's been going. I haven't asked. Maybe I should have. "Come on." I grab his upper arm and yank him to his feet. "Let's go."

"I'm not going anywhere with you." He tries to pull away from me, but I keep hold of him.

"Yeah, I'm taking you to rehab."

"Fuck that!" he shouts, starting to fight me harder, but he's still too weak. I picked him up off the floor at the Airport. He had two fights tonight and got his ass kicked both times. Trey Mason, the youngest of the three brothers, had to help me get Ethan to my car. "You never stopped him from doing drugs."

I grip his face with my free hand. "Your sister has been through enough."

"She made her choices," he spits out.

I'm going to fucking kill this kid.

Bones pulls me away from him and shoves his back in the front door. "Get the fuck away from here. I don't care if you go to rehab or go get fucked up. But stay the fuck away from April and Grave, or I'll kill you myself."

He shrugs off him, turns around, and slams the front door shut on his way out.

"He needed rehab," I bark at Bones.

"You can't force someone to choose sobriety, Cross," he snaps. "You of all people should know that."

I do, but ... "She just lost her child. How do you think she'll feel if she loses a brother to an overdose?"

He shrugs. "Looks like she'll be better off."

Alexa gasps at his words, but I'm not surprised that's how Bones feels. And I can't say that I disagree. But I'm also thinking of Grave here. April is his everything. What will he do if she leaves him? If she loses a child and a brother? How will that affect her? And then their relationship? I'm trying to make sure I do my part to keep all sides together. I hate to admit it, but I was never there for Grave like he needed me to be. I enabled him. I'm trying to do better. Be a better friend for him now. And I'll be damned if I let myself fail.

"How did you know it was Ethan?" Jasmine asks me.

I look up at her, and a conversation I had with Grave comes to mind.

"YOU LOST THEM AGAIN?" I ASK GRAVE AS I STAND IN HIS *bedroom up in our Royal Suite at Kingdom.*

"*I had them in a bag," he growls, shuffling through his closet.*

I'm not sure what he's looking for exactly. I fall on the end of his bed. "And you didn't take them?" How do you lose a bottle of pills?

He snorts. "I would know if I had taken an entire bottle of pills last night."

I shrug, flipping my Zippo open and closed. "Maybe April took them." I reach, trying to think of the options. I don't know anything about this woman. Maybe she does drugs. He does them all the time with his go-to fuck—Lucy.

Grave shakes his head. "One, she didn't know they were there, and two, she wouldn't have had the chance. She sucked my dick on the way to her house, and the moment we arrived, we went upstairs to her room. After we were done, she passed out and never left. It had to have been her brother."

WHAT WAS IN THE PILL BOTTLE WASN'T WHAT GRAVE USED TO keep in there. It's obvious that Ethan had finished off the pills he stole and then refilled it with whatever he wanted, keeping the bottle.

"Cross?" Alexa speaks, reminding me that Jasmine asked me a question, but I ignore them. Instead, I kick the jackass's bag across the foyer that he left behind and turn to the door. Yanking it open and slamming it shut behind me, I head to my house. I'm tired and need a shower. We have a compound here in a cul-de-sac right outside of Las Vegas. It's been a while since I've stayed at my house, but right now, I don't want to take the time to go to Kingdom.

"Cross?" I hear Alexa call out behind me, running down Grave's stairs.

"Not now," I say, not wanting her around. I want to be alone for the night. "Go home, Alexa."

"Cross!" she shouts.

I enter my house and slam that door as well, but it instantly swings open behind me. I should have locked it, but since we live in a gated community that only we Kings have access to, I never do.

"I'm fucking talking to you!" she shouts.

I spin around to face her. "And I told you to go home!"

She crosses her arms over her chest. Things got intense, and my blood pressure is still rising. My anger is far from faded. How long would Grave had let April think he was using again? She would have left him. All because he wanted to spare the truth of her brother. Pitiful. What the fuck was he thinking? I yank off my jacket and turn, walking down the hallway to my master suite at the back of the house.

"We need to discuss this," she states.

I snort. "There's nothing to discuss."

"That is her brother."

"Bones was right," I say, entering the bedroom.

"Did you do that to Grave? Huh?" she demands, causing me to pause and turn to face her. "Did you leave him to overdose?"

"You have no idea what the fuck has happened!" I shout. "What he went through. What I allowed to happen. None of us could have stopped him!" I believe in my heart that April was the only one to make Grave want to sober up. "What do you expect from me?"

"How about a little human decency?" she screams in my face. "Some compassion. He needed help, not to be kicked out of the house and left on his own on the streets. He'll just go find more drugs."

I laugh at that, and it just fuels her hate for me at the moment.

"You Kings say that you're all brothers. But you allowed Grave to get high. What if he had overdosed? Huh? Then what ...?"

"Don't act like you know what happened, Alexa. Because I promise you, you don't know shit." I step into her, glaring down my nose into her green eyes. "This is the last time I'm going to say this. Get the fuck out of my house."

Her jaw sharpens, her nostrils flare, and I think she's going to slap me, but instead, she spins around and marches out of my room, slamming the front door on her way out.

"FUCK!"

ALEXA

I DIDN'T SLEEP at all last night. After arguing with Cross, I stormed out of his house and had Jasmine take me home since I had arrived with her because Cross and I had to "pretend" we weren't seeing each other—if they didn't already know, they do now after the way I followed him out of Grave and April's house—I showered, then laid in bed while I tossed and turned until my alarm went off this morning. I wanted to call April so bad, but I refrained. She already had so much going on, and I wanted her to spend that time with Grave. They had a lot to talk about.

Jasmine came and picked me up, and we met Bones at a private hangar. We boarded what I'm guessing was Bones's jet. The plane ride was silent. Bones was on his phone the whole time, either emailing or texting someone. Jasmine didn't even try to talk to me. Usually, she's the first one to try to cheer me up, but we were all still reeling from last night. I found myself falling asleep here and there during the flight.

A Cadillac Escalade is waiting for us at the private hangar once we touch down in New York. Jasmine and I get in the back, and Bones drives us to our hotel. I rest my forehead against the window and take in all the tall buildings. I've never seen anything like it. I was looking forward to seeing the city, but now not so much. It just doesn't feel right.

He brings the car to a stop in front of the hotel. "I'll pick you girls up here at midnight." Bones finally speaks.

I look down at my watch to see it's a little after four. I'm actually glad we have some time because I'd like to get some sleep before we go out tonight. I'm exhausted.

"You're not coming up?" Jasmine asks.

He shakes his head. "No. I have some business to take care of while in town."

She nods before she and I get out of the car. A couple of guys grab our bags for us and help us into the hotel. It's exactly what I expected a classy and expensive hotel to be in Times Square. It's open, allowing you to look up and see all the floors from the inside. It's so tall that I have to lean my head all the way back to see the top. Everything is pristine—white with gold trimming. The floor a white and black marble design. There are white leather couches to the right and a bar to the left. Looking inside of it, I can see TVs on the wall and people sitting at round booths. A massive chandelier hangs five stories tall, the crystals wrapped in a circle making it look like it's raining down on the guests.

The guys help us onto an elevator, and my stomach rises in my throat as we climb, looking out the floor-to-ceiling windows while the lobby gets farther and farther away.

It finally comes to a stop, and we enter the door of the Presidential Suite. We thank the guys and tip them.

I look around in awe. My shoes sink into the rich carpet. There's nothing but floor-to-ceiling windows showcasing Times Square. "This is amazing," I whisper, wishing that April was here to see this with me.

"Right?" Jasmine agrees, walking over to the bar area.

I sit down at the piano in the middle of the living room and wish my mom would have made me commit to my lessons when I was younger just so I could say I played the piano in our hotel while visiting New York.

"I'm going to take a nap," Jasmine informs me.

"Okay," I wave her off, knowing I won't be long behind her.

My cell vibrates in my pocket, and I pull it out, hoping it's Cross. But I'm disappointed when I see it's none other than my ex.

> CUNT: Alexa, quit fucking ignoring me! I
> need to talk to you!

While I'm reading over it, my cell begins to ring, and it's him. Pressing decline, I pocket my cell and decide to go lie down for that nap.

I wake up, and it's dark outside. The clock on the nightstand reads nine o'clock. I yawn and stretch out my heavy limbs before checking my cell. Thankfully, there's nothing from Mitch, but sadly nothing from Cross either. Not sure what I expected. Cross and I are just fucking. It was nothing serious, and I don't see him as the apology type. I'm sure as hell not ready to swallow my pride and apologize for what I said. In a way, he was right. I don't know what has gone on between the Kings over the years, so I should have just kept my mouth shut. Rolling off the side of the bed, I make my way to the adjoining bathroom.

I jump back, screaming when I flip on the light and find Jasmine in the bathtub. She and I are sharing a suite. Bones got his own.

"Come on in." She waves a bubble-covered hand. "Can't see anything. Even if you could, I wouldn't care." She winks at me. "It's all the same."

I laugh and enter because I really have to pee. "Why are you in the dark?" I ask, noticing that she has candles lit all over the room. The black shades above the large jacuzzi bathtub are pulled closed, hiding her from the city.

"I prefer candles over bright lights."

I notice one sitting by the sink and pick it up. It's a dark purple candle in the shape of a ... "Are these dicks?"

"Yes." She smiles, rubbing bubbles on her upper chest and up her neck. "I find it very therapeutic to set a dick on fire. Not as much as a real one"—she shrugs—"but it still makes me feel good."

I laugh, shaking my head, and make my way to the toilet. "I'll have to try that," I mumble. The fake ones, of course.

———

THREE HOURS LATER, BONES PULLS UP TO THE BACK OF A RED brick building. Exiting the car, I can hear music pounding from inside the club. I'm not sure what I was expecting, but this is not it.

I start to walk to the right, but Bones goes left. Jasmine takes my hand and pulls me after him. A black door opens, and a man dressed in a three-piece suit steps out, holding it open. He lifts his right hand to his ear. "They're here, boss," he speaks. Then smiles. "Bones!" He shakes his hand and pulls him in for a man shake/hug. "How're you doing, man? It's been a while."

"Busy. As usual," Bones answers.

I frown, and Jasmine leans into my ear, whispering, "Bones is a member."

My lips make an O shape. My eyes drop to his shiny Hermes shoes and run up over his black dress slacks and his dark gray button-up. He's got the sleeves rolled up his tatted forearms. His shoulders are pulled back, and his hands are tucked into his pockets. I can see Bones demanding total submission from a woman. He just seems like someone who has to be in charge all the time, of every aspect of his life.

"Well, he's inside waiting for you." The man steps to the side, keeping the door open for us.

Bones grabs Jasmine's hand, and she continues to hold on to mine. Bright, flashing lights momentarily blind me. I reach out my right hand and find a wall. It vibrates from the bass of "Buttons" by The Pussycat Dolls. Bones continues to pull us down a long hallway until we enter an opening. Looking up, I see the crowd of people. I'm not surprised to see it's packed. But it looks like any other club. Nothing special or kinky to it. We walk past the bar and a dance floor to the other side of the club, down another long hallway. A man stands guard of a door at the end.

Bones reaches into his back pocket and pulls out his wallet. He holds up a card, and the guy looks it over, then to us. His eyes sweep over Jasmine and me in a way that makes me question why I even agreed to do this. But then he steps to the side and opens the door.

It's a dimly lit staircase. We follow Bones down it, and he opens the door at the bottom. Fuck, it's a maze. Is this the only way to enter? Or is this the only way they are allowing us to get in? We walk through the door, and my mouth drops while my eyes widen.

The lights remain dimmer down here than the flashing neon lights upstairs. Soft music plays, unlike the blaring noise above us.

Men and women are in the center of the room on a dance floor. Most are dressed in leather outfits. One man is crawling on his hands and knees while another leads him around by a leash. A guy walks by us dressed in what looks like a red latex one-piece.

Kink—makes total sense to me now. It's like night and day compared to what I just saw upstairs. This place is hidden? But why?

"Bones!" A man dressed in a white three-piece suit approaches us, and Bones releases Jasmine's hand to shake the guy who said his name. "Ladies." He nods to us, placing his hands behind his back. And I wonder why he didn't shake ours.

Jasmine pulls her shoulders back, obviously noticing it too. "Hooke," she acknowledges him.

His name is Hooke? That's gotta be a fake name, right? Maybe a last name? He looks young. Maybe not my age, but late twenties, early thirties at the oldest.

"Bones, you've been here enough to know how it all works. But let me show you ladies around." He turns, giving us his back.

Now that I know Bones is a member, I understand why Jasmine brought him in. He knows the ins and outs. But my concern is what kind of restrictions they have with a member buying in?

The man takes a right at the end of the dance floor, and we come to a hallway. Nothing but glass. You can see into the rooms on either side. You can see the people inside the rooms having sex. So many props. One that looks like a cross with a naked man strapped to it. Another that looks like a black leather bench—a woman bent over it.

One room we walk past has two men and a woman in it. She's bent over a table, her hands tied behind her back, legs spread wide tied and restrained. One man is behind her, the other in front of her.

"This is heaven," Jasmine says excitedly.

He takes us into a room that has a black leather couch and two chairs. A coffee table sits in the middle with a stack of papers. Not a single window on the walls.

Jasmine still holds my hand so when she sits down on the couch, I plop down beside her. Bones takes the chair across from us, and Hooke unbuttons his suit jacket before sitting beside him in the other one. "I'm not going to lie; I was excited when you called me, Bones. I think Kink will be great for you. We're honored to have a Vegas location."

I'm not much of a fan of this Hooke guy already. Jasmine said we needed Bones, and the more he talks, the more I understand why. I hate sexist pigs.

"It was Jasmine's idea." Bones looks at her, giving her the credit. "It was an opportunity I couldn't pass."

"Yes ..." He lets out a long breath. "Well, Kink is thrilled to have two women partnering."

Liar. Even I could hear the sarcasm in his voice. Like someone is forcing him to let us in. I wonder if Bones is that person? It makes me want to do this even more.

"I've done some research," I say, finally speaking. "And I find it interesting that you have twenty-five locations worldwide and not a single woman owns a Kink. Why is that?"

Hooke lifts his right leg to place his ankle on his left knee and settles back into his seat. His eyes meet mine. "Look around Kink. Most of your dominant participants are male. Women choose to follow, not lead."

Jackass.

"And then, of course, men are more reliable. More dominant in the business field ..."

"Excuse me?" Jasmine asks, sitting up straighter. "What does that mean?"

He looks at her. His eyes drop to her cleavage before returning to hers. A smirk grows across his face as if he's imagining tying her up in one of those rooms we just passed. "Women prefer the family life. Babies. They have responsibilities at home that keep them permanently tied there. Whereas men choose to devote their lives to their careers." He reaches his hands out wide. "The statistics back up those facts."

"That—"

"We're getting off topic," Bones interrupts Jasmine.

"Look ..." Hooke places his foot on the floor. Adjusting his suit jacket, he obviously has more to say. "We're thrilled to have you two joining Kink, but I'd be lying if I said I'd be sitting here with you ladies without Bones."

Even though Jasmine had already told me we needed Bones, Hooke's words still piss me off. How dare this motherfucker tell us what we can do with our lives? With our money. Women are capable of anything, but we're looked at being weak because we carry a child for nine months.

A silence falls over the room. I can feel Jasmine's stiff body next to mine. She wants to say something. Hell, I want to say more, but the look on Bones's face is telling us both to shut the hell up. Maybe Hooke wants us to take his words personally and make a scene—then he'd have a reason to turn us down when we lash out at him. He's probably recording us at this very moment.

I run a hand down my black dress. "How many members do you have?" Screw this guy and what he thinks he knows of us. I'll show him how committed I am. I've read the paperwork.

"A little over five hundred at the moment," he states proudly.

I almost choke on fucking air. *Five hundred?* The contract said the member buy-in is fifty grand a person. Each year. At fifty thousand a pop, it's twenty-five million dollars. That's insane.

"Are the memberships your only source of revenue?" I ask. The contract didn't state anything other than the original buy-in for the members.

He shakes his head. "The fifty thousand per membership only gets them in the door. If they bring a date, it costs them. If they want bottle service, it costs them." He gives a cruel smile. "If you want a room ..." He holds his hands out wide. "Well, you get it. Everything costs you here."

"Forgive me for being skeptical, but why would they pay for this?" I ask.

He looks at me. "Men like to show off what they have."

"You mean to parade their sex slaves around," I counter.

He chuckles softly. "If being a slave is your kink, then yes."

"So, all of your members are men?" Jasmine asks.

"Not a hundred percent of them. But the majority, yes."

"Why is that?" I go on.

He gives me a smile that makes my skin crawl. I wish men like him could be a woman for one day to know what it's like. "A man will come five times a week and bring a different woman each time."

"Getting his money's worth," I say with disgust.

He goes on as if I didn't speak. "A woman will come ten times a year and bring the same man. So, it's hard for a woman to justify that kind of ... commitment."

He means financially. He's already said men make more money than women.

The door opens, and a woman enters dressed in black leather pants with a red crop top. She has her jet-black hair up in a tight bun. "Hooke, may I see you for a second?"

He stands and buttons his suit jacket. Bones stands as well and shakes his hand. "Thanks for taking the time to meet with us."

"Of course." He turns and nods to us just like before. "Ladies." Then he exits the room. The door softly closing behind him.

I fall back onto the couch and let out a long sigh.

"Well, that actually went better than I thought it was going to," Bones says, sitting back down.

"He's a fucking prick," Jasmine spits out and turns to face me, taking my hands in hers. "But it doesn't change what I said, Alexa. Just give me the word, and we will show him how wrong he is."

I search her green eyes. I trust Jasmine, and she trusts Bones. I have no doubt that she will devote her entire life to this club. She wants it to be a success. And I want that too.

Fuck Hooke and his view on women. We can be dominant and rule over men. "I'm in."

THIRTEEN

CROSS

I PACE MY office back and forth with my cell in my hand. I should call her. But I'm not sure what I would say at this point.

Sorry? Somehow that just doesn't seem like enough. I've had some time to think about last night, and she wasn't wrong. I just didn't want to admit that.

I hate how much she's on my mind. She was supposed to be a fuck, but she consumes me. Why did I allow it to get to this? And how do I stop it?

"You busy?" Titan asks, entering my office.

"What do you want?" I ask, flipping my Zippo open and closed.

"Still pissy, I see?" He laughs softly.

I roll my eyes and turn my back to him.

"Just thought I'd let you know that I just got off the phone with Bones."

"And?" I spin back around to face him. "What did he say?"

"The girls took the deal."

I knew Alexa would. It was too good to pass up. I'm happy for her. Nodding, I tell him, "Thanks."

"How long are you going to beat yourself up over this?" he asks, plopping down in the seat across from my desk.

I ignore that question and ask my own. "Why are you avoiding going home?" It's almost midnight. He hasn't stayed this late in a while.

"I'm not avoiding anything. Emilee is over at Haven and Luca's right now." He checks his watch. "I'm picking her up in an hour."

I nod and fall into my seat behind my desk. "Have you heard from Grave?"

"No."

I place my elbows on my desk and run my hands through my dark hair, releasing a sigh. "I haven't either."

"He'll let us know if he needs anything," he states, standing to walk toward my door.

"Thanks," I say, making him stop.

He places his hand on the knob and turns to face me. "Just thought you'd like to know. Since she's not talking to you right now."

My jaw tightens. Getting in a fight with your girl in front of your friends is never good. "It's complicated," I say.

He snorts. "Been there. Good luck figuring it out." Then he turns and leaves.

I sit back and let out a sigh. This is why I fuck and move on. To avoid this bullshit.

ALEXA

I SIT ACROSS from Bones and Jasmine in his private jet. My mind is going a hundred miles an hour trying to figure out everything that needs to be done once we get back.

"Here you go, sir. Ladies." His flight attendant stops beside us with a bucket full of ice and champagne.

"Thanks, Nicki," he says, reaching over and grabbing it. He pops the cork and pours it into three flutes, then hands us each our own. "To you, ladies, and your success." He lifts his glass.

"Thank you," I say, smiling up at him. "For helping us out."

"I don't believe a person should have a set of balls in order to do what they want," he states.

I like Bones. The guy has this air about him that totally screams *don't fuck with me*. But he also just signed away his life to a two-million-dollar contract to help me and Jasmine start our own business.

"To the three of us and our future." I lift my glass.

We both look over at Jasmine. She stares down at her champagne; it bubbles in the flute. Her green eyes are intense on the drink, and I wonder if she thinks we've made a mistake. If she has doubts about going into business with me.

"Depend on a man to feed you, and you give him the power to starve you." She looks up at me. A slow and devious smile spreads across her face. "Here's to us—two women who are going to feed our-fucking-selves." She throws back her drink, and Bones laughs.

I drink my champagne in one gulp and know what I just did was the right thing for me. For her. For the three of us.

Things are about to change, and I couldn't be more excited to be a part of it.

Bones cell rings, and he gets up to move to the back of the plane to answer it. Jasmine looks out her window at the dark sky, and I pull my cell out. Hovering over Cross's number, I think about texting him, but I'm not sure what I'd say at this point. Plus, I've never been a coward. I'd rather talk to him face-to-face.

I go to pocket my phone when it beeps. I look back down at it to see it's a message from Mitch. I don't even open it. Turning it off, I lean back and close my eyes to get some sleep on our flight home.

FOURTEEN
CROSS

O N MONDAY MORNING, Titan, Bones, and I are sitting in the conference room when the door opens. We all get to our feet when Grave walks in. He messaged us an hour ago wanting a meeting this morning, and it's the first time he's ever done that.

"Grave ..."

He holds up his hand to stop Bones. "I'm not staying." Running his hand through his hair, he swallows nervously. "I just wanted to tell you all that I'm taking some time off."

"Of course," Titan acknowledges him first.

"Whatever you need," I add.

"Good." Bones nods once.

"I ... uh, April and I are going to get away. After the baby ..." He pauses, collecting himself with a deep breath. "We need some time away. Together."

"You don't need to explain yourself, Grave," I tell him.

He places his hand in the pockets of his holey jeans and averts his eyes. "It'll only be a week. Maybe two at the most."

"Take as long as you need." Bones goes to step toward him, but Grave steps back, moving to the glass double doors, and Bones stops.

"I need to grab a few things from my office." Grave turns and leaves.

Bones rushes after him. I plop down in my seat and run a hand down my face. Leaning back, I stare up at the white ceiling, trying to get my head on straight. I'm not in the game. Between Grave, April, the baby, her brother, and then Alexa, I'm totally fucked. I'm not sleeping at night, which isn't unusual, but it's worse than normal.

Titan leans forward, placing his elbows on the table, and runs his hand through his hair when Bones returns. He slams the glass door shut, surprised when it doesn't break. "Fuck!" he hisses.

"He's not going to talk to you," Titan states.

"Nothing new. He never has before," Bones hisses.

Titan stands, straightening his shoulders, and turns to face Bones. "You may be able to lie to yourself, but not us. This time is different whether you want to believe that or not." Then he too exits the conference room, stomping off to his office. Fuck, it's going to be a long day.

I hang my head when I hear Bones throw the coffee pot, and it shatters against the wall.

"Sir?"

"What?" Bones shouts at Nigel as he enters the conference room.

Nigel is unfazed by our outbursts by now. He's seen us at our worst. Placing his hands behind his back, he rocks back and forth on his heels. "Luca is down in the meat locker, sir. And he has brought a visitor."

Bones's eyes go from Nigel to mine. I stand, nodding my head. This is what I need—what we all need. To bury our heads in work. Get our hands bloody.

"We'll be right there," Bones tells him.

He turns and exits the room, to go get Titan, and I stand from my chair, pocketing my Zippo. The three of us step onto our private elevator and head down to the basement. Walking off the elevator, we make our way down the hallway to the metal door. Bones opens it, and we enter to find Luca Bianchi at the head of the room dressed in his black three-piece suit with his arms crossed over his chest. His adopted brother, Oliver Nite-Bianchi, stands behind the man tied to the metal chair in the center of the room.

"Didn't know you made deliveries, Luca," I say, letting the door close and lock behind me.

"Well, I just couldn't pass this up," he jokes.

"What is it that you found?" Bones asks.

Luca reaches into the pocket of his suit jacket and pulls out a handful of something. Then he drops them onto the table. Bones walks over to them and picks one up.

It's a diamond! "Where was he?" I ask.

"Glass." The strip club that Luca and Bones own together. "He owed one of my girls three grand, and when he couldn't pay in cash, he offered her one of these."

"Where did you get this?" Bones asks him, handing me one of the diamonds. It's one we're looking for. The special order was for black diamonds. They're not as rare as red ones, but still hard to find.

The guy remains silent.

"Did you purchase them or steal them?" I wonder. We're not sure if Kale fucked over our client or not. We just know our client is pissed and wants what he paid for. You can't ensure a transaction that is illegal in the first place. So, he's out ten million.

"Fuck you." The man sneers at me.

I hand the diamond over to Titan. "How many did he have on him?" I ask Luca.

"Six," he answers.

Bones sighs. "The order was for twelve." Then he asks the man, "Is this all you have?"

"Fuck you!" He shouts this time.

"Here, make sure these are returned," Titan tells Luca, handing them to him.

"Maybe he swallowed them," I offer. People will do stupid shit to hide what they want no one else to have.

Bones smiles. "Let's find out."

Nite produces a pocketknife from the inside of his leather jacket and hands it over to Bones, who cuts the ropes tying the man to the chair.

I walk over and yank it from it, throwing his back onto the table. I pin his legs down while Titan holds his shoulders down. Luca comes over and rips the guy's shirt open, exposing his hairy chest.

The guy begins to scream, and Luca slaps his hand over his mouth to quiet him. Not because we don't want anyone hearing him —the room is soundproof—but because we don't want to have to listen to him. Like the others, he has made his choice.

Bones pushes the blade into his flesh right below his sternum, cutting the skin and dragging it downward. The guy's muffled screams turn to outright sobbing while blood pours out and onto the table as we play operation on him, knowing we'll be burying a body later.

It's a quarter till three when I pull up to her bar. Hers is the only car left in the parking lot. Getting out of mine, I walk up to the back door and enter. Grinding my teeth, I'm irritated that she leaves it unlocked. That's not fucking safe.

I walk down the long hallway and come to a stop when I see her standing behind the bar, cleaning it off with a towel, softly humming to herself. She turns and jumps, letting out a scream when she spots me. "Jesus, Cross." Her hand goes to her chest. "What the fuck are you doing? Creeping?"

"Well, if you'd lock your door ..."

"Don't start with me." She slaps the towel on the bar. "I'm not in the mood." Then she disappears into the cooler.

I make my way over to the bar and sit on a stool, waiting.

130

"What do you want?" she asks when she returns.

"I thought I'd tell you congratulations to your face."

She snorts. "You spoke to Bones."

"Not exactly," I say vaguely.

"Well, thanks. you may leave now." She points in the direction of the back door. "You know your way out."

I stand and am about to do as she states, but something stops me. I knock my knuckles on the bar and turn to face her once again. "Listen. I came here to apologize."

"Apologize?" She arches a brow, crossing her arms over her chest. "For?"

"Grave ... April's brother." My arms go wide before dropping them to my thighs. "All of it." I fall back down onto a barstool. "I never once tried to help Grave. Bones was so hard on him. Grave pushed him away because of that. Titan just did his own thing. But me? I enabled him. I partied with him. Did drugs with him. Covered at Kingdom for him. I didn't know how to help him. And I didn't want to. If I didn't have him, then I had no one to help me bury my problem." I slam my fist on the bar, hating that I'm admitting to her that I have my own issues. "I knew it was wrong but just didn't seem to care."

She looks like she wants to question that slip I just made about my problem but thinks better of it. Instead, she sighs. "I'm sorry too. I shouldn't have said anything. It's not my place." Reaching across the bar, she places her hand on mine. "Just like you said, he's not that person anymore."

"Yeah." And I guess I'm not either. I haven't done anything in weeks.

They helped me forget about all the bad memories of my father. My mother. How he would remind us that we live for God. I still have the scars to go along with them. So, even if I was lucky enough to forget, the reminder will forever be there. Just like he wanted. In a way, the bastard won. Even after all these years, he's still in my head.

. . .

"PLEASE, MOM. MAKE HIM STOP," I BEG HER AS I LIE ON MY stomach.

She sits next to me on my bed, rubbing cream on my burn marks as tears slowly run down the side of my cheeks to wet my pillow.

"Forgiveness must be earned," she says softly.

"Forgiveness from what?" I ask. I haven't done anything wrong. Not yet anyway.

"Being born," she answers.

She makes it sound like I asked for this life. Who would want to live a life of punishment? "I didn't ..."

"Shh," she tells me. "It won't be like this forever, son. But power comes with a price. He's preparing you for what's to come."

"I don't want it." I'm not even sure what she's talking about, but I know it's not what I want.

"A King is powerful. He rules his Kingdom. He must be able to endure the darkest of days. He must be able to conquer the biggest threat. You are too young to understand now, but one day you will see. You will find strength in the crosses that you bear."

"Cross?"

I blink and look up to see her now standing next to my barstool.

"You okay?" She reaches out to cup my face, but I'm faster. My arm lashes out, gripping her wrists and stopping her. She sucks in a breath at the tightness of my grip. Instead of releasing her, I yank her closer to me.

She practically falls into my lap. I stand quickly and grip her hips. Picking her up, I plant her ass on the bar and move to stand between her legs. I need her right now. I want a fucking hit. I hate that I can't get high to erase the memories, and she's the closest thing I have to a drug.

She doesn't hesitate. Alexa lets me take control. I kiss her desperately. My lips bruising hers. My fingers dig into her soft yet firm skin. A growl comes from deep in my chest. The need to control is strong.

I never had control before of any aspect of my life. I was conditioned to like fire, to learn from it, and that's what she is—my fire. She burns me in a way that leaves scars. The kind that I won't be ashamed of and hide with tattoos.

She pulls away, throwing her head back, sucking in a breath. I kiss my way down her neck as I shove her shirt up and over her head before tossing it to the floor.

Her hands run through my hair before gripping it.

"God, I've missed you." I let go of her long enough to undo her jeans.

"Me too," She breathes, lifting her hips so I can yank them down her legs. They meet her shirt on the floor as well. "I've missed you."

I jerk her from the bar and carry her over to the closest round table. I bend her over it, facedown. Her hands flatten out over the surface, and I pull my hard dick out before running my fingers over her pussy. She's wet, which is good because I'm in the mood to fuck.

Sliding into her, I feel everything fade away. She's my fire. They say love should be your shelter from the storm, but that's not even close to what I feel for Alexa. She's everything I was taught to need. Crave.

She's my altar, where I kneel and repent for all the sins I've committed over the years. The souls I've taken.

Her pussy tightens around me as I fuck her, and I look down to watch my hard cock slide in and out of that sweet fucking cunt I can't get enough of. My hands grip her hips, holding her in place while her body rocks back and forth on the table, making it rattle with each thrust.

Her hands reach out above her head, and she grips the edge of the table, needing something to hang onto. "Oh God, Cross ..." she cries out as I slam into her.

Letting go of her hips, I lean over her back, and my right hand grips her hair. Yanking the side of her face off the table, I kiss her. Needing to taste her lips while I'm inside her. Needing more of her than she could ever offer.

A sinner is a man who takes what he wants without question. I want her. Right now. Tomorrow and the next day. I need her like I need a hit that I haven't had in weeks. Like the cigarettes that I gave up because I didn't need another death trap in my life. I've already got enough enemies for that. Why try my luck?

Her pussy tightens around me again, and I feel her try to pull away from my lips. I let her go just enough so I can watch her come. Her green eyes heavy, lips swollen and wet. Hair stuck to her slick face. She's absolutely gorgeous in a forbidden way.

A person will always want what they can't have. But my question is, what do we do once we get it? She will be the one to give me that answer.

ALEXA

THE FOLLOWING NIGHT, Jasmine and I stand behind the bar. I closed it down over an hour ago, but we're still here due to Kink. The number of members we have joining Kink is unreal. We can't keep up with it all.

They say that information travels the fastest by word of mouth, and I never understood that until now. You can't just put an ad out for Kink. So Jasmine said she made a couple of calls, and that's all it took. Those two calls turned into more calls. And bam, we're on our way to guys signing up for our sex club.

I look up when the door opens to the bar. A man dressed in a pair of jeans, a plain white T-shirt, and black leather jacket walks toward us. His dark hair is slicked back, and I don't see any visible tattoos from here. He looks well put together—almost a GQ lookalike with a touch of bad boy on the dangerous side if you know what I mean. All he's missing is a cigarette behind his ear while sitting on a motorcycle.

"Tanner Mason." Jasmine smiles at him. "Why am I not surprised to see you here?" She crosses her arms over her chest, looking him up and down.

He says nothing. Instead, he reaches into his leather jacket and produces an envelope, slapping it on the bar counter. "Fifty grand."

She leans forward. "Will we be seeing Trey and Turner as well?"

He stares at her intently for a long moment. I think he's going to walk away without answering when he speaks. "Trey?" He shrugs. "Maybe. But Turner?" He shakes his head. "That boy is selfish with his toys. He prefers to keep his pets in cages where only he can play with them."

"Well ..." She picks up the money. "We're glad you could join us." Reaching over to the right, she picks up a form and slides it to him. "An NDA."

He nods and picks up the pen, clicking it. Without even looking it over, he signs his name and slides it back over to us.

I want to ask him why he didn't even read it but bite my lip to keep quiet. I don't want to look stupid. If Jasmine doesn't have a problem with him signing it without reading it, then neither do I.

He nods once and knocks his knuckles on the bar before turning and walking out.

"Who was that?" I ask once the door closes behind him.

"That was the eldest of the Mason brothers."

"Who?" Was that supposed to mean something?

"They own the Airport and Mason Towers."

Ah, now I remember. I look over at her. "He was joking, right? About the guy named Turner and cages?" Can't help but ask. Rumors are just that—rumors. But they have to hold some truth to them, right?

She laughs. "Doubtful. The Mason boys are seriously disturbed. Their father did a number on them. They each have their own level of being a sadist."

That thought makes my chest hurt. I don't believe evil is born; I believe it's made. And people like the Mason brothers just prove that theory. "Did he ... abuse them?"

"I'm not sure, but rumor has it their father sold their souls to the devil in exchange for power."

"You don't believe that shit, do you?" I can't help but ask, laughing.

"I believe there's a heaven and a hell." She shrugs. "And I believe there is evil in this world that even God can't cleanse."

I place my hands on my hips. "Yeah, but come on …"

"The Airport and Mason Towers sit in the middle of the desert. The address is 666 S. Mason Boulevard."

I frown. "That's … odd but doesn't mean anything."

"Maybe, but I go there all the time."

I've only ever been that one time, and I was pretty drunk. I didn't really pay that much attention to my surroundings. Especially since we had Cross watching out for us. "And?"

Her green eyes meet mine. "And I see things that take place there. Only evil would allow such vile things."

"Then why do you go?" I wonder. "Why put yourself in that position? Who wants to willingly go to hell?"

She tilts her head to the right, a red strand of hair falling across her face before she tucks it behind her ear. "Because I've always been drawn to the darker side of life."

Just then, my brother enters the bar. He spots Jasmine and snorts. "Shouldn't you be working your corner?"

"Derek," I snap. *Why is he such a dick to her?* I think he secretly has a crush on her but knows she'd never give him the time of day.

Before she can say something sarcastic back to him, his eyes drop to the money counter. "What the fuck are you two doing? No way your pussy brought that much in," he says to her as she puts Tanner's envelope of cash in her purse.

I don't miss the fact that he's still ignoring me. "Derek!" I slam my hand down on the bar. "Quit being a fucking piece of shit!" I'm so tired of men like Hooke and my brother. Derek is a man-whore, but God forbid a woman has sex with more than one guy in her lifetime.

He just laughs it off like I'm joking, the first time acknowledging that I even exist since he saw Cross and me in the office.

The front door opens again, and Bones enters, wearing his usual fuck-off face. His pretty blue eyes glare at my brother instantly. He looks him over once and then dismisses him like he's not a threat. Which he isn't, but Bones made it an insult. I refrain from smiling. Derek's body stiffens, and his eyes narrow. "We're closed."

"I'm not here for a drink," Bones responds flatly.

"Sis, may I see you for a second?" Derek grabs my upper arm and drags me into the cooler before I can protest. "What in the fuck are they doing here?" he snaps.

I jerk my arm free of his hold. I was going to tell him what I'm doing tomorrow, but I guess now is as good a time as any. "I'm going into business with Jasmine and Bones."

He blinks a couple of times, glaring down at me before he manages to get any words out. "What do you mean?"

"We're opening a bar. Down in the basement." I'm not going into detail at the moment because it doesn't fucking matter. I own Lucky's and allow him to work for me.

"The fuck you are!" he commands.

My teeth grind. I'm not arguing about this. It's not up for negotiation. "It's done, Derek."

"How could you?" He gives me his back, running his hands through his hair aggressively. "That is the stupidest fucking thing you've ever done. And you've done some dumb shit."

"Derek ..."

"He's a King, Alexa," he growls in my face. "Connected to the Mafia. He can't be trusted. None of them can. Didn't you learn your lesson when April started dating Grave?"

He doesn't know that April lost their baby. I haven't had a chance to tell him, and honestly, it's none of his business. "You don't know anything about them," I point out.

"Neither do you," he fires back. "They're fucking criminals."

I roll my eyes. "They're not—"

"And not to mention druggies," he interrupts me.

It just pisses me off that he judges them. "Oh, just like your friend Ethan." Derek and I grew up with April and her brother. He was never as close to Ethan as I am April because Ethan was quite a bit younger than us. But they're still friends.

He purses his lips. "No, he isn't."

Derek either doesn't know Ethan like he thinks he does, or he's a good liar. "Yes, he is. He was over at April and Grave's the other night fucked up. Cross dragged him in. April was crying when she found out."

He shakes his head, not believing it. "Well, if he is, Grave got him started. Hell, he's probably his dealer. That piece of shit ..."

I slap him across his face, cutting him off. He stands there glaring down at me stunned. "Don't you accuse Grave of that. Ethan is responsible for his own actions!" I scream, my blood pressure rising with each second.

"You're going to do this. Pick them over me?" he asks through gritted teeth.

"It's business," I snap. "Not a competition." Derek has always been happy with where he's at in life—single with no ambition—but I want more. I want what Jasmine strives to have. A career. A woman can do more than lie on her back and push out kids. We just have to work harder, and I'm not afraid to do that. Men like my brother and Ethan hold us back. They make it harder than it has to be.

"If you do this." He points at the closed door of the cooler. "If you go into business with them, I quit," he threatens.

No one will give me an ultimatum. "It's a done deal, Derek."

"Alexa ..."

"The papers have been signed," I clarify, letting him know it's too late. Not like I'd change my mind anyway.

"Fine." He spins around and storms out. I follow him, but he exits the bar just as fast as he did the cooler.

"Are you okay?" Jasmine asks me.

I nod my head, but my heart is heavy. I never can win with Derek. He's always making my life about him. It's a never-ending battle that I'm tired of fighting.

"Anything I can do?" Bones asks me.

My eyes meet his, surprised by that question. "You're offering to help me do what exactly?" If he's as bad as Derek seems to believe, then that could be endless possibilities. I'm not discrediting my brother's concern for the Kings, but I trust Jasmine. If she says they're okay, then I believe her. She's known them all of her life while my brother only knows what he's heard.

Bones crosses his tatted arms over his chest, lifting his chin just a bit. "I'm asking if there's a problem that needs to be solved regarding the business."

"No." I shake my head. "I handled it. He quit."

He nods, satisfied with that answer, and a silence falls over the bar before Bones speaks again. "You ready to close up?"

I nod. "Yeah. Everything is done for the night."

He stands. "Come on. I'll walk you ladies to your cars."

I look at the front door my brother just stormed out of and think of my next step. It's been on my mind ever since I signed the papers for Kink in New York. I want more, and I know what I must do in order to get it.

FIFTEEN
ALEXA

T HE FOLLOWING MORNING, I meet Jasmine for breakfast at Kingdom. I must say that it's nice staying the night here up in the Kings Royal Suite. Cross was right. No one has been here, so we've had it to ourselves.

"You're being really quiet today," Jasmine observes while I push around the eggs on my plate.

April has been heavy on my mind. I wonder where she is. Are she and Grave okay? Relationship wise? When she got pregnant, she was prepared to do it on her own because she knew Grave had demons. But he changed for her. And then when they lost the baby, she was afraid once again. That losing their child might bring them back for him. I haven't messaged her, not wanting to bother her. I know if I was them, I'd have my cell off anyway. They left to be alone and grieve in their own way.

"Earth to Alexa?" Jasmine orders, snapping her fingers in front of my face.

"Hmm?" I look up at her.

She chuckles, shaking her head softly. "I said you've been really quiet. Everything okay?"

"Yeah." I wave her off. "Fine." Picking up my fork, I take a bite of my eggs. "Actually, there is something I want to talk about with you."

"I'm all ears."

Dropping my fork, I say, "I want to find another job." I might as well tell her my plans. We're partners after all.

She frowns. "Why would you want to do that? I told you that Kink ..."

"It doesn't have to do with Kink. Well, yeah, I guess it does."

She pushes her plate away, giving me her full attention. "I don't understand what you mean."

"I want to remodel the bar. And in order to do it how I want, I need to close it down," I state. "So, I need another job while it's under construction."

She tilts her head to the side for a second. "Well, first off, please don't do this because of me and Kink. Do not think you need to change Lucky's for our new business."

I figured she'd think this. And honestly, if I hadn't gone into business with her for Kink, I probably wouldn't be doing it. "I've wanted to do it for a while now. The fact we're going to remodel the basement for Kink just makes this the perfect time."

"Okay then." She starts digging into her Chanel bag and pulls out a checkbook and pen, clicking the end she asks. "How much do you want me to make it out for?"

"No, no, no," I say, quickly throwing up my hands. "I don't want your money, Jasmine. This isn't about that."

She frowns. "Why not?"

I run a hand through my hair in frustration. I don't want her to think I'm using her. That is not what this is about. "I have money saved up. I just need a job in the meantime to keep funds flowing," I explain.

She puts her pen and checkbook away and smiles. "Well, I can help with that too. Ever heard of Glass?"

"The strip club?" I question. "Who hasn't?" It's the classiest one on the Strip. They have the best girls and the strongest security.

"What about it?" Not sure what that has to do with me. I've never been inside, but the girls from the club come into Lucky's. They're great tippers.

"I can get you a job there."

I begin to laugh. "I'm not going to strip."

"Not as a dancer. A cocktail waitress," she clarifies. "They make bank there. Plus, they might be able to put you behind the bar."

"Okay." I could do that. It's just serving drinks. I've worked in a bar since before I was even legal. It's all I know really.

"Come on," she says, taking one last sip of her orange juice, and scoots out of the booth. She throws some cash down on the table and grabs my hand, yanking me out.

"Where are we going?" I ask as she takes me across the casino floor and to the elevators.

"To get you that job," she says vaguely.

I'm not sure what Glass has to do with Kingdom, but she takes me over to tower one, and I wave at Nigel when he sees me.

"Jasmine. Alexa. What can I do for you two ladies today?" he asks, coming around from behind his desk. He seems to always be here.

"We're here to see Bones," she answers.

"Is he expecting you?"

She shakes her head, and he picks up his phone that sits on his desk. After a few seconds, he speaks. "Sir, you have Jasmine and Alexa down here wanting to speak to you ..." A short pause. "Yes, sir." He hangs up. "Right this way, ladies." He steps up to the private elevator and scans a key card, taking us up to the thirteenth floor.

We follow him down the hallway to a room that reads BONES on the door. "Thank you," Jasmine and I say at the same time as we enter.

"Ladies." Bones nods, standing from his desk. He comes around to the front and leans back against it, crossing his ankles and arms over his chest.

I step over to the wall to see pictures hanging on it. There's one of

Titan, Bones, and Cross standing on a baseball field wearing deep blue and white Wildcats uniforms. They each have baseball bats in their hands, and none of them are even smiling. They look young, and they're not covered in as many tattoos as they are now. It's weird. Almost as if I'm looking at them naked without them. I've only ever known them covered in ink. It's strange, but they don't look any less approachable without them. Like they've always been intimidating.

It's odd seeing them doing something so common. I would have never expected them to play sports. Especially college level. I'm guessing that's where they are, considering the size of the stadium behind them.

"Alexa wants a job," Jasmine states.

"Uh, no ..." I spin around, eyes wide. *What is she doing?* He just signed a contract with us. Why would she go to him for this? Laughing nervously, I add, "That's not what I ..."

"And you came to me?" he asks, sounding just as confused as I am at the moment.

I don't want him to think I'm using him. Or her. "No, that's not ... I never said—"

"Yes," she interrupts me. "You said if she needed anything to let you know."

He looks at me and nods once. "I did. What were you thinking?"

I bite my bottom lip confused and scared. Jasmine mentioned Glass, so why are we here talking to Bones?

"Glass," Jasmine says, obviously doing all the talking here since I can't get a sentence out. "I told her you could get her a waitressing or bartending job at Glass. It's just while she remodels the bar."

"Yeah, sure, I can do that," he agrees without giving it another thought.

"Really?" I ask wide-eyed. "Thank you." That seemed almost too easy. I wasn't sure what the hell Jasmine was doing, but I'm going to owe her dinner for this.

"Of course." He nods once, uncrossing his arms. "Whatever you need."

Who knew Bones could be such a nice guy?

CROSS

I PUSH OPEN Bones's office door with a stack of papers in my hand but come to a stop when I see Jasmine and Alexa standing in front of his desk. The girls turn their heads to look at me over their shoulders.

"Alexa? What are you doing here?" I'm guessing it has to do with Kink. They are all partners now.

"Bones just gave Alexa a job at Glass," Jasmine announces.

The smile drops off my face, and my eyes go from her to Alexa's. "Excuse me?" I ask, blinking.

"It's just for a couple of months," Alexa says, turning to fully face me. "Hopefully," she adds quickly.

"You can have the job for as long as you need it," Bones states, walking back to sit behind his desk.

"Bones, may I speak to you for a second." I made it sound like a question, but it wasn't.

He leans back in his chair. "Ladies, if you would give us a moment, please."

"Yeah, sure," Alexa says, bowing her head and pushing blond hair behind her ear. "Thanks again, Bones."

I step to the side, allowing them room to exit. Once they walk into the hallway, I slam the door shut and turn back to Bones. "What in the fuck are you doing?" I demand.

He frowns, tilting his head to the side. "She came to me for help. You expected me to deny her?"

I step forward, pointing a finger at him. "And you thought that Glass, of all places, is where she is best suitable?" She's not a fucking stripper.

"Listen, Cross. I was doing her and you a favor. I know you're seeing her and thought I'd help her out. She came to me and asked for a job specifically at Glass. What was I supposed to do?"

I snort, ignoring the fact he recognized I'm seeing her. I thought he, of all people, would keep what I'm doing a secret. He's the most secretive person I know. Bones is very private in everything he does. "Say 'fuck no.'"

He sighs. "I told her yes, and I'm not going to fire her just because you don't want her there. Alexa is an adult and can make her own decisions. If she wants to quit, then she'll quit." With that, he drops his eyes to his computer screen, dismissing me.

I slap the papers onto his desk and rush out of his office to find her and Jasmine standing in the hallway. I grip Alexa's upper arm and pull her away. "I need to speak to you."

"Cross—"

"Now," I interrupt her protest, yanking her into my office and slamming the door shut behind us. "You will not work at Glass," I state immediately.

She arches a brow, pushing a hip out. "Excuse me?"

I shake my head. "Absolutely not. I won't allow it."

"Good thing I didn't ask for your permission then." She laughs like I'm joking.

"It's a fucking strip club!" I snap.

"If you would have asked, then you'd know I'm going to waitress or bartend, not dance naked!" she shouts.

She's right, I didn't know that, but that doesn't mean it's any better. I remove my Zippo from my pocket and start flipping it open and closed. "I don't want you to ..."

"This has nothing to do with you, Cross." Her eyes glare at me, and her body is now stiff. Just like the fight we had at my house the other night.

"Why do you want to bartend at Glass all of a sudden?" She owns a fucking bar, for Christ's sake, and she's opening up a sex club. Why add Glass to her already full schedule?

"I'm closing Lucky's down to remodel it," she snaps, still pissy. "I need a job in the meantime."

"Well, Glass is not it!"

Her nostrils flare. "I will work wherever I damn well please!"

I slam both of my fists on the desk. "No. You. Won't."

"Why the fuck not?"

"Because I won't allow it!" It's as simple as that. I used to practically live there with Grave. I know what kind of shit goes on there, and it's a no for me. Even the waitresses and bartenders will go home with guys for the right price. I'm not saying Alexa's that type of girl, but where there's opportunity …

"You don't get to make decisions for me!" she snaps.

"You're my woman!" I didn't mean for it to come out like that, but by the way her face turns red, I can tell I've hit a nerve.

"Your woman?" she questions with a laugh that was not humorous.

Fuck! "You know what I mean."

"Obviously, I don't," she argues. "Because we're not exclusive, Cross. We're not even dating."

Her reasoning doesn't sit well with me. "Are you saying you're seeing someone else?"

She crosses her arms over her chest, pushing her already perky tits up even more, and looks away from me, staring out my floor-to-ceiling windows that showcase the Strip. Mitch enters my mind, and if he was right here in front of me, I'd knock his ass out just because I can.

"Alexa?" I snap.

"No!" she shouts. "But that doesn't mean I'd turn a date down if offered."

"Abso-fucking-lutely not!" I growl.

She rolls her beautiful green eyes. "We said this was just sex. That it would be our secret. That way, when it's over, no one would feel awkward when we hang out."

I can't argue that she's wrong. But we've been fucking for what, a month now? She's more to me than that. "And is that what this is to you?" I question.

She throws her hands out to her side before they hit her bare thighs. "What do you want me to say, Cross? That I like you?" She steps closer to me. "Hmm?" She takes another step closer. "Do you want me to confess my undying love for you so that you'll feel superior over me ..."

I grip her face in my hands and yank her forward, closing what little space is left between us, and kiss her. She opens her lips for me immediately, and I take the opportunity to deepen the kiss—my tongue dancing with hers. Her hands grip my T-shirt, and I press my hips into hers so she can feel how hard I am for her right now.

She pulls away all of a sudden. "Cross ..."

"I'll give you a job, but you have to quit Glass," I offer before we go back to a yelling match that I know I can't win. Those two days without her after I kicked her out of my house were miserable. I'm trying not to make that mistake again.

She frowns. "I own a bar. That's what I know."

I push some loose blond strands behind her ear. "I know. Grave runs one of the nightclubs here in Kingdom." Who knows when he'll come back? And if it's soon, he'll still want his nights free to spend time at home with his girl. "While he's gone, I've taken it over. It's yours."

"What?" she asks, stepping back, and I let her go to give her the space.

"It's yours. You can run it." Kingdom really has whatever you could possibly need—it has three nightclubs, over ten restaurants. Twenty sports bars. Tattoo shop—Tit-for-Tat. A shopping mall that connects all four towers. Golf course, bowling alley, wedding chapel, five pools, and its own theater with ten screens. They play movies twenty-four seven. And not to mention the largest convention center. It sponsors anything from UFC fights to sold-out concerts.

"Cross. No. that's not ..."

"It's a perfect solution. You can manage it. Your brother can work there too. However many employees you need to hire from Lucky's, you can. We can always use more help." I know she keeps a small staff at her bar. We have over sixty-five waitresses and thirty bartenders that are in rotation at Crown. We don't have requirements on how often they work. Some are three nights a week, and others are five times a month. That's why we employ so many.

She shakes her head. "Derek quit the bar. And he would never work for anything here at Kingdom. He thinks Bones is in with the Mafia." She laughs but stops when I don't and swallows nervously. Lowering her voice, she asks, "Is he?"

"Yes," I say honestly.

She gasps, her eyes widening.

"We all are." I don't feel the need to lie to her. I trust Alexa. Plus, this is something that she could find online if she just did some research. I hate to admit that her lack of knowledge about the Kings and our friends hurts my feelings. I thought she'd have looked me up by now. And honestly, I'm surprised that April hasn't already filled her in on this. Or Jasmine, for that matter. I know she's hung out with Haven before. She's met Luca. Not like he introduces himself as mafia royalty, but still. The information is right there if she wanted it.

She starts to pace. "Cross? This is ... He was right." Her hands fist. "I hate when Derek is right. Now what do I do? You're friends with the Mafia."

"Technically, you are too," I add to her rambling.

"No, I'm not," she says defensively, coming to a stop.

"Yes ..." She shakes her head. "Haven."

"What about her?" Her voice has a high pitch to it. "Oh my God, is she okay?"

"She's married to Luca Bianchi, who runs the Italian-America Mafia here in Vegas."

She just stands there and stares at me, looking surprised and terrified at the same time. So, I step into her once again, placing my hands on her shoulders to keep her in place since she looks like she's about to bolt any second. "Luca owns Glass." I'm not going to disclose that Bones owns half of it as well. That's his secret to tell, not mine. "That's how Bones was going to get you the job."

"And Jasmine knows all of this? That's why she took me to

Bones." Her wide eyes search mine like she's waiting for me to say gotcha.

"Yeah." We grew up with Jasmine, Haven, and Emilee—those three women know more about us than any other women ever will.

"I, uh ..." She pulls away from me.

"Alexa ...?"

"Need a moment." She spins around and rushes out of my office.

SIXTEEN
ALEXA

I CAN'T BELIEVE it! How did I not see it? Was I that blind? Or just stupid? A conversation I once had with my brother and April comes to mind when she first found out that Ethan was hiding something from her.

She sits across the bar from me up at Lucky's.

"Anything you need me to do?" Derek asks. "Want me to talk to him about something? Is it girls?" he asks referring to Ethan.

She shakes her head. "I found a key card of some sort from Kingdom at the shop today. I think it fell out of his jacket pocket."

"What?" I ask. "How the hell would he get in there?" Her younger brother isn't even old enough to gamble.

She shrugs. "I'm not sure what the hell he would be doing with that."

Derek's dark eyes look around before he leans forward and whispers to her, "Kingdom is bad fucking news, April."

She waves him off. "It's just a casino."

"No. I hear shit in here. Kingdom is into some bad shit."

"Like what?" She frowns.

"Yeah? Like what?" I ask Derek. How the hell does he know about what goes on there? I've never heard talk in here about Kingdom before.

"I hear that the guy, Bones, is in big with the Mafia. Whatever they want, he gets them. Vice versa. And they bury bodies in the desert."

"Mafia? Really?" She laughs. "Since when do you believe in that shit? And what could this Bones guy get them?"

He shrugs. "I don't know exactly. I just know that anything goes there. I guess there's some sort of black market that the guys run."

"Illegally?"

He rolls his dark eyes. "That's what black market stands for."

"What would Ethan have to do with that?" She wonders, still skeptic.

He shakes his head. "You need to find out. And better hope that it's not too late to get him out of it."

Bodies? Isn't that what Jasmine mentioned to Haven that morning at breakfast? How in the fuck did Derek know about all that? And who did he hear it from? Who is he hanging out with that would have that kind of inside information?

"Alexa?" I hear Jasmine call my name, but I jump onto the elevator. Before the door can close, she jumps in. "Hey, what happened?"

I spin around on her. "Luca runs the Mafia?"

She sighs, her shoulders sagging.

"Derek was right, and you …"

"It's none of Derek's business what others choose to do with their life," she snaps. "Sometimes it's either you do what you're told, or you die." She turns away from me, all of a sudden regretting getting in the elevator with me. "I don't expect someone like you or Derek to understand that."

The elevator dings, and the door opens. She steps out, and I go to reach out for her, but she pulls her arm away just in time to avoid it. "Jasmine?" Now I'm the one hollering at her, but she's gone.

I run my hands through my hair, aggravated. *What in the fuck just happened?*

"Problem?"

I jump when I hear the man behind me. Spinning around, I come face-to-face with another King—Titan. All the Kings have one thing about them that's the same—intimidation. They are all covered in ink, have muscles, and a pretty face. It's truly unfair. Like they were all made in a lab. Titan is by far the largest of them. He has tattoos like Bones that run up and around his neck.

"Something like that," I mumble.

He looks over at their private entrance where Jasmine ran out of the double doors. "She'll come back."

She can't run too far. We're partners now. "Yeah," I agree.

"There you are, babe." I hear a woman say and then see Emilee step up next to him. "Thought you were meeting me outside." She looks at me, smiling. "Hey, Alexa. How are you doing?"

"Good," I lie. I'm confused as fuck, and I hate that my best friend is away. But even if April was here, I still wouldn't be able to talk to her about what's going on. Not with what she's going through right now. It sucks feeling alone.

Emilee frowns. "Titan, I'll meet you up in your office," she says, dismissing him.

"Okay." He leans down and gives her a quick kiss on the lips, and then he turns, getting back on the elevator.

"Come on. Let's take a drive." She links her arm in mine and escorts me out the glass double doors and down the steps to a white Rolls-Royce Phantom coupe parked at the curb. I fall into the passenger seat, and she starts it up. "Talk to me."

I glance out the blacked-out window, not really looking at anything as she pulls away from the Kings' private entrance. "About?"

"Whatever it is that's bothering you," she says simply.

"It doesn't matter." Everything I've known is a lie. Or maybe I was just stupid and naïve. Bottom line—I only have myself to blame.

"Of course, it does. Tell me. Maybe I can help you out with it."

She did grow up with them. She's married to a King. Why not? I'll give it a try. "I just found out that Bones is in with the Mafia."

"Ahh." She nods, pulling onto the Strip. "I see."

"And I guess Haven is married to it."

"Yep. Poor girl never stood a chance." She chuckles. "She dated Luca while we were in school. She fell for him before she even knew what the Mafia was."

Not surprised about that part. "Jasmine is mad at me," I add, seeing where it gets me.

She sighs heavily. "Jasmine is going through something right now."

"Like what?" I ask, worried for her.

"Her dad."

I frown. "What about him?" I don't know much about Jasmine's family. She never talks about them.

"Well, he found out about Kink, and he is pissed. Told her to back out. She refused, of course. Jasmine isn't one of those women who can be told what to do, ya know? Even by her father."

That's why she was snappy with me. I've never seen her that way before. She's always smiling. Even when I know it's fake. She's good at that—making things look okay. "So, what happened?"

"Last she said to me was that she told him to fuck off and to stay out of her business." Emilee shrugs.

"Why would he care that she opens up a Kink?" I wonder.

"Jasmine's dad is a big deal ... or so he thinks. And he takes his reputation very seriously." She rolls her eyes so hard her head moves. "He's a piece of shit. Always has been. Always will be."

"So, what's going to happen when she chooses to go against his demands?"

"I'm guessing he'll cut her off. Who the hell knows? Jasmine has

154

always been very independent. Well, I don't have to tell you that. You're her friend. She'll figure it out."

I sit back and let out a sigh. I never stopped to think about what others would think once they see we are opening up Kink. The members that will come in and out. I'm guessing most, if not all, will be high profile. I mean, some average Joe Smith won't be able to afford fifty grand to join.

I DIDN'T HAVE MUCH TO SAY TO EMILEE. WE DROVE AROUND IN silence after she informed me of Jasmine's situation. So, when she took me back to Kingdom, I jumped in my own car and headed to her house. I wasn't ready to speak to Cross just yet. Not sure what to really say to him anyway. I was afraid I'd just make myself look stupid again.

I stand on the front porch of her mansion and ring the bell. Seconds later, the door opens to Jasmine standing before me. Her eyes drop to the bottle of Fireball in my right hand before they return back to me. "Figured we'd have a drink."

I half expect her to slam the door in my face, but I'm hopeful when she takes a step back, holding it open for me instead. I notice the boxes sitting in the foyer immediately. Not hard to miss. "Are you moving?" I joke.

"Yes," she deadpans.

The smile drops off my face, and I go to ask why she hasn't already told me this but her doorbell rings.

Jasmine yanks it open. "Lauren," She sighs. "What can I do for you today?"

"Your dog is in your backyard." The older woman places her hands on her hips.

"Yes. I know this may come as a shock, but dogs have to piss and shit like humans do."

She pulls her lips back at Jasmine's choice of words. "She's barking at me through your fence."

"Dogs bark. Just like Karen's bitch," she states dryly.

The woman gasps.

"Have a nice day, *Karen*." Then she slams the door in her face.

"You got a dog?" I ask confused.

"Yeah," she answers, walking from the foyer.

I quicken my pace behind her as she heads to her kitchen. "Wait. What?" Let's go back to her moving. "Are you serious about moving?" How did I not know this?

"As a heart attack."

We enter the kitchen, and I place the Fireball bottle on the counter and turn around to face her as she gets two shot glasses out of the cabinet. "Since when?"

Grabbing the glasses, she turns back around and places them on the white marble counter and unscrews the lid before pouring us both a shot. She stays silent, fills her glass, and then throws it back, not even bothering to wait for me. Once done, she refills it.

Before she can take this one, I reach out and grab it from her hand. "What the hell is going on, Jasmine?" I demand this time.

Placing her hand on the counter, she bows her head and takes in a deep breath. Then she looks up, her eyes on mine. "I was a Queen."

I've heard of that before.

"Hey, girlie."

I look up from behind the bar to see Jasmine sit down next to April. "Hey. What are you doing here?" April asks her.

She shrugs. "Was on my way out for the night and thought I'd stop by and see Alexa. Have to support my friends." She drops a couple of hundreds in the glass tip jar that sits on the bar. "What are you up to tonight?"

"Nothing," April answers, taking a sip of her Corona.

"Come out with me. I'm going to a party," Jasmine offers, fixing the thin shoulder straps to her little black dress.

"Nah—"

"Hey, you work at Kingdom," I interrupt her, joining their conversation. I'm not sure exactly what she does, but I've heard her mention it. Maybe she can help April out with her Ethan problem. "We have questions."

"What? You work at Kingdom? What do you do there?" April wonders.

Jasmine chuckles, shaking her head. "Sorry, ladies. I can't discuss that."

April frowns as my brother jumps in while he pours a Miller Lite into a frosted mug. "See, told you some bad shit goes down there."

Jasmine squares her shoulders. "You know nothing about Kingdom. Trust me."

He tops off the mug and sets it down before placing his forearms on the bar and leaning into her personal space. "I know that Bones is in with the Mafia. I know that a lot of illegal shit goes on there." He pulls back and looks her up and down the best he can since she's sitting, and adds, "And I know you're a Queen."

"What's a Queen?" April whispers to me.

I shrug. No fucking clue.

Jasmine places her hands on the bar and stands, leaning over it. They're nose to nose. "You seem to know a lot about nothing."

His eyes drop to her breasts that are poking out of her skintight dress. He licks his lips before his eyes meet hers again. "I know enough." Reaching out, he takes a piece of her red hair, freeing it from behind her ear. "How much does a Queen go for these days?" he asks her.

Her red-painted lips turn up at the corners before she runs her tongue along her upper lip. "More than you can afford."

He lets go of her hair, his finger trailing down over her neck. "I don't know. I've heard pussy comes pretty cheap."

"Not the good ones."

"Hey, Derek? Where's my beer?" a guy shouts from the end of the bar.

He ignores him as he looks at her. It's like they're in a staring contest. Whoever looks away first will lose. "Let's just say our opinions differ on what's good," he finally says before pulling away from her and delivering the beer.

"What was that about?" I ask Jasmine, wide-eyed and confused.

"I gotta go," Jasmine states, picking up her clutch while completely ignoring my question. "We'll do lunch next week." Then she walks away without another word.

"Which is?" I ask again, hoping she fills me in this time. I tried to ask Derek, but he blew me off. Then I just forgot about it. I can't ask him now. He won't even speak to me. And I can't go to him now that I know about Bones and Luca. I can't let him know he was right.

She walks over to the bar and sits down at one of the high back stools. I sit down next to her. "Titan runs the Queens at Kingdom. The Queens are high-paid escorts for the worldwide elite."

"Oh." Not what I was expecting, but that conversation she had with my brother makes much more sense now.

"I couldn't talk about it then because it involved an attorney and an NDA. Even now, I'm not supposed to say anything, but ... Titan wouldn't mind me telling you because I know you won't say anything." She runs a hand through her hair. "A ... friend was in a hard place and needed a job. I knew about the Queens, so I went with her, and Titan hired us both. My father found out and demanded that Titan fire me, but he wouldn't. My father is a member." She rolls her eyes. "A man buys you a few tacos from a taco truck, and you're expected to fuck him in the back seat of his truck. How dare a woman fuck and actually get paid for it? Anyway, now my dad is threatening to take everything from me if I don't stop Kink."

I reach out and place my hand on top of hers. "We can put it on hold." I shrug. "Do it another time. Lucky's isn't going anywhere."

She shakes her head. "What my father doesn't know is that the money I put down for Kink didn't come from him. He has no control over that. While I was a Queen, I met a guy who paid me a lot of money to just hang out with him. He was newly married, but his wife refused to do anything with him. I was supposed to spend an entire week with him in New York, but something fell through, and he had to head back home early. He found his partner's son in bed with his wife."

My eyes widen. Not where I saw that story going.

"She's a year younger than me, and he's fifty-five. She didn't know that she had been caught with her boy toy. So he flew to Vegas, and we spent the rest of that week here in town at an attorney's office."

"Doing what exactly?" I ask, trying to keep up. I'm still processing everything I've found out in the past hour.

"He sold me several properties he had for really cheap. He was going to wait a few months and then file for a divorce. His parents are dead. He no longer trusted his business partner, especially if he knew his son was fucking his wife. And he didn't have any kids."

"That's where you got the money for Kink?" I start to piece it together.

"Yep." She nods. "Even though he had a prenup, he still didn't want to take any chances of her getting anything. After his divorce was final, I offered to sell them back to him at the same price as I bought them, of course, but he told me to keep them. I sold one of them last month when I decided I wanted to open Kink with you. I went to Bones first, explained the situation, and asked him to help us because I knew we weren't going to be able to do it on our own."

"But your dad ...?"

"I don't care about him." She averts her eyes to her hand on the bar. "He's on this house with me. And that's why I'm moving out and selling it." Her eyes come back to mine. "He'll hold it over me for the rest of my life, and I refuse to live like that."

"You know you can stay with me, right?" I say. "I mean, it's not a mansion, but I've got a spare room."

She smiles at me. "Thank you, but I've got somewhere lined up. And I've already made an offer on another house. If I'm lucky, I'll be moving in shortly."

I nod my head once, not digging into that. She's already told me enough about her life tonight. I'm not going to question who she's sleeping with. Hell, for all I know, she plans on moving in with Titan and Emilee in the meantime. "Well, if there is anything that I can do, just let me know." And as I say the words, I already know what I can do for her.

As she's pouring us both a shot, I send a quick text to Emilee.

CROSS

I'm SITTING BEHIND my desk the following morning when I hear a knock on the door. "Come in," I growl, hoping it's not Bones. I'm not in the mood to do shit today.

The door opens, and I look up to see Alexa is back. She softly closes the door behind her and comes to stand in front of my desk. I'm surprised to see her here. Again. After what was said yesterday. I've wanted to call her a hundred times but refrained. Not sure what to say or how to say it. "Have a seat," I offer at her silence.

She steps forward and sits down in the empty chair across from my desk, crossing one leg over the other and pushing her hair behind her ear. She's nervous.

"What do you need, Alexa?" I ask, my eyes falling to the manila envelope in her lap. Wonder what's in it?

"I just wanted to say I'm sorry for snapping at you yesterday." She runs her hands over the envelope. "I heard rumors and figured there were some truths to them. I just hated that Derek was right."

Derek was right? Just what does her brother know? I already don't like the guy. He's a punk-ass bitch if you ask me. But I won't tell her that because I'm pretty sure she already knows. So, I just stare at her.

"Anyway, I wanted to come up here. I just spoke to Bones and quit Glass. Do you still have an opening at the club?"

"Of course." I want to fist pump the air right now but refrain from looking like a jealous bitch. I wasn't going to let her work at Glass, no matter what she said. But I'm glad she made that decision on her own. Things would have been awkward when I stepped in to destroy that job for her.

"Lucky's is going to be open through Sunday and then shut down for the remodel. I'll start here at Kingdom on Monday if that's okay with you?"

I nod. "Absolutely."

She stands, taking the envelope into her hands. "Thank you." And without another word, she turns, and I let her walk out of my office, knowing that more needed to be said.

My door opens, and I smile, expecting it to be her coming back, but it falls when it's just Titan. "What?"

He closes my door. "We've got a problem."

Of course, we do. "What is it?"

"The man Bones carved open?" he questions.

"Yeah, what about him?" We didn't find any more diamonds in his body or in his car parked at Glass. He only had six on him, meaning we are still missing six. We did, however, return the ones we found. The Mason brothers better hurry up and do their job, or we'll own Kale's business and share it with Luca and Nite. If they don't produce on their end, we won't hold up ours.

"Well, he worked for Kale." He sits down in the chair.

I frown, tilting my head. "So, Kale fucked over our client. It wasn't stolen or anything like that?" I question.

He shrugs. "As far as I know, no. But if that's the case, why didn't he have all of them?"

"Maybe they distributed the diamonds out?" I offer. "It'd be harder to find them if they're scattered."

"Or maybe that guy had all of them at some point but sold some." He leans back in the chair, linking his fingers behind his head.

The guy didn't have a cell phone on him or in his car. We found that odd. Who doesn't have a cell these days? Especially if he's buying and selling product. They have to communicate somehow. "Have you told Bones this?"

"Nope. I wanted to have more concrete evidence before I went to him."

"Has Luca found the guy's address?" His wallet was in the center console of his car, but it didn't have a driver's license, and the car wasn't even registered to him. It was another dead end. No surprise there.

"He told me he's got Nite working on it when I spoke to him an hour ago."

I sigh. Well, there's nothing else we can do other than wait and see who gets answers first.

ALEXA

I'm CLOSING DOWN the bar later that night when my door opens, and I see Jasmine enter. "Don't you ever sleep?" I ask her.

"Sleep is for the weak. Only those willing to sacrifice will ever make it." She sits down across from me. "I've always preferred the night over the day."

"Well ..." I slap the bar. "I'm actually glad you're here because I have something for you." Walking to the other end of the bar, I pull my purse out of the cubby and remove the paperwork that I picked up on the way to work earlier this evening. Bones and Cross weren't the only two Kings I spoke to while at Kingdom this morning. I had messaged Emilee yesterday when I went to Jasmine's house, asking her if Titan could help me out with something. Jasmine mentioning an NDA and an attorney gave me the little information I needed. I don't know any attorneys, but Titan does. After I explained to Emilee what I needed one for, she told me Titan would meet with me this morning. "Here you go." I slap it down in front of her.

"What's this?"

"This is me paying you back." I say the same thing she said to me when she showed up here with the papers for Kink.

True to his word, Titan called his attorney while I was sitting in his office this morning, I explained what I wanted, and he had the papers drawn up within an hour.

She frowns but opens it up and pulls out the contents. Her green eyes scan over it quickly. Then they snap up to glare at me. "You're kidding, right?"

"Nope." I shake my head with a smirk on my face. "One hundred percent. All in."

She sets it down and sighs. "This is not what I meant ..."

"I know. This is what I want to do."

"Alexa ..."

"You and me, Jasmine. I trusted you. Now you trust me."

She drops her head, running her hand through her hair. Then she flips it back and stands with a big smile on her face. I added her to Lucky's as a partner. I want her to know that I have as much faith in her as she does me.

SEVENTEEN
ALEXA

T HE NIGHTCLUB AT Kingdom is more stressful than I thought it would be. I've run my small bar for one year now, and I don't think I've ever seen this many people in a week at my bar who are here in just one night.

Crown has three stories, two dance floors, four bars, and bottle service. The place is like nothing I've ever seen before, and I love it.

The rush. The demand. I like being on my toes. I've been working here for two weeks, and it never lets up. There are no slow nights. Just busy and busier. Plus, they stay open until four in the morning. I've always closed Lucky's at two because it just doesn't have the crowd to stay open the extra two hours. My schedule is thrown off, making me extremely tired.

"I'm going to use the restroom really quick!" I yell in the barback's ear. I've held it for too long, waiting for it to slow down, but it's not going to happen.

He nods his head and shouts, "Okay!"

I take off and rush out from behind the bar and down the left hallway. Thankfully, there's not a long line. Once done, I wash my hands and step back out into the hallway just as the men's door opens across from me, and I come face-to-face with my ex Mitch.

It's deja vu that night at the Airport.

"Alexa," he says, surprised. His dark eyes drop to my Kingdom sleeveless crop top that I wear, and the smile disappears. "You're kidding, right?"

I've ignored every text and call he's sent me since I saw him at the Airport. I thought avoiding him was enough. That he would eventually let it go. But as luck has it, here he is. The cockroach that just won't die. "What?" I cross my arms over my chest. Bitch mode activated.

"You're working for him now too?" he growls.

I don't like the way he says it. Like I'm Cross's little bitch.

"What happened to Lucky's?" He digs when I don't confirm what is so obvious.

"That's none of your business," I state.

He laughs. "Your brother did say it was going under."

"What?" I demand. My brother was talking to him about the bar? What the fuck? "When did you see him?"

He smiles. "That's none of *your* business," he says, throwing my own words back in my face.

I slam both of my hands into his chest, catching him off guard and shoving his back into the wall. "Stay the fuck away from my family."

"What are you going to do, Alexa? Sick your new boy toy on me?" He shakes his head once. "Have him light me up?"

Light him up? "What does that mean?"

He laughs, gripping my wrists. I flinch when his fingers tighten to the point they'll bruise. "Your man has some kind of sick obsession with fire. Haven't you looked him up?"

"No," I answer honestly. You can't believe all the shit you read online. "I'm sure it's all lies anyway."

"Oh, yeah?" He arches a brow. "Why don't you ask him what happened to his dad."

I frown. "What do you ...?"

"Everything okay here?"

I take another step back from Mitch at the sound of Cross's voice and turn to see him standing a few feet from us in the hallway with Bones next to him. "Yeah," I say, all of a sudden uncomfortable. Why do I feel like I was doing something bad? What if Cross heard what he said to me, and he thinks I'm asking around about him? I haven't asked him anything personal about his life. I hope he knows that I definitely wouldn't go behind his back to my ex and do so.

"You sure?" Cross asks, but his eyes are glued to Mitch. His right hand holds his Zippo, and he's flipping it open and closed. Like always.

"Positive," I try to reassure him. Walking over to him, I place my hand on his hard chest.

He finally looks down at me, his green eyes looking clouded under the neon lights. I give him a soft smile, trying to ease the tension even though I can feel the heat coming from Bones. If Cross doesn't knock Mitch out, I have a feeling Bones will. "I just needed a quick bathroom break." Then rising up on my tiptoes, I give Cross a soft kiss on his lips, not caring if Mitch and Bones are watching us.

CROSS

I DON'T KISS her back. I'm too focused on her ex. He still stands against the wall, now glaring at me. She pulls back and walks away, heading to the bar, leaving us alone.

He reaches up and wipes the corner of his mouth while his eyes are on her ass.

This fucker. "You know you're not the only dick that wants her."

His eyes meet mine, and he pushes off the wall, straightening his shoulders like he's ready to pounce. Bones goes to step around me to beat his ass, but I place my hand on his chest to stop him.

"She won't stay once she finds out about the real you," Mitch states.

"She knew the fake you and still left." I shrug. I haven't asked what happened between the two of them. Honestly, I didn't think he was an issue, but the fucker just keeps showing up. But I'm going to tonight after she's off work and in my bed.

His lips thin, and his nostrils flare. *Good.* I want him to give me a reason to beat his fucking ass.

"Enjoy it while it lasts." He walks up next to me. "Because when she leaves you, she'll be crawling back to me. And well, let's just say— I loved it when she was on her knees."

My hands fist down by my sides at that. Any thought of her with someone else is enough to make me want to put someone's head through a wall. But I don't know where they stand right now, and I'm not about to fuck things up with her. That's what he wants.

He just chuckles, and I allow him to walk away. For now.

"You should have let me handle him," Bones growls. "That way, his blood isn't on your hands."

"I'll take care of it," I inform him.

———

"Any word on when Grave and April will be back? I still haven't spoken to her," Alexa states as we enter the Royal Suite. A quick look at my watch tells me it's five thirty in the morning. I'm exhausted. The fact that she's been working at Crown has me staying up all night because I want to make sure everything goes smoothly for her.

"No." I haven't heard from him either. But I have it on my list of things to ask Titan tomorrow if he has any news.

"I'll send April a text tomorrow," she adds. "Just to check up on her."

"What happened between you and Mitch?" I blurt out, not in the mood for anything else at the moment. Although I'm concerned about Grave and April, they will return when they're ready. It's only been two weeks, and I don't think that's nearly enough.

She stops and spins around to face me as I close the door. "It's not important."

"It is," I argue, needing to know. "I want to know. Please tell me." I resort to begging. I've realized that demanding anything gets me nowhere with Alexa. So, I have to try something different.

Looking away from me, she runs her hand through her blond hair. "Long story short, he cheated on me. And I left."

"When was the last time you were with him?" I dig.

Her head snaps to face me, and her eyes narrow. "Excuse me?"

I step into her. "You heard me. When was the last time he fucked you?"

She slams her hands into my chest. "Fuck you!"

Turning, she goes to stomp off, but I grab her upper arm and spin her back around to face me. "Answer the question, Alexa."

"You think I sleep around?" She arches a brow, challenging me while avoiding my question at the same time.

I want to say that she did fuck me that first night, but even I know that would be a fucking bomb blowing up in my face. "I think you two have a past, and I don't doubt he's tried lately." She was surprised to see him that night at the Airport. And he seems to be trying harder since he found out that we're together. Do I think it's a coincidence that he showed up at the club tonight? No! Someone he knows has seen her there since she started earlier last week, and he stopped by to check on her. I'm not an idiot. My question is was tonight the first time? Or was it just time for him to show his face to her?

"Don't worry about it, Cross." She yanks away from me. "I haven't fucked anyone else since you."

"Then why won't you tell me?" I chase after her into my bedroom.

She lets out a huff entering my bathroom. I'm not going to drop this. I will get the answers that I want, one way or another. "Alexa!"

"Before I met you," she snaps, turning to face me once again, now standing in the middle of my bathroom. "Hmm? Is that what you were looking for? It was months before the night I saw you at the

Airport. I was out with the girls, and I met up with him afterward." Placing her hands on her hips, she pushes her right one out. "When was the last time you fucked someone who wasn't me?"

"That night before the Airport," I answer.

Her eyes widen as her lips part. She didn't expect me to be honest with her. Why would I lie about that? I understand that we both have a past and that we're not virgins. How was I supposed to know that I'd see her that night? That we would be standing where we are right now?

"With who?" she asks.

"Rachel," I say. I fired her from Tit for Tat weeks ago, and I haven't seen nor heard from her since. She understood what we were doing—just fucking—was over, and there was no future there for her.

"Of course." She gives a hard laugh. "I knew you had. It was obvious, but I didn't want to even know."

Stepping into her, I cup her face. "But I haven't been with anyone else since then, and I don't want anyone else," I remind her. "But I need to know if I need to force Mitch to back off."

"No," she says softly. "He's a prick but harmless. He didn't know that I was working at that club. He looked just as surprised as I was seeing him there."

That's what she believes, but it's not the truth. It can't be. "And now?"

"What do you mean now?" She huffs.

"Do you think he's going to start showing up because he knows you're working there?"

She shrugs. "I'm not sure. But I do know that if I see him there, I will let you know. Okay?"

Oh, I'll know if he shows up. I have cameras all over that place. I'll make sure that I watch them every second when she's working. But I say. "Okay."

EIGHTEEN
ALEXA

CROSS IS SLEEPING next to me in his bed, and I've got my cell out. It's down to three percent, but I need to know what Mitch meant about the fire and his dad.

I go to google his name and realize that I don't know it. I've only ever heard people call him Cross. So I type that in.

Kingdom pops up, along with the other Kings. Cross is the third article down. I click on it.

It shows pictures of him playing baseball in high school and college. It shows a picture of Kingdom and Tit for Tat. Then I see an article titled "Oak Grove." I click on it, and it's a church.

It's on fire. A once gorgeous white structure is up in flames. The picture is taken from the front. Fire trucks are to the right, lining the side street.

I enlarge it. Red and orange flames engulf the church, lighting up the dark night.

Scrolling down, it says Father James was killed in the fire.

I look over the top of my cell at Cross as he moves, rolling onto his other side. My eyes go back to my phone. *His wife and son were thankfully not there at the time of the fire.* It doesn't say how it started, just that it was accidental.

I clicked on the next article. *Father James—beloved priest and member of the Three Wisemen—was a loving father and doting husband. Survived by wife, Genevieve James, and son, Hoyte James.*

Hoyte? Cross fits him better. I'm surprised he doesn't have a biblical name due to his father and religious background.

A passerby called 911 a little after two in the morning when they saw the church up in flames. The fire department arrived and entered the building. They retrieved the body of Father James, who was found in his office. The cause of the fire is still unknown, but no foul play was suspected.

"What are you doing?" Cross asks through a yawn.

"Nothing!" I answer, slapping my phone facedown on the sheets so he can't see it. It was dying fast anyway.

He sits up and runs a hand down his unshaven face, yawning again. "What time is it?"

"Late," I offer because I have no clue, and I'm not going to pick up my cell to look since I didn't exit out of the article I was reading.

He throws the covers off and gets out of his bed, heading toward his adjoining bathroom. I quickly pick up my cell, exit out of the news article, and look at the time. Placing it on the nightstand, I get up too and walk into the bathroom. He's standing at his sink, washing his hands in nothing but a pair of black boxer briefs.

I walk up behind him and look over his back. I've never had the chance to really look at his tattoo. It's a cross—it starts at the base of his neck and runs all the way down, the end dipped inside of his boxers. It spans from shoulder to shoulder. It's outlined in black ink. Looks like any other cross, but it's what's around it that makes the hairs on the back of my neck stand up. Fire. His entire back is covered in red, yellow, and orange flames. As if the cross is burning. It reminds me of the cross that stood high on the spire of the church his father was found dead in.

Stepping closer to it, I squint to get a better look at it. Like the fine print you should always read before you sign something, there's a story here. Or maybe it's the fact of what Mitch said to me and the article. But I see something there. The outline of the cross looks to be running. As if the heat of the flames is melting it down. But that's not what's really catching my attention. It's the scars that the tattoo hides. I spot one, two, three. They run up and down his spine.

Reaching out, I place my hand on his back to touch one, but he quickly spins around and grabs my wrist.

I jump and try to take a step back, but he doesn't let go. "Cross ..." My words die off as I get a look at him. His hard and muscular body is tense. His breathing has picked up, and his pretty green eyes are drilling holes into mine.

My heart pounds in my chest, trying to think of what to say. What to ask. "I ..." The ringing of his cell phone in his room cuts off whatever bullshit I was about to come up with.

Letting go of me, I rub my wrists as he walks out of the bathroom to go get it. I lean my head back and close my eyes, letting out a long breath.

You're being paranoid.

This is what every girl does when she starts falling for a guy—overanalyzes everything.

I'm not going to let Mitch get to me. What Cross and I have is a good thing. We sleep together yet still have our own lives. We're not dating. We're not living together. Just fucking. And now, he's my employer.

I read the article about his dad, and it was clearly an accident. As for the scars? That doesn't mean anything. Hell, I have them on my knees from when I wrecked my bike. The scars don't mean they have anything to do with the church. The fire. The tattoos ...

"Get dressed," he orders, making me jump when he comes back into the bathroom. Walking past me, he marches toward his closet.

"Where are we going?" It's like three in the morning.

Coming to a stop, he turns around and lets out a long sigh. His eyes no longer angry. They almost look sad. A darker green. "To Lucky's. There's been an incident."

CROSS

I PARK MY car behind Oak Grove and enter through the back door. "Dad?" I call out. He had sent me a message earlier while I was at baseball practice to meet him here. A quick look at my watch shows it's almost midnight. "Dad?" I yell this time.

No answer.

Making my way down the hallway, I open the door on my right and step into his office.

"Son," he says, looking up at me from behind his desk. My mother kneels on the floor to the right of it. Her palms on her thighs, head down. Mr. Reed—Bones and Grave's dad—lounges on the couch.

"Mom?" I go to walk over to her, but my father stands and side-steps his desk, blocking my view of her.

"I called you here ..."

"What in the fuck are you doing?" I demand, placing my hands on his shoulders to move him, but he doesn't budge. "Mom?" I call out to her, but she stays silent.

"I brought you here to repent," he states.

"Fuck that shit!" I've grown to where I need the pain. His punishment to me is my acceptance to his world. But why is my mother here? I can hear her softly crying.

"Don't talk to me that way!" he shouts, shoving me backward.

"Mom!" I bark at her, and she flinches. "What the hell are you doing? Get up!"

She stays still, and my father throws his head back, laughing. "She knows her place, son. Do you need a reminder of yours?" Before I can respond, he reaches out and wraps a hand around my throat. He pushes me backward through the office, taking away my air and practically lifting my feet off the floor. He knocks my back into the door, throwing it open in the process. He drags me down the rest of the hallway and into the chapel with Mr. Reed behind us. He then shoves me forward, making me trip and fall over a pew.

With a quick look around, I see that the candles are already lit, and he starts undoing his cuff links and then sliding his sleeves up his forearm.

"What in the fuck are you doing with Mom?" I demand. I've never seen her like that before. I mean, I'm twenty-one. I'm not a virgin. I know my father fucks around on her, but I don't think they're into BDSM shit and stuff like that. So, why was she kneeling on his office floor as if she's a submissive? Does he treat her the way he treats me? Worse?

"What I do with your mother is none of your business," he states and removes the cross from around his neck. He takes a candle and heats up the precious metal that he cherishes so much.

I fist my hands. "I will not bow down to you." Not today. I will not kneel for him to burn me. Not until I know what is going on. This is different than all the other times. Why now? Why her? What has happened that he wanted me to see that?

He looks up at me, and a bone-chilling smile spreads across his face. "Genevieve," he calls out.

Seconds later, my mother comes walking into the chapel. Tears run down her face, and I see that her right eye is swollen. He hit her.

"Come here, Gen," he calls her, and like a dog, she tucks her tail and slowly walks over to him.

"Mom." I step forward. "You don't have to do this."

She says nothing and doesn't even look my way. Once she gets close to him, he grabs her by the hair, and she cries out. He grips the back of her neck and shoves her facedown onto the floor that I've kneeled at so many times before. Kneeling beside her, he pins her down.

"Come over here, Cross. It's time."

"No," I state. I will not do whatever sick shit he's wanting from me.

175

"You will do this!" he growls. "It's time your mother pays for her sins."

He's lost his goddamn mind. "I won't do it."

Mr. Reed steps toward me, and I take a step back. "Leave him be." My father huffs. "I'll do it myself." While he holds her down with one hand, he holds up the cross to a candle, heating it up and then pressing it to her back.

She screams, thrashing against him.

I go to run over and rip him off, but Mr. Reed holds me back.

She sobs as he does it again. And again. Scarring her back with crosses to match mine. Once he decides he's done, he stands, and she falls to her side crying.

"Take her home," he orders Mr. Reed. "I'll finish this later."

Finish? What else is he going to do to her?

He lets go of me, and I stay where I am, not wanting to make it worse for my mother. "You piece of shit," I say through gritted teeth once they are gone. "How long have you been doing this to her?"

"Whenever she needs a reminder," he answers ominously.

"I won't allow you to do this," I growl.

He laughs at that. "What are you going to do to stop me?" Arching a brow, he lifts the cross and begins to heat it up again.

I charge him.

ALEXA GETS MY ATTENTION, SITTING IN MY PASSENGER SEAT, legs bouncing up and down while she bites on her fingernails. I've tried to avoid letting her see my back. The tattoos I've gotten over the years cover up most of my past, but she saw them. She touched them. I tried not to freak out, but I couldn't help it. The way it felt when she touched them had memories rushing back. Ones I buried long ago.

She sits up straighter and gasps as I pull up to her bar. Firetrucks surround it, and black smoke rolls from what's left of the burning structure. Stopping my car, she jumps out before I can even say anything to her.

I get out and walk over to her as she stands there crying with her hands to her face. I got the call that a 911 call was made and that it was on fire. I have an idea who did it and why, but I just need a way to prove it.

Reaching my arm out, I wrap it around her shoulders, and she turns into me, her hands gripping my shirt. "It's going to be okay," I tell her.

It'll be better than ever.

WE ALL SIT UP IN OUR ROYAL SUITE. WELL, EVERYONE EXCEPT for Grave and April. They are still away.

Titan stands at the kitchen island. Bones stands over by the floor-to-ceiling windows while Jasmine and Alexa sit on the couch.

"What are we doing here?" Alexa asks. "Shouldn't we be at the police station?"

"That's not needed," I inform her. I've got something better than the police.

"Then what—?"

Her voice is interrupted when there's a knock on the door. I walk over and answer it.

"Well, maybe you should just put me on a monthly salary." The guy winks at me as he enters.

"Seems that would be best, Jeffrey," I agree, closing the door behind him.

He goes to the center of the room and removes his shirt up and over his head and undoes his jeans.

"Uh …" Alexa scoots farther back in the couch cushion as the guy gets down to his boxers.

Once done, he spins around in a circle with his arms out wide. I nod my approval. And he gives me a "when are we going to stop doing this" look. Never is the only answer. We were raised not to trust anyone. A person can have your back a million times, but someone could get to them to backstab you once. I'll never give anyone that kind of trust. Especially someone who can be bought.

"It was arson," he states, bending down to pick up his shirt.

"What?" Alexa jumps to her feet. "Lucky's? Are you saying someone set it on fire?'

"Yeah," he says, buttoning his shirt and then pulling his pants on.

"How do you know?" she asks, moving her head back and forth to look from me to him.

"I know what to look for," he answers vaguely. "And they weren't even smart. The bar area was covered in an accelerant and lit by a match."

She falls back down onto the couch.

"Who all has a key?" he asks her. "There was no sign of forced entry."

"Me and my brother," she answers, bowing her head.

"And me," Jasmine speaks. "Alexa just gave me one yesterday."

"I know you didn't do this." She waves her off.

"You think your brother did?" Jasmine goes on.

"No." She shakes her head. "Maybe he lost his key."

"Or maybe he gave it to someone," I offer.

Everyone's head snaps up in my direction.

"He's framing you." Bones is the one who speaks to me, mimicking my thoughts.

"Who?" Alexa demands. "And why would they frame you by catching my bar on fire?"

"Because this is what I do," I answer, flipping my Zippo open and closed.

Her eyes widen at my honesty. "I don't understand," she mumbles.

That's because you don't know me. Not the real me. I walk over to the side of the couch and pick up my duffel bag. Dropping it onto the coffee table, I look at Jeffrey. "It's all there."

He nods. "As always, it's nice doing business with you Kings." He picks up the bag, and Titan helps him out the door.

NINETEEN
ALEXA

My bar was burned down. Well, thankfully, it didn't ruin everything. It's salvageable. Thank God. The structure is still there from what I saw. The police wouldn't allow me to walk through it. Said it wasn't safe. I'll go back tomorrow and see what kind of damage was really done.

Titan closes the door and comes back to the living room with us. Leaning forward, I place my face in my hands. "I'm confused." I look up, and my eyes land on Cross. "Tell me what is going on," I demand, getting irritated.

"Do you remember the burning of St. Mary's Cathedral last year?" Jasmine asks me.

I whip my head around to stare at her sitting beside me. "Yeah?"

I STAND BEHIND THE BAR, CLEANING IT UP AFTER CLOSING WITH the TV on. I normally never watch it but was tired of silence while being here alone.

A reporter stands in front of the once St. Mary's Cathedral. Smoke fills the night while firefighters try to put it out behind her. At this point, it's a total loss. "At this time, some are throwing speculation out regarding arson, but nothing has been confirmed yet." *It goes to a commercial, and I turn it off and throw my towel onto the bar, ready to go home.*

IT WAS HARD TO MISS. IT WAS HEARTBREAKING BECAUSE IT WAS so pretty. "What about it?" I ask Jasmine. What does that have to do with my bar?

She looks over my shoulder for a quick second and then back to me. "That was Cross. He set that fire."

I slowly stand and turn to where I can face him. He leans against the bar in the kitchen, looking at me unphased. "You set the cathedral on fire?" I ask slowly, expecting him to laugh at me. That's absurd, right?

He doesn't answer. Just fucking silence.

"Why would you do that?" I demand, still thinking it's impossible.

"Because a friend needed him." Titan is the one who answers.

"What kind of friend has you do that?" I snap.

"One who loves his wife," Bones answers.

"What—?"

"We had some friends who were to be married there," Jasmine interrupts me. "Someone wanted them dead, and we had been told that it was going to happen while at their wedding. The Kings were going to attend. It would have been mass casualties," Jasmine says softly, staring down at her hands in her lap. "Cross set it on fire and saved all of us that would have been there in attendance." She swallows. "He paid off the fire marshal then too so the report would show no foul play."

Foul play? My heart picks up at those words. They're the same ones I read online about the fire that killed his father. But I don't have time to think about that right now. I'll circle back. Right now, I need to focus on Lucky's.

I run a hand through my hair, not understanding. "This has nothing to do with my bar. Who was that guy?" I point at the door. "Why didn't he tell the police it was arson? And why the fuck did you give him money?" I'm not an idiot. There was cash in that bag. "And why the hell did he strip down." My mind wonders out loud.

Where does that leave me? Because now I can't go to the police and file a report. No matter if it's arson or not, they'll want a statement, and Cross wouldn't let me tell them anything. Said he'd take care of it.

"He was the fire marshal. I needed to make sure he wasn't wearing a wire." Cross finally speaks, and the answers knock the wind out of me because a part of me already knew who he was. I just didn't want to admit it to myself. "I paid him off to lie on his report."

"Why would you do that?" Tears sting my eyes. Lucky's is my livelihood. I was in the process of remodeling it, and then Jasmine and I were doing Kink. Now what?

"Because if he told the police the truth, then they'd only get in my way," he answers flatly.

"That is their job, Cross. What could they possibly get in the way of?" I snap at him.

"Making him pay."

"Who is he?" I ask, hands start to tremble. Everything is falling apart, and nothing makes sense.

"Mitch," he answers.

I start shaking my head. "He wouldn't ..." I trail off before I can even finish that sentence. Why would Mitch set my bar on fire? I never confirmed I'm with Cross, but I also never told him I wasn't. He was the one who brought up Cross's dad, and the news article said that Oak Grove caught fire. But the statement said no foul play or arson.

Swallowing nervously, I plop back down on the couch next to Jasmine. That's what Bones meant by *he* is setting Cross up. Whoever it was wanted me to suspect Cross. But I was with him. If it was Mitch, he had to have known I was with Cross at the time, right? It couldn't have been him.

CROSS

BONES STEPS FORWARD to speak at the same time the door to our suite flies open.

"What in the hell is going on?" Grave demands, entering the room, holding April's hand.

"Oh, thank God." She sighs when she spots Alexa sitting on the couch. April lets go of Grave and runs over to Alexa. She pulls her up from the couch and hugs her tightly. "I've been worried sick. I was praying you weren't there."

"I'm fine." Alexa pats her back; her eyes meet mine briefly over April's shoulder. "I wasn't there." She pulls away. "How did you—?"

"Someone sent me the news footage of your bar up in flames," Grave growls, interrupting her. He looks at me. "I'm not asking again. What the hell happened?"

Jasmine stands as well. "Someone caught the bar on fire. We think it was Alexa's ex."

"Why would he do that?" Grave digs.

No one answers him, and it just pisses him off even more. "Kings." He snaps his finger. "Office!" Then he's storming off out of the living room and down the back hallway.

Letting out a long breath, I follow him with Bones and Titan on my ass. We enter the office, and he's pacing in front of the desk. The curtains are open, showcasing the Strip lit up at night.

"Grave, it's okay," Bones starts. "No one was there. Someone saw it and called it in. It's not a total loss—"

"We need to call the fire marshal," Grave interrupts him. "Get him there right now. To find out what happened." He nods to himself.

"It's taken care of," Titan states.

Grave comes to a stop, his head popping up, and he stares at us. "How so?"

"He was already here," I answer. "He confirmed it was arson."

He leans back against the desk, crossing his arms over his chest, and bows his head. Silence falls over the office while we let him process this. "Alexa can come stay with us. She'll be safe—"

"That won't be happening," I say, interrupting him.

He slowly lifts his head, and his blue eyes meet mine. Tilting his head to the side, he says. "If her ex is after her, she can't go home. She needs to be somewhere safe."

"She will be safe," I say vaguely.

His brows pull together. "Her ex is after her. He obviously wants to hurt her."

"We don't think that's the case," Titan states, leaning up against the wall.

"Then what do you think?" Grave snaps.

"We think—"

"We think that he's trying to frame me," I interrupt Titan. Grave needs to hear it from me.

He pushes off the desk, squaring his shoulders. "What would make you guys think that?"

"Because he knows that we're together," I state. Okay, so it's not official, but I've decided for the both of us.

He stares at me, his eyes narrowing slightly while he sucks in a long breath. "Uh, what?" he finally asks.

"We've been—"

"Behind my back?" he shrieks, not allowing me to finish.

I can't argue with him because it would be a lie. Alexa and I chose to keep it a secret from him for this reason. So, he wouldn't overreact. But I do understand the situation has changed. There's an unpredictable new player. And her life is in danger. Along with Jasmine's. What if she had been there in the basement preparing for Kink? Would she have been able to get out? Would she have burned to death? The what-ifs are staggering.

"It's not like that," I say.

"Then what the fuck was it, Cross?" he demands. "I told you she was off-limits."

"You don't own her!" I shout back at him. "You can't tell her who she can and can't date."

"Date?" He chuckles roughly. "You mean who she fucks!"

"It's more than that!" I argue.

"Oh, really?" He arches his brows. "So, you're telling me you love her?"

The door swings open, and April enters the room. "We can hear you guys in the living room," she whisper-shouts. "Lower your voices."

Grave doesn't listen. "Your best friend has been fucking Cross." He points at me as if there's another guy who goes by that name in this room.

She looks at me. Her ice-blue eyes are sympathetic before they go back to him. "Grave ..."

"You knew?" he states breathlessly, taking a step back like she hit him.

"Yes." She doesn't even bother to lie.

His face falls and so do his wide shoulders. "You kept another secret from me?" Before she can answer, he looks around the room at each of the Kings. "Did everyone know?"

"Yes," Bones and Titan answer at the same time, not wasting a breath.

His blue eyes drop to the floor, and he nods once before heading to the door.

"Grave ...?" She reaches out to him, but he shrugs her off and exits the office while she chases after him, calling out his name.

I go to follow them to try to help calm the situation, but Titan stops me, grabbing my upper arm. "One problem at a time." He gestures to the hallway. I know he means Alexa and the situation we are now in. "Grave is upset, but it's not all because of you and Alexa." He lets go of my arm, and I understand what he means. April and the baby. That's not something you get over just because you go on a two-week vacation.

Grave is looking for something to be mad about. Something else to project his anger on. Right now, he hates the world and all of us in it.

TWENTY

ALEXA

"APRIL?" I ASK, standing from the couch when I see her and Grave rush through the living room. She stops, turns to face Jasmine and me placing her hands up, and nods once.

"I'm glad you two are okay. Lunch?"

Before Jasmine and I can even answer, they're out the door. I look at the clock on the wall and see it's already past eight in the morning. I haven't even been to bed yet. I'm exhausted.

Titan, Bones, and Cross re-enter. "What in the hell happened in there?" I demand. We could hear somewhat of what they were saying, but it was mainly just loud shouting. You couldn't really make out their argument word for word.

"I told him about us," Cross answers, pulling the Zippo from his pocket and starts fidgeting with it.

"Us?" I step forward. "Why would you do that?"

"Because he needed to know." Titan is the one who answers me.

"No, he didn't," I argue. *Fuck!* April must be so mad at me. "Shit!"

"Yes, he did," Cross argues.

"There is no us!" I snap. "We are fucking, and that's none of his business." We had an agreement. What made him sell me out? I almost roll my eyes at myself. They're the Kings. I'm a nobody. Of course, he wouldn't keep his part of the deal.

Cross looks at the other Kings, and they get the hint. He wants to be alone with me. Jasmine pulls me in for a hug, whispering, "I'll see you at lunch."

Once we're alone and the door closes, I sit back on the couch, burying my face in my hands, and silence follows. My knees bounce and my heart races from anger and embarrassment over this shit night. I look up at Cross. "Do you have any idea how mad my best friend is going to be at me if Grave finds out she knew?" I had April promise to keep my secret. I'd hate for him to be mad at her because she kept something from him.

"He knows that she knew," he states, staring down at me with no remorse.

Motherfucker! I shoot to my feet. "How could you?"

"What did you expect me to do?" he shouts, pointing at the door.

"Keep your mouth shut!" I argue.

"That won't help us."

"There's that us again." I roll my eyes, giving him my back.

He grabs my upper arm and jerks me back around to face him. "Why is *us* such a hard concept for you to comprehend?" he snaps in my face.

I shove his chest, but he doesn't even sway. "Fucking doesn't mean us. You're lying to him."

He moves both of his hands into my hair, grabbing a handful, forcing my head back so I have to look up at him. "Why is it so hard to comprehend that I want more from you than just your body?"

His words make me pause. My eyes search his, looking for any indication he's lying. I wait for him to laugh, but instead, he licks his lips and steps in closer to me. His body presses into mine while his grip loosens. "Cross ..."

"I'm serious about you. About us." He runs his hands through my hair. "So, if you don't want that, I'll let you leave. But just know I want you to stay."

I ignore the butterflies in my stomach that he wants more than just a fuck. I've had the same thoughts, but I've refused to try to decipher them. But I've been doing this a lot lately—jumping without thinking twice. That's how I ended up with Kink. And the same way I added Jasmine to Lucky's. Why not do the same with him? He told me that timing was rarely on our side. And that seems to continue to prove true. "I want to stay," I say softly. The more I learn about Cross, the more I can't walk away. He's exactly what I thought he would be —all consuming.

Letting go of my face, he runs his knuckles down over my neck, feeling my pulse race. "I was lying," he whispers, his free hand wrapping around my back, holding me in place.

My stomach drops. He was baiting me to see how I felt just so he could say it's over.

A slow smile spreads across his handsome face. "I wasn't going to let you leave." Then his lips are on mine. Desperately, demanding all of my attention.

"Don't you have to go to work?" I ask, not wanting to keep him, knowing he has a lot to do. The poor guy never stops.

"I can be late," he answers against my lips.

I jump up into his arms and wrap my legs around his waist, suddenly a little less tired. Nothing a Monster drink can't fix later. He starts walking up to his room and then we're on his bed. Clothes are being ripped off.

WE LIE IN HIS BED, AND I STARE UP AT THE CEILING. I'M currently trying to avoid the elephant in the room. I'd much rather him roll me over, shove my face into the mattress and fuck me again than talk about my feelings. I guess I could start lightly snoring and pretend to be asleep, but the curtains are open and it's light outside.

"We need to talk," Cross speaks, his voice still rough from the sex we just had.

So much for avoiding this. Who knew a King would ever utter those words. "About?" I play dumb because let's face it, it could go one of two ways.

"What happened before I carried you off into my bedroom," he answers, turning onto his side, curling his arm around me.

That doesn't answer my question. "Fine. You can join the girls and me for lunch later." I dodge the conversation.

"Alexa." His arm wrapped around me, forces me to turn to face him. Removing his arm, he reaches up, running his thumb over my still parted lips. "You. Me. Us. Grave."

I sigh.

"It's important that you understand things have changed now."

"It doesn't have to," I say softly, unable to meet his eyes so I look at his skull tattoo on his chest. Even though it has no eyes, I swear it's staring into my soul.

Gently gripping my chin, he forces my eyes to meet him. "I want it to."

My breath catches at his words.

"Grave asked me if I loved you."

My eyes widen. "Why would he ask you that?"

"I didn't get to answer him. April stormed in." He doesn't answer my question.

"That's a good thing," I breathe.

"I was going to say yes."

I swallow nervously. He shifts onto his left forearm and looks down at me. His right hand cups my cheek. "I didn't realize it until this morning. When I received the call that your bar was on fire. For a moment, I forgot you were standing in my bathroom." His eyes search mine. "I understood what I'd be losing. If someone hurt you." His hand drops to my chest, and he places his palm on my skin, feeling my heart race. "If someone took you from me. Alexa ... I don't need you to feel the same way." He gives me a smile as if he won a bet.

"But I want you to understand that ..." He leans down and tenderly kisses my parted lips. "I'm in love with you. And when a King finds his queen, he's one hundred percent committed." Pulling away, he cups my face.

I open my mouth, but his lips find mine again, and before I know it, he's back on top of me. I'm desperate for him.

His touch.

His words.

His love.

I never thought it would feel like this. Like I'm the only woman in the world. Nothing before him ever mattered.

CROSS

I SHOVE MY *father back, and he hits the podium, knocking it over.*

He stands, rubbing the blood off his chin with the back of his hand. "Is that all you've got, son? I've been training you for years now, and you're still a weak little boy."

I rush him again, this time, bending my knees and picking him up over my shoulder. I throw his body down onto the floor and hear bones break.

His laughter bounces off the cathedral ceilings, and they make my skin crawl. "You're fucking pathetic," I spit at him. I walk away, giving him my back. Going home. My mom needs me there. If that's where Mr. Reed even took her. She needs to know that she can leave his ass. Why the fuck has she stayed this long anyway, money? Money isn't everything.

"You know." He laughs roughly, "She never once stood up for you."

My feet come to a stop, and I slowly turn around to see him still sitting on the floor, leaning up against the fallen podium.

"It was her idea, actually." He pulls a cigarette out of the inside of his leather jacket and lights it up. Putting it to his lips, he takes in a big drag and then lets it out. "Do you know why you were born, Cross?"

He calls me by the nickname I was given when I was younger due to the kids who saw the scars on my back that he gave me. "You were born for a purpose, son."

I snort at that. "No one was born to burn."

"You were born because your mother wanted a baby who would pay for our sins."

I look away from him, not wanting to believe what he says, but deep down, I know it's true. She has never tried to stop him from hurting me. She's never been nothing more than a doting wife and a pathetic fucking mother.

"You don't live in this world without paying debts, son." He gets to his feet once again. "Get used to it. The debts will get too big to pay with your own flesh." With that, he drags himself back to his office.

I've fought him a lot over the years. Most ended in me getting my ass kicked. But he's gotten older, slower, weaker. Where I've grown bigger, stronger, angrier.

I go to leave but stop staring up at the front of the church. I've been a prisoner to this place ever since I was born. The crosses, the burns and the humiliation.

"Men don't kneel for forgiveness. They kneel for humiliation." He once said to me.

My hands fist and I know that if I don't stop it now, it'll never end. Not today. Not tomorrow. Not until he's dead. I've been praying for years he'd die. God never listens. If my father can stand in front of a congregation and pretend to be God, so can I.

I make my way to the office and storm in. He's sitting at his desk, looking at his computer. "Go home, son," He dismisses me without looking up. "You can repent tomorrow."

"That won't be happening." I state, pulling my Zippo out of my pocket that my mother gave me all those years ago. "It's time you pay for your sins father."

"What are you doing?" He jumps to his feet.

Picking up a book off his bookshelf, I rip the pages out, then toss it to the floor. It's all ancient biblical shit that he doesn't even believe in.

"Everything must look perfect," my mother always tells me. They're just props.

"Cross! Stop!" he snaps.

I do it to another one.

He rushes me, slamming me into the bookshelf, but I lift my right arm, elbowing him in the face. He cries out, holding his nose and falling onto the couch.

"You must learn to endure pain, Father," I say the same thing he once said to me while I kneeled in this church. "It's time you pay your debt." I light some papers on fire and toss them to the floor next to the ripped books. They catch fire immediately. Then I light a few more on the shelf for safe measure. I don't want him putting it out. Then I'd have to start all over.

"Cross." He reaches out to me from the couch. He coughs, as smoke is already filling the room, the fire growing bigger with each second. "Son, stop this."

I walk over to him and rip the chain that holds the cross from his neck. Pocketing it, I turn to the door not even looking back. "Learn to like the fire, Father. I hear it's hot in hell." Slamming the door shut, I lock him inside.

I sit straight up, breathing heavily and looking around aimlessly. Blinking, I remember it's just a dream. Well, it was very real back then. Now it's technically a memory. I can still smell the smoke and feel the heat. I hope the motherfucker is still burning.

Getting out of my bed, I make my way to the bathroom and turn on the sink. I splash some water on my face. Then cup my hands, taking a drink of it. I've maybe been asleep for an hour. After the night we had, I had to get some rest. I needed to lie with Alexa in my bed, knowing she was with me and safe.

"You okay?"

I spin around to see her standing in the doorway. Still naked from when we passed out earlier after we were done with each other.

"Fine." I lie.

She walks up behind me and wraps her arms around me. "Thought things were different?" She questions. "If that's true, then why are you lying?"

I turn to face her. Spinning us both around, I pin her back to the counter and pick her up, setting her ass on it. "It wasn't a lie."

"It wasn't the truth," she counters. "I want to see you."

"You're looking right at me."

"No," she says softly, placing her hands on my forearms and slowly running them up my arms. "The Dark King known as Cross." They continue up to my neck, and she brings them around the front and grabs hold of the cross that hangs around my neck.

Instinct has my hand shooting out and gripping her wrist tightly, but she doesn't flinch. Instead, she gives me a soft smile, her head tilting to the side as if she was testing me and I failed.

"Are you afraid I won't love the real you?"

"No," I say honestly. "I'm afraid that you will."

She pulls back, and I let go of my hold on her, knowing this is it. She's had her fun, but it's over. I've been too honest with her and how I feel.

I step back to give her space, and she jumps down off the counter. But instead of leaving the bathroom, she steps into me. Placing her hands on either side of my face, she stands up on her tiptoes. "I'm not so innocent, Cross. I don't need you to protect me."

But I have to. No matter what I do now, I promised myself years ago I would never be my father—If I ever fell in love, I'd cherish her. I'd burn the world to protect her from people like him and myself.

She drops to her knees before me. My cock is instantly ready for her, and I let out a growl as she takes it into her hands. Mine find their way into her already knotted hair, helping hold it back from her face.

She opens up for me and licks up my shaft. I throw my head back and moan when she gets to my piercing. Her tongue gently plays with it, making me weak in the knees. "Alexa," I call out her name, not even sure why. Other than just needing to say it.

Her hand grips the base of my cock while her mouth swallows it, setting my body on fire and fulfilling that craving I always have. I touch the back of her throat, and I lean forward, one hand having to hold the counter while the other remains in her hair. She picks up her pace, and I allow her to take control, letting her do whatever she wants to me.

Slow, fast, deep, or shallow, it doesn't even fucking matter. This woman is my damnation. I've always known I was going to hell; now I know it'll be her who sends me there. Because I will do absolutely anything for her. She doesn't even have to ask.

TWENTY-ONE
ALEXA

"**G**OOD AFTERNOON," I sing, falling into my seat at the booth for lunch at Empire, downing what's left of my second Monster.

"Afternoon." Emilee is the first to greet me. Haven gives me a smile, and Jasmine didn't hear me because she is too wrapped up typing out a text.

"I'm so sorry to hear about your bar," Emilee tells me, giving me a sympathetic look with her amber eyes.

"Do they know who did it?" Haven asks curiously.

I've never really spoken to her, but she's the girl's best friend, and now that I know who she's married to, it makes me a little nervous to even be around her. What if she goes home, tells her husband she hates me, and he offs me? The guy has some major pull in this town. I bet he'd make it look like an accident. Like I slipped and just happened to fall on a knife to the chest. Or maybe my car would conveniently lose a wheel while I'm driving down the highway. I mean ...

"Alexa?"

"Hmm?" I blink, looking up at Emilee.

"Do they know who did it?" she asks what Haven had, and I realize that I never answered.

"I believe so." I keep it vague. I'm not sure what Cross would want me to say. I guess we should have had the discussion last night instead of fucking multiple times. So many things needed to be discussed, but I craved that connection with him more than answers. Or maybe I just really don't want to know. Love does make you stupid.

"I'm so sorry I'm late," April states, falling down next to me.

"You're just in time. We were about to order mimosas," Jasmine tells her.

"I'm not drinking." Haven waves her off.

"What? Why not?" Jasmine snorts.

"Because Luca and I are trying for a baby," Haven answers with a smile on her face, but it quickly drops when she looks at April. "I'm so sorry," she rushes out. "I didn't think …"

"There's nothing to be sorry for," she says, giving her a kind smile in return.

"Yeah, I'm fucking a lot too," Jasmine jokes, trying to lighten the mood, and I snort while trying to take a drink of my water.

"Jasmine …" Haven shrieks. She always seems to be the most proper of the girls. A little more uptight than the rest.

"What?" She shrugs. "It's the same thing."

"I'm married," Haven says, flipping her hair over her shoulder.

"Us single girls can fuck too, ya know?" Jasmine rolls her eyes.

"Are you still seeing Nite?" April jumps into the conversation, looking at Jasmine.

Emilee and I look over at the redhead. Both of us wide-eyed. That is … surprising. And what's even more is that Emilee didn't seem to know about it. We need to have these get-togethers more often. I learn so much about these girls.

"We had plans to fuck tonight, but he sent me a text earlier informing me that he had to cancel." Jasmine looks around, trying to catch the eye of a waiter to order those mimosas.

"He's out of town. Luca had to send him to Italy ..." Haven quickly stops speaking and averts her amber eyes to the table like she just told us all a secret that none of us were supposed to know. The way she starts nibbling on her thumbnail makes me think it's a big one.

"For what?" Emilee digs, placing her elbow on the table, her chin in her hand.

"Doesn't matter," Jasmine states, and Haven's shoulders literally sag as if she just dodged a bullet. Damn, now I really want to know what the hell is going on there. "We don't explain anything to each other. It's just sex." She laughs it off.

"Speaking of sex, Emilee, are you still fucking Bones and Titan?" Haven wonders, making sure to change the subject to anyone else other than Nite and Italy.

Not going to lie. When I first heard she was sleeping with both of them, I choked on my popcorn that I was eating while up at Roses. It was one hell of a shock. I guess she dated Bones through high school and college. Not sure what the details on that were. But she didn't get with Titan until last year.

"No." Emilee shakes her head once. "It was fun. Actually, it was awesome, but I got married. And my body is for my husband. If I wanted to fuck multiple guys, I would have stayed single." She goes on. "Plus, Bones will find a woman and settle down one day. It just wasn't something that was meant for forever."

Haven snorts. "Bones settle down? That's hilarious. That man will never find someone to tie him down."

"I don't know. I believe there's someone for everyone. It just takes time to find them," Jasmine offers. "Not everyone marries the only person they've ever fucked." She looks over at Haven.

"Wait a minute." I hold up a finger. "You've only ever been with Luca?"

"Yeah." She chews on a chip from the bowl that sits in the middle of the table. "I was young when we got together. We had a breakup after college, but I never got with anyone else. I'm glad I didn't, although there was one time I hated him so much that I wish I had because he knew he was the only guy I had been with."

"I wish Grave was my only," April adds, sighing. "I mean, when you find your someone, the others never seem to have existed, ya know?"

"Not me." Jasmine shakes her head. "I like sex too much to limit myself to one man." She shudders at that thought, making us all laugh. "Plus, I've slept with some men who had no fucking clue what they were doing. I couldn't imagine being stuck with either one of them forever. I'd never know what a good fuck really is."

The woman does have a point.

CROSS

I SIT AT the Kings conference table, flipping my Zippo open and closed. Titan sits across from me, twirling his wedding band around his ring finger. Bones stands at the front of the room, arms crossed over his chest.

The glass double doors open, and Nigel shows Luca into the room along with the fire marshal.

"Find out anything?" I jump to my feet. I've had Jeffrey digging ever since he left our suite this morning.

He shakes his head, and I fall back into my seat. "No." He pulls out the chair next to Titan and sits down. "No witnesses."

"Then who called the police?" Bones wonders. "Whoever made the call saved it from burning to the ground."

"A Derek Milner.".

I sit up straighter. "Her brother?"

"Well, this changes things." Bones sighs. "Maybe it wasn't her ex after all."

I run a hand through my hair. "That doesn't make sense."

"She did say that he had a key. Maybe he and Mitch were working together?" Bones offers.

"Or he did it on his own," Titan adds.

Alexa did say that he quit Lucky's. Mitch saw her at Crown. He could have told Derek, and it pissed him off even more.

"I've got some calls in," Jeffrey says vaguely. "In the meantime, I need to keep the scene cleared."

I run a hand down my face and let out a sigh of frustration. "How long?" The girls were already getting things ready for Kink and the remodel. This is going to set them back.

"At least a week." He shrugs, clearly a fucking guess. "But I'll keep in touch and let you know as soon as I do."

I nod. "Thanks."

He turns and exits the conference room. I lean back in my chair, fisting my hands.

"You really think her brother did it?" Luca asks, looking at me.

"Either her brother or her ex," I explain. "Or maybe both of them. I'll find out."

"Looks like we need to make a visit tonight," Bones offers. "Take care of them at the same time. I don't know her brother, but we all know that Mitch is a little bitch. All we have to do is scare him, and he'll tell us everything."

The door opens, and Grave steps inside. He stops, looks around, and then turns, leaving just as quickly as he was entering.

"Grave?" I jump up from my chair and rush out of the room. "Grave?" I run to his office and throw his door open, but he's not in there. Walking out, I go to head back toward the conference room but see him standing at the end of the hallway with his back to me looking out the floor-to-ceiling window. His hands in the front pockets of his jeans. Stance wide and body tense.

Running a hand through my hair, I swallow nervously. I hate that I've hurt him. "Grave, I ..."

He turns around, glaring at me. "How long?" he asks.

"That night we went to the Airport," I answer honestly.

His face falls, and he take a step back, leaning up against the window.

Grave never knew how to hide what he feels. It's always written all over his face. "I'm not going to say I'm sorry for what I did."

"I didn't expect an apology." He snorts. "That requires you admitting you were in the wrong."

"I was going to tell you." I step forward. "I wanted to tell you."

"When were you going to do that, Cross?" He chuckles, like I'm joking.

"The night …" I pause, unable to go on with that sentence that I started.

"When Cross?" he yells, getting irritated. "When were you going to tell me that you were lying to me?"

"I never lied to you!" I shout back. "I fucked your girl's best friend. There's a big difference there." It's not like it was April or some girl he had once been with. The only tie he had with Alexa was April. And I don't think I should be punished for that.

"And you felt guilty. That's why you never told me!" he screams, his face turning red with anger.

"No." I shake my head. I won't regret or feel guilty for what Alexa and I have been doing.

"Then what was so important that came up that kept you from telling me?" he demands. "Huh, Cross?"

I shake my head, unable to answer that.

He quickly takes a few steps forward until he's in front of me and pokes his finger into my chest. "What happened that you couldn't be my friend and tell me the truth?" He spits in my face. "You were my best friend, and you lied to me!"

"You lost a child!" I scream, and silence follows as his face falls, realizing the truth.

His eyes drop to the floor, and he takes a stumbling step back. "Grave …?"

"Don't," he mutters almost brokenly, and I close my mouth. Giving me his back, he turns to look out over Sin City again. "I know it doesn't matter what the two of you do," he admits quietly. "You were right. You're both adults and can do whatever you want."

I don't really know what to say. Somehow over the past month, I've lost my best friend, and I don't know how to get him back. If that's even a possibility. Over a woman of all things. I feel other factors apply as well, but this is the one thing he wants to cling to. Maybe he wanted to push me away. "You asked me if I loved her. And I didn't get to answer you."

He slowly turns around, his blue eyes meeting mine.

"I do," I say, and a smile spreads across my face. "It didn't start out that way of course. But that's what it is now."

He looks away, staring at the black-painted wall, and sighs heavily. "I'm pretty sure I fell in love with April the moment I saw her. But now ..."

I frown as he trails off. "Now what?"

"Nothing. It doesn't matter." He goes to walk past me, but I reach out, grabbing his arm and stop him.

"It does matter," I tell him. "What is it?" I want to be here for Grave. He hasn't even given me a chance to be a good friend to him, but I want to help him.

He drops his head to stare at his feet. "It's ..." He sniffs, unable to look at me. "She kept her feelings from me. Afraid I'd turn to drugs if I knew how much pain she was in over ... the baby." His voice breaks.

I let out a long breath.

"And I hate that I can't be what she needs." He takes in a shaky breath. "She thought I was too fragile to handle the truth. Such a weak man, that she felt she had to hide that from me," he chokes out.

"Hey?" I let go of his arm and grip his face, making him look up at me. Tears silently run down his cheeks. "Don't do this to yourself, Grave. You are what she needs. Do you understand me?"

He nods and sniffs again. I pull him into me, and he hugs me. "April is lucky to have you." I slap his back. "And she knows that." I know she thought she was doing the right thing. There's no manual when it comes to helping a recovering addict. They can relapse for no reason other than they just want a hit. A relationship can be a lot and then a pregnancy ...miscarriage? She just wanted to protect him.

He nods, hugging me tightly before he pulls away quickly, as if our manly hug had timed out. He rushes to wipe the tears from his face and clears his throat. "I hope that Alexa is what you've been looking for, Cross."

I give him a soft smile. "She is, Grave. She is."

TWENTY-TWO
ALEXA

"OH MY GOD, I'm stuffed." Jasmine sighs, leaning back in the booth.

"What are you ladies doing this Friday night?" April asks.

"Nothing." I groan, also feeling like I ate too much. It's my one night off this weekend from Crown. The great thing about the nightclub is that I make so much that I don't have to work every damn day. But then a thought hits me and last night might have been my last night now that Grave and her are back. Another thing to add to my list of questions for Cross.

"I'm free. What's up?" Emilee wonders.

"I could really use a girl's night," April answers. "Not a get dolled up and go out kind of girls night. But one where we wear pajamas, drink wine, and eat pie in the living room while watching a movie kind of girls night."

"Count me in." I raise my hand.

"Yes!" Emilee agrees. "That sounds amazing."

"Sure." Haven nods.

Jasmine sucks down what's left of her mimosa. "I'll bring vodka too."

We get up and start to say our goodbyes. Everyone needing to get on with their day. "April, may I speak to you?" I ask nervously.

"Of course." She says, sitting back down in the booth as the girls walk out of Empire. "Everything okay?"

I push my hair behind my ear. "I just wanted to apologize."

"For what?" She frowns.

"Cross told me that Grave knows you lied to him." She sighs heavily. I reach out and grab her hand. "I'm so sorry. I should have never asked you to lie to him. I know that was a mistake now."

"Alexa ..."

"I was being selfish and ..."

"Alexa!" She stops me. Her ice-blue eyes soften, and she gives me a smile. "You have nothing to apologize for."

"I just don't want him mad at you. Or to cause a fight between you two," I rush out.

"You didn't. I promise." She pats my hand. "Grave and I have some things to work through, but they have nothing to do with you or Cross."

I nod, pulling away, not feeling any better at that statement. I just pray that they can get through this. Grave and April were made for one another.

I PULL UP to my house and walk inside. I'm exhausted. Those two energy drinks are already wearing off, and my body is fading fast. I haven't stayed here in two weeks. Ever since I started at Crown. After I get off, I go to the Kings Royal Suite to be with Cross. And the nights I don't work, I've stayed there, and he wakes me up when he gets off. It's exhausting dating a King. The sex is too good to pass up even when you're running on fumes. I had to run by here after breakfast to grab some new clothes and a few other things. I've tried not to be that girl and just move myself in with him over the past two weeks, but I think I have more of my clothing in Cross's closet than my own.

"Alexa?" I hear my name being shouted from the front door.

"What the fuck ...?"

"Alexa?" I see my brother rushing into my house.

"What are you doing?" I ask concerned.

"Where in the hell have you been?" he snaps. "With that bastard?"

I roll my eyes and turn my back to him. "I don't have time for this, Derek." He hasn't spoken to me in weeks and he shows up at my house out of nowhere throwing insults at my boyfriend. That's no way to get on my good side.

He grips my upper arm and spins me around. "Did he do this? Did you break up with him or something?"

"No." I rip my arm from his hold and roll my eyes. "Go home, Derek. You haven't cared about what's been going on in my life. Why now?"

"Because Lucky's was set on fire," he snaps at me.

His words make me pause. He said set on fire. As in on purpose. I watched the news. They said it was accidental. Even though the fire marshal said it wasn't, they want the public to think so because Cross wants to take care of it himself. How would he know ...

Cross and Bones suspected it was Mitch, but Mitch said that Derek told him Lucky's was in trouble. So, what if my brother did it? What if he's the one trying to frame Cross because he hates the Kings so much? He knows I went into business with Bones and Jasmine. Derek knows more than Mitch has to.

"I'm fine," I say gently. "See?" I spin around, with my arms out wide. "I wasn't even there."

"Thank God." He pulls me in for a quick hug. "Where were you?" he asks, pulling away.

"With Mitch," I lie. I don't want him knowing I was with Cross. Right now, I have to tread very carefully with him.

He frowns but doesn't question it.

"Here, sit down." I pull him over to the couch. "Let me get you a drink. What would you like?"

"Water," he says, running a hand through his hair. "Please."

"Okay. Give me a second." I exit the living room and head toward the kitchen. But I sidestep into the hallway and run to my bedroom. I gently close the door and pull my cell out of my back pocket, dialing up Cross's number.,

"Hey, gorgeous," he answers on the first ring.

"My brother just showed up at my house, and when I asked why he said because Lucky's was set on fire. He thinks you did it." I rush out but make sure to keep my voice quiet.

"We're on our way."

CROSS

I PULL UP to Alexa's house with Grave. Titan and Bones are behind us. I don't even bother knocking on the front door. I shove it open so hard that it hits the interior wall with a thud.

"What the hell?" I see him jump up from the couch.

I rush him, my hand tightens to a fist, and I swing, knocking him out with one hit.

"Oh my God, Cross," Alexa squeals rushing over to her brother, who now lies on her living room floor, but Bones grabs her. Wrapping an arm around her from behind, he pulls her back.

"Take her to Kingdom," I tell him.

"No!" she shouts, fighting in his arms. "What the hell are you doing?"

Bones suggested we bring her brother and Mitch to Kingdom tonight. Play with them in the meat locker, but we can't move him there right now. We don't have the trunk space to get him back there and I don't want to use her car just in case I have to bury him later. So, I'll have to take care of him here instead. That means she must leave.

"Take her to Kingdom," I repeat at Bones as he just stands there with her. This isn't up for debate. I dig into my pocket and throw my keys to Titan. "Pull my car into her garage and load her into it. Don't want the neighbors to see her leaving kicking and screaming."

He nods and takes off through the kitchen toward the garage.

"Cross ..." she cries. "Please don't do this," she begs. "What if it wasn't him?"

I can't blame her for holding on to the hope that her brother didn't try to burn her dreams down. "Then I won't hurt him," I answer simply.

"And if he did?" she asks nervously.

I look at Bones. "Leave. Now." He picks her feet up off the floor and starts to carry her out of the room. She screams my name, but he must cover her mouth with his hand, muffling it. We don't want the neighbors hearing her and calling the cops.

"What do you want to do with him?" Grave asks, looking down at Derek.

I wanted him to stay here with me. Grave deserves to blow off some steam. Right now, it's the only thing I can give him.

"I'll see what I can find."

I SIT DOWN ON THE COFFEE TABLE IN FRONT OF THE COUCH AND slap Derek's face. "Wake up."

His head jerks to the side and then snaps up. He opens his eyes, blinking rapidly. "What ...?" He tries to move but realizes his wrists are tied behind his back with a piece of rope I found in the garage. Along with his ankles as he sits on the couch. "Alexa?" He shouts, starting to regain consciousness.

"She's not here." Grave informs him, entering the living room, pocketing his cell.

Derek shifts on the couch. "Where is she?" He swallows nervously. "What have you done with her?" His voice rises.

"She's safe." Is all I give him.

SHANTEL TESSIER

He sucks in a deep breath. "I told her to stay away from you." His eyes go to Grave. "And you ... you fucking ..."

I slap him across the face. "Pay attention. I'm only going to ask this once. What do you know about Lucky's?"

"I know you set it on fire!" he shouts at me. "I know that you want to hurt my sister. You Kings are fucking evil!"

I make a tsking sound with my tongue and teeth. I lean forward and rip his shirt down the middle, exposing his chest.

"What are you doing?" he shouts, trying to pull away from me unsuccessfully.

I reach inside my shirt and pull out the cross and remove it from my neck. Then I adjust my ass in order to dig into my jean pocket and retrieve my Zippo, lighting it up.

"What the fuck are you doing?" he screams.

"This is going to hurt," I tell him.

Grave walks behind the couch and shoves a dish towel into Derek's mouth. Then he leans over the back and wraps his tatted arm around his neck from behind, pulling his ass off the couch just a little, holding him in place for me.

Derek struggles but can't do much when he's tied, gagged, and in a chokehold.

I let the cross hang from my hand while my other holds the lighter to it. When it gets as warm as I want it, I press it to his chest.

His screams are muffled due to the gag. When I remove it, he sucks in deep breaths through his nose, and Grave takes a step back, letting him go.

I remove the gag. "You son of a bitch!" Derek snarls at me. "You better not have hurt her. I'll rip your head off," he warns.

I almost laugh at that. Instead, I say, "I would never hurt her. You, however ..." I hold up the lighter and cross again, heating it for round two.

"What?" he asks, his dark eyes wide. "No. No. No. You think I did it?" He shakes his head quickly. "I didn't do it. I swear."

210

I pause and shut the Zippo closed. "You knew it was set on fire," I state.

"Yeah, because that's what Mitch told me." He rushes out, trying to adjust himself on the couch to sit up straighter.

Grave and I exchange a look. "When?" I demand.

"This morning. He told me that he spoke to Alexa. She told him it was arson." He licks his lips. "I may be mad at my sister, but I would never hurt her."

I pull my cell up and dial Bones's number. He answers on the third ring. "Hello?"

"Ask her if she spoke to Mitch this morning," I demand.

Has she been talking to him this whole time? If so, why? We haven't seen him at Crown since that one time. Maybe she told him I've been watching out for him and to stay away.

I hear him ask her but don't hear her response. Seconds later, he's back on the phone. "She said no. She hasn't spoken to him since that night at Crown."

TWENTY-THREE
ALEXA

I PACE THE Royal Suite back at Kingdom. It's been two hours since Bones dragged me out of my house and brought me here. He and Titan haven't left my side. They even took my phone from me.

"How long are you going to keep me here?" I demand to anyone who will answer me.

Titan sits at the table, glaring with his arms over his chest. Bones stands in the kitchen, ignoring me while typing away on his phone.

"I'm not staying here." I shake my head and start to walk toward the door.

Titan gets up from his seat and puts himself between me and the door, forcing me to a stop. "You aren't going anywhere, Alexa."

I give him my back and grip my hair. I want to scream. I know they aren't going to hurt me, but I can't say the same about Derek. My brother can be a pain in the ass, but that doesn't mean I want him dead.

Cross just knocked him out like he was nothing. I didn't think of what would happen when I called Cross and told him Derek was at my place. I just acted; afraid he knew something. Now I'm terrified Cross will kill him.

I sit down on the couch and bury my face in my hands. How long will they keep me here? How ...?

The door opens, and my head snaps up to see my brother enters the room, followed by Cross and then Grave.

"Derek." I rush over to him and jump into his arms. "Oh my god." I sniff with relief that he's not dead.

"I'm fine." He says softly, hugging me tightly.

I pull back, and he lets me go. I gasp when I get a look at him. His shirt is ripped open, and he has a mark on the left side of his chest. "What is that?" I touch it, and he jumps back, hissing in a breath.

What...? I take another look, and it's a cross. Is it ...? I reach out, and he grabs my wrists to stop me from touching it again. The skin is raised and irritated, and I instantly realize what it is. I've seen it before.

Pulling away, I turn to face Cross. My hands fisted by my side. "You branded him?" I snap.

He leans back against the bar top, crossing his ankles and arms over his chest, but he stays silent. His once pretty green eyes are now dark and clouded like a storm.

"Sis, I'm fine." Derek grabs my arm, forcing me to face him. "Are you okay?" He asks gently, his eyes running over my body. He reaches up, cupping my face.

"She's fine." Titan is the one who answers Derek, but my brother ignores him.

I shove him away and storm over to Cross. "Why would you do that?"

"I needed answers." Comes his clipped response.

"Then just ask him," I shout, shoving his chest, but he doesn't budge.

"I did. He refused to answer." Cross shrugs. "Hence the reason I did what I did."

"You son of a bitch." I start to hit him, but I'm grabbed from

behind and pulled away. Then I'm spun around. I expect to come
face-to-face with Bones like last time, but a soft pair of dark eyes meet
mine. One already bruised from the hit he took to the face earlier.

"Calm down, Alexa," Derek says, grabbing my face.

"He hurt you." I cry out. He hates the Kings, so why is he taking
their side on this?

He sighs, looking at someone over my shoulder for a quick second
before his eyes come back to mine. "And someone's trying to hurt
you. The Kings were just doing what they thought needed to be
done."

"But ..."

"I'm fine." He gives me a soft smile. "Promise."

"I want to go home," I tell him.

"You're not going anywhere." The familiar voice comes from
behind me.

CROSS

I watch her spin around. Her green eyes stare at me with
disgust, but I can see the tears pooling in them. I hate it. Where we
are right now. But I won't budge on this. I won't go soft because I fell
in love with her. She has to understand the severity of the situation.

"I'm not staying here with you," she states and starts to head to
the door, but Derek grabs her hands, stopping her.

"As much as I hate it, Cross is right. You need to stay here."

Her mouth drops open. "He knocked you out ..."

"I know." He nods once.

"He then branded you ..."

"Too bad you started talking. I was in the mood to fuck you up,
D." Grave winks at him, interrupting her.

"I know," he growls, acknowledging what she said and ignoring
Grave.

"Why are you taking his side?" she demands, pulling away
from him.

He runs a hand down his face. "Because this has nothing to do with them and everything to do with you."

"Take me home, Derek. Please?" she begs, gripping his shirt.

"Listen." He gets angry, grabbing her shoulders. "I can't protect you. Don't you see that?"

She goes to speak, but I say. "Derek was at Lucky's. He was the one who called the police," I inform her. I've held onto this information. I didn't want him to know that I knew. That would have given him time to think of a lie. When I mentioned he knew it was set on fire—that was his chance to confess. But instead, he told me he'd spoken to Mitch, and although I believed him, he wasn't going to willingly tell me that he was the one who called the cops because then that would have put him at the scene of the crime, ratting himself out.

He throws his head back, sighing at the ceiling.

Her wide eyes look at him with disbelief. "What? Derek, did you do it? Did you set that fire?"

"No," he growls.

"Then why ...?"

"I went over there, okay? I wanted to apologize to you. I pulled up, and it was already on fire. I didn't realize it until I walked inside. I smelled the smoke the moment I entered and called 911." He looks at me. "I promise that's the truth. I did not set that fire."

A part of me wants to believe him. Another part tells me not to fall for it. He hasn't proven himself to be loyal to her. He's turned his back on her. Why would he care now?

She says nothing to his confession. Her mind trying to decide if she should believe him or not either.

I clear my throat, getting both of their attention, and I arch a brow at him. "Either you tell her or I do." There's more to this story.

"What?" She looks back at him.

He steps back from her, needing the space.

"What is it?" she demands, wanting to know what I'm talking about. Wondering just how many more secrets he's been keeping from her.

"I've been talking to Mitch," he admits.

"I know," she states.

I push off the bar at the same time as his eyes narrow on her. "You knew?" we both ask in unison.

She steps to the side so she can see both of us before she speaks. "Yeah. When I saw him at Crown, he told me that you informed him Lucky's wasn't doing well."

He reaches up, running his hands through his hair aggressively. "Alexa ..."

"When I asked him what he was doing talking to you, he said it was none of my business." She frowns. "I told him to stay away from you, and he just laughed."

He drops his head and shakes it. "Jesus."

"Wait?" She looks from him to me. "Are you mad at me?"

"Why didn't you tell me this?" He demands.

Her brows rise at his tone. "You weren't even speaking to me. Why the fuck would I come to you? Plus, I never see Mitch. I thought that he could be lying just to piss me off."

"You told me you spent the night with him last night." Derek fires at her.

"What?" I ask, blinking. "You spent the night with him last night?" My blood pressure rises instantly, and my need to burn something is strong. I'm going to need a bigger cross.

She rolls her eyes at me and snaps, "I was with you last night, you dumb ass!"

"But you—"

"I lied to you," she interrupts her brother. "You were yelling at me and talking shit about Cross. I wasn't going to tell you that I've been practically living with him and make the situation worse."

"What?" He gasps. "You're living with him? When were you going to tell me it's this serious?"

I look over at Grave, and he arches a brow at me as if to ask the same thing. I told him I love her. What did he expect? "We're getting off topic," I interrupt their conversation. "Derek, tell her what you told me," I growl, getting back on track.

He plops down onto the couch and looks up at her. "I never told him that Lucky's was in trouble. I ran into him at the Airport, and he asked if I knew you were fucking Cross." He shudders. "I told him I didn't give a shit who you were fucking. He laughed it off and asked how Lucky's was. I said I had quit."

"What were you doing at the Airport?" she asks. "Nothing good goes on there, Derek."

"I was there with Ethan." He shrugs.

I never thought to ask him that question when he confessed; he had spoken to Mitch. And I'm wishing she hadn't. Grave drops the banana he was eating and steps into the living room. I move quickly, stepping in front of him. My hand on his chest. "Don't," I warn. "We'll take care of it. One problem at a time." I say the same thing to him that Titan had said to me.

His hard eyes go from mine to Derek, and his jaw sharpens. No one has seen or heard from Ethan since Bones kicked him out of Grave's house the night of our celebration dinner for the girls. Guess that's another problem Grave and April are having. He didn't go into much detail but mentioned it to me in the car on our way to Alexa's house earlier. April is scared because he's gone MIA. And Grave just wants to find him to kick his ass.

"I promise," I tell my best friend. "We'll figure that out."

"Were you doing drugs with him?" I hear Alexa bark at her brother.

"No." he snaps as if that question was absurd. "I'm not a druggie. I'm not like him." He points at Grave.

He shoves me out of the way and runs for him but I'm quicker. I grab his shirt and push him back. "Stop!" I shout.

Alexa has put herself between her brother and Grave. As if she was going to be able to stop him. Derek is up and jumped over the back of the couch, needing it for protection. Bones is now behind his brother while Titan stands beside him.

"One problem at a time." I repeat, rubbing my temples. I'm fucking getting a headache.

"I'm going to kick your ass." Grave warns, pointing at Derek.

"What's the problem, Grave?" Derek smirks, feeling cocky. "April finally come to her senses and leave your ass?"

Grave runs for him again and I jump in front of him while Titan and Bones both grab him. "He's not worth it man," Titan tells him.

Grave shoves us all off and storms toward the door, picking up a glass bowl that sits on a shelf in the foyer, and turns throwing it right at Derek's head. He ducks just in time, and it hits the marble floor shattering to a million pieces. Then he storms out, slamming the door shut.

"Jesus." Derek breathes, relieved he didn't just get knocked out for the second time today. "What the fuck is his problem?"

Bones runs after his brother while Alexa turns on hers. "What the hell is wrong with you?" She shouts at him.

"I was just joking about him and April." He points at the door. "Not my fault he can't take a joke."

She just shakes her head at him, and I see tears start to build in her eyes. "April lost the baby, Derek."

His face falls, turning white and his mouth forms an O shape. "I didn't ... I didn't know. You didn't tell me."

She holds her hands out wide giving out a rough laugh. But I see it's to hide her sadness. "Why would I tell you anything to do with the Kings? April? Or myself at this point? You hate all of us." Sniffing, she pushes some loose strands behind her hair. "Just go."

"Alexa." He comes around the couch and reaches out to her. "You know that's not all true."

But she lifts her hands. "I'm tired, Derek. Just leave." And with that, she turns and heads to my bedroom, softly shutting the door behind her.

TWENTY-FOUR

ALEXA

I SHUT OFF the light to Cross's bedroom and fall face-first down onto it just as the first sob hits. I bury my face into his comforter, hoping it drowns it out. I don't want them to hear me breaking.

I'm so fucking tired. Everything seems to continue to pile on, and I can't breathe. Plus, with the lack of sleep I'm getting just makes it all worse. I need to go home and get some rest. When I'm here, I spend my time working at Crown and fucking Cross. My body needs rest. But Cross already said I can't leave. Now I'm stuck here because my psycho ex probably set my bar on fire. Who knows why?

My boyfriend punched and branded my brother. Grave wants to kill him. I can't say I blame him. Grave is already fragile, and I know Derek's words hurt him. I could see it on his face, let alone the actions that followed.

I haven't been able to talk to my best friend for weeks because she's dealing with her own problems that she won't discuss with me.

And Cross? I'm in love with a King. And even though he just showed me who he really is, I still love him. I should hate him, but I can't. He was protecting me. Even if it was wrong.

I saw the burn mark that was on my brother's chest. It matched the ones that I saw on Cross's back the night in his bathroom. Someone used to hurt him. The tattoo of the burning cross is to try to cover the scars.

It makes my chest hurt but explains so much about him. It makes me love him even more. I just want him to know that he's loved and that someone cares.

Pulling away from the comforter I take in a deep breath trying to calm my breathing. Then I crawl up to the pillows and lie down on my side, curling up into the fetal position, I close my eyes and yawn.

I OPEN MY HEAVY EYES TO A PITCH-BLACK ROOM. SITTING UP, I pat down my shirt and jeans, looking for my phone but feel nothing. Reaching out, I run my hands over the cool comforter and realize I won't find it. Bones took it from me.

Getting out of bed, I make my way to the adjoining bathroom and use the restroom. After washing my hands, I walk back through the bedroom and decide it's time to join the shit show. At least I got a nap. I feel recharged for at least two more screaming matches.

Stepping out of the bedroom, I come to a stop when I see Cross standing in the kitchen at the stove.

He looks up at me and comes over. Cupping my cheek, his eyes search mine. "Hey, gorgeous."

"Hey," I say softly.

"How do you feel?" He asks, trying to run his hand through my wild hair.

"Rested."

He nods once. "Good. You're just in time for dinner. Come eat." Leaning down, he kisses my forehead and walks back to the kitchen.

"Dinner? What time is it?" I smooth out my wrinkled shirt. Like he gives a shit what my clothes look like. Looking out over the floor-to-ceiling windows, I see the lights of the Strip illuminating the night.

"Almost nine."

I gasp. "Cross I have to go. I was supposed to be at Crown ..."

"I had someone cover your shift." He interrupts me.

"What? No."

"You needed the rest, Alexa." He points at the bar. "Sit."

I plop down not wanting to argue. Looking around I see the TV that hangs on the wall is on but muted. The place is quiet. "Where is everyone?"

"Your brother went home. Bones never returned from running after Grave and Titan left."

I drop my head and sigh. "I'm sorry for what my brother said."

"Don't be." He blows it off.

I look up at him. "It was horrible." I was embarrassed, pissed and hurt all at the same time for what Derek said to Grave. I wanted Grave to knock him out just to make a point.

"You can't control what he does or says, babe."

"Have you spoken to Grave? Is he okay?" I wonder.

"No. I tried calling but he didn't answer. I spoke to Titan after he had left here, and he mentioned Grave had asked Titan to take him to a meeting sometime this evening."

I nod.

"Here," He pulls my cell out of his pocket and places it on the bar in front of me.

"Why did Bones take it from me?" Who the hell was I going to call to come and get me? Jasmine? April? None of them would have been able to help me. I sure as fuck wasn't going to call Mitch.

"He just needed to turn it off so no one could track it, knowing where you were at."

I snort. That sounds ridiculous. "I promise you; no one is that determined to get to me. You're being paranoid."

He leans across the bar, placing his elbow on the marble and cupping my cheek. His eyes search mine before he leans forward and gently kisses my lips. "That's a chance I wasn't willing to take." Letting go, he pulls away and turns back to the kitchen.

"Cross," I sigh his name. "We need to talk." There's so much that needs to be discussed.

"I know." He agrees "After you eat."

TWENTY-FIVE
ALEXA

I PLACE MY plate in the sink and make my way into Cross's bedroom. He came in here a minute ago to plug in his phone and get ready for bed. For once, he's going to bed at a decent time and I'm going to be up all night because of my damn nap.

He stands on his side of the bed, removing his shirt up and over his head.

"I Googled you." I blurt out. If I don't do it now, I'll never have the courage to.

He pauses and looks over at me. "And?"

I lick my lips. "I found Kingdom, Tit for Tat, baseball ..." I trail off and take in a deep breath adding. "Oak Grove."

If it bothers him that I brought that up, he doesn't show it. He just stares at me as if I should have more to say. At his silence, I shuffle from foot to foot. Dropping my head, I look at my hands. "I saw the scars on your back, Cross. They looked like the exact same branding you gave my brother." Lifting my eyes, I peek at him through my lashes.

"Are you asking me a question?"

The hard tone in his voice has my heart rate picking up. "How did you get them?" I can only manage to whisper it. And I fist my hands mad at myself for being so afraid. It's not that I think he won't tell me. It's that I'm terrified of the answer.

He reaches up and removes the cross that hangs around his neck and sits down on the bed. "My father believed that kneeling was originated for humiliation, not for forgiveness."

I frown, confused with those words. "Your dad was the priest," I say, remembering what I read online. Did he mean in reference to people who kneel to pray? There's nothing wrong with asking for forgiveness.

He gives a rough laugh. "My father played that role." He looks up at me. "He believed as long as the congregation saw him as a savior, then he was one." Opening his nightstand, he pulls out a ring. "My father was a Three Wisemen."

"What's that?" I've never heard of that before.

"My father, Titan's father and Grave and Bones's father were all members. They started Kingdom. And they raised us to take over."

A chill runs up my spine at his words. *Raised them to take over?*

"He would say 'you must repent for your sins.' I didn't understand him at first. I mean, what nine-year-old commits sins that are unforgiveable in the eyes of the Lord?"

"Nine?" I whisper, horrified, feeling my knees shake.

"That's when it started. My punishments—repenting."

"Cross ..." I choke out his name, not sure what I was going to say. No words will heal those scars I've seen. "What? He'd use that?" I look at the necklace in his hand, sitting down on the bed next to him, my knees now too weak to hold myself up.

"He told me that I must repent. And he would take a candle, heating up this Cross and he would burn my back with it."

Tears sting my eyes at his confession.

"I thought it was for the wrongs I did, but as I got older, I understood it was a sacrifice. He was righting his wrongs through me."

"Cross, I'm so sorry," I manage to choke out.

He smiles at me. Reaching out, he cups my cheek, wiping away the tears.

"One night, he called me to the church, and my mother was there. He told me that it was her turn. He told me to burn my mother."

I swallow a gasp, not wanting to interrupt him. This man has endured more than I could have ever imagined.

He rubs the back of his neck while staring down at the cross still in his hand. "When I refused, he made me watch while he did it."

My hands tremble, and I sniff as my nose runs due to silently crying.

"He had my mother taken home. And ... we argued. Fought a little. Then I locked him in his office." He sits up, reaching into his pocket, and removes the Zippo. "I took the present my mother gave me on my thirteenth birthday and lit the church on fire with him in it and stole his cross that he used on me."

Fresh tears run down my face, and I try to control my breathing.

"I stood on the other side of his office door and listened to him curse me, damn me to hell, scream for help. And I never thought twice to try to save him." He licks his lips. "The fire grew bigger, got hotter. I made my way through the church and tipped over the burning candles to make it look accidental. Then made my way to the front lawn where I stayed and watched. Until there was nothing left of it."

CROSS

STANDING UNDERNEATH *the black sky, I watch the smoke pour out of where the stained-glass windows were only minutes ago. You can still hear the ones in the back of the church shatter as the fire gets to them.*

The flames lick the walls and heat the cold night.

I can hear his lingering screams. His words. I still feel his hands on my back, holding me down. I thought burning it to the ground would take away the pain. The memories. But it's not helping. Instead, it makes it all more real. Years I've prayed he would die. God never listened. So, I did it myself. I did his job, erased another evil person from this world.

A new king is born. And I understand what must be done.

I hear sirens in the distance, and I turn to walk away, when I see him standing there. His once black hair is now smoke and what was ashen skin, now burns red, yellow, and orange like a sunset.

"You will burn in hell for what you've done." He growls.

I give him a smile as I flip the Zippo that my mother gave me for my birthday open and closed, my other hand holding the cross. "You've been burning me for years; you think I'm afraid of the devil?" I shake my head. "I am hell."

"There were so many different stories by the following morning. Not one was true. They thought he was missing for a while because there was nothing left of him. Then the rumor was suicide." I shrug. "Someone had said they saw us enter together, but I came out alone. It didn't matter what the story was. He was dead, and they had nothing to pin on me. My mother left the next day. Said she couldn't forgive me for what I did to my father. That I'd be a constant reminder of what she lost." I look at her, and she's crying.

I could tell that story a million times and not feel a damn thing. But that's who I am. How I was raised. I forget that not everyone is as cold as I am. "I'm sorry." I wipe away the tears. "I shouldn't have told you." I wanted to open up to her. The fact that she even admitted she googled me made me excited. This is what I wanted. Her interested in my life. My demons. I'm a horrible person for even wanting to share them with her. Those aren't her burdens to carry.

She leans forward, wrapping her arms around my chest. Her wet face touching my bare skin. "Thank you," she whispers. "For telling me." Pulling away, she sniffs. "I'm so sorry, Cross."

"I'm sorry too," I say.

She gives a rough laugh and starts wiping her face clear of tears. "For what?"

"Derek," I say, and she looks up at me, her laughter fading. "For making Bones drag you out of your house. For ... everything that I've done wrong since I met you." *And for all I'll do wrong in the future.*

She cups my face and I lean into her soft hand. "I love you, Cross. Nothing you could do will change that."

"You love me?" I smile, lightening the mood. I don't want to see her cry. Those three words light that fire in me that I need to survive. "After all that, you still find a place in your heart to love me?" How could she be so perfect? What did I ever do to deserve her? Maybe I paid for enough sins.

She laughs, shoving my chest, and I grab her arm, pulling her to me. She climbs on top of me, straddling my hips, pressing my back into the headboard. I kiss her. My hands tangle in her hair while hers are on my face.

She all of a sudden pulls away, panting. My eyes fall to her wet lips. "I want you to be honest with me."

"Anything." I'll tell her whatever she wants to know.

I lift my eyes to hers, and they look sad. I wrap my arms around her waist, holding her tighter. "What is it?" I ask the loaded question. After what I just told her, I didn't expect our talk to be over.

"I ... I don't want to not share things with each other." She sighs, running the tip of her nails across my Kingdom tattoo on my chest. "I can handle it. Whatever it is, Cross."

She's referring to Grave and April, and all the secrets they've kept from one another. "I promise."

My phone beeps, and she starts to get up off my lap. "It can wait," I say, holding on tighter.

"Look at it. I have to use the restroom anyway." She kisses my lips and gets out of my bed.

I smile, picking up my cell. I feel ... lighter. Like a weight has been lifted. This is how I wanted to feel after I burned the church, and it never came.

Alexa Jade Milner is the fire I've always craved and never want to put out.

Opening up my messages, I read over the text in our Kings group chat from Grave.

"What is it?" Alexa asks, sounding worried.

I look up to see her staring at me nervously from the doorframe to the bathroom. "We're going out tonight." So much for me going to bed early.

"Oh." Her face lights up. "Where to?"

TWENTY-SIX
ALEXA

"WHAT ARE WE doing here?" I ask Cross as he pulls into the parking garage at the Airport. After he told me we were going out, I didn't have time to ask questions. He informed me I had one hour to be ready to leave.

"Grave messaged the group, saying that he was meeting Derek here."

"What?" I shriek. "Oh God, Cross. You can't let him fuck him up. I understand he's an ass, but he is my brother. And if Grave breaks his legs, I'll have to take care of him." That's all I need—add babysitting to my already very busy schedule.

Cross chuckles at my concern. "Calm down. The message that Grave sent said he spoke to Derek and is meeting him here. I guess Derek is helping Grave find Ethan."

"Oh, okay. Whew." I reapply my lip gloss, thinking that doesn't sound so bad.

"Don't get too excited. I said he won't touch Derek. That doesn't mean he won't beat up Ethan," he adds dryly.

Well ... shit. That wouldn't be good. Then he'd be hurting April.

Cross gets out of the car and walks around to open my door to help me out. I see Titan's candy apple red Maserati pull up next to us and park. Then he's helping Emilee out of the car too.

"Hey, sexy," I say, looking her over. She wears a pair of black booty shorts and a white sheer crop top. She's got her dark hair pulled up into a high ponytail and her makeup done heavy with red lips. They match his car.

"Look at you." She looks me up and down. "Fucking hot, girl." Coming over to me, she gives me a kiss on the cheek that I return. As I'm turning around, I see Titan and Cross are standing over by his car whispering.

I can't make out what they're saying. Cross just happens to look up and see me watching. He turns, giving me his back, and continues talking.

What the fuck? We said no secrets.

A white BMW i8 pulls up next to Titan's car, and Jasmine gets out. "Look at you two hot bitches," she announces, pulling down her black mini skirt.

Emilee laughs, and I smile, but it drops the moment that I see her passenger door open and who exits. "Derek?" My arms fall to my sides.

I notice that Titan and Cross pause their secret conversation to look over at us.

I look at Jasmine. "Why would you bring him? He's been nothing but mean to you."

She smiles. "Yeah, but he called me and apologized. So, I offered him a ride."

"May I talk to you for a moment?" I grab his upper arm and pull him across the parking garage.

"Alexa ...?"

"I got it, Cross!" I snap at him.

"What is your problem?" Derek asks, yanking his arm from my grip once we're away from the others.

I point my finger in his face. "I don't know what you're doing ..."

"I'm trying to make things right." He sighs. "After today, I understand the dick that I've been."

"This better not be a joke, Derek," I warn.

"Look." He looks over my shoulder, I'm guessing to make sure Cross and Titan aren't on their way over here, then back to me. "I love you. No matter who you are with. I still think they're fucking insane." He presses his hand to his chest where he was burned. "But I understand that the Kings are someone to have on your side. I want to make things right. Not only for you but also for April. If Ethan is in as much trouble as you say, I want to make sure he gets the help he needs."

"Thank you." I give him a small smile, and he pulls me in for a hug. "But just so you know, they will kill you, so don't fuck this up." I pat him on the back.

I now know a little of what Cross and the other Kings are capable of. I'm sure the fire marshal in their pockets is just one person of many that they have for resources.

"And don't mention the baby to April. No matter how much you want to give her your condolences," I add quickly, trying to think of everything I want to say.

"I wouldn't. Never." He shakes his head.

"Everything okay?" Cross asks me when I walk back over to the cars.

"Yep," I answer.

"Alexa." He grabs my arm, bringing me to a stop. His green eyes search mine before he speaks. "What's wrong?"

"You're keeping secrets from me." I arch a brow, daring him to lie.

He lets go of me and looks over at Titan who is now talking to Bones, who just arrived in his blacked-out Lamborghini Reventon. "Yes, but it wasn't intentional. We just started sharing an hour ago," he whisper-shouts, getting irritated about something.

True, but he could have told me while we were in the car on the way here. "Will you tell me later?" I challenge.

233

"Of course." He leans in, kissing my forehead, and I let him grab my hand, pulling me over to everyone.

Just then, a Dodge Challenger SRT Demon pulls up and parks. As expected, Grave and April get out of the car. She's dressed in a white off-the-shoulder sweater dress. She's got her dark purple hair braided down the center and all pulled up in a big messy bun high on her head. Her lipstick matches her hair, and she's got smoky eyes with thick black liner. She looks stunning.

"Racing tonight?" Titan asks Grave, looking over his car. "She stays in the garage otherwise."

"No. Just thought I'd drive her," Grave answers. He holds his hand out for April, and she takes it, cuddling into his side with a soft smile on her face as she looks up at him adoringly.

They seem happier. Better than when I saw them together last in the Royal Suite. Grave looks over at my brother for a quick second and then dismisses him.

I have a feeling tonight isn't going to go how the Kings are planning. That's just not our luck lately.

"Are we ready?" Bones asks, looking around as if he's counting everyone.

I'm not sure where Haven and Luca are, but they must not be coming.

"Yeah," Cross answers, taking my hand, and we lead the way into the Airport.

CROSS

WE STAND AT the bar getting the girls drinks. It's a weekday, so it's not as packed as the usual weekend crowd. Thank God. I really wasn't in the mood to go out at all tonight. I wanted to spend my evening in bed with Alexa, but I needed to be here for Grave however I can. Even if that means looking for Ethan.

"He's got about thirty minutes!" Titan shouts over the song "Raging on a Sunday" by Bohnes.

234

"Gives us plenty of time." I sip on my rum and Coke, pulling my cell out with my free hand. Setting the glass on the bar, I send a quick text.

Me: We're here.

He reads it immediately, and I look up at the black domes hanging from the ceiling, knowing they're watching us. We're here to kill two birds with one stone tonight.

My phone vibrates, and I read the incoming text.

Turner: Come on down.

Pocketing my cell, I lean into Titan. "They're ready." He walks over to get Bones and Grave while I grab Derek's neck, yanking him to me.

"Hey ..."

"Don't leave your sister's side," I growl.

He nods quickly. "I know the plan."

I lied to Alexa. We are here for Ethan, but we're also here for other reasons. We didn't want to leave the girls at home, so I made sure Derek came along to be the babysitter. "We won't be long." I shove him away. Just because he's decided to kiss our asses doesn't mean I have to like him. I love his sister, not him, but I might as well make him useful. He'll be family one day since I'm going to marry Alexa. If I have it my way, someday soon.

"Let's go," I say, throwing what's left of my drink back.

"Cross ...?"

"I'll be right back," I tell Alexa. "Do not leave this bar. You understand?"

She nods. "Of course." Leaning up on her tiptoes, she kisses my lips, and a growl forms deep in my throat at the reminder this is the last place I want to be tonight, but business calls.

"Hurry back." She smiles up at me. "I'll be waiting for you."

The Airport sits on two-hundred-and-fifty acres, has five stories of the original airport, and turned the Mason Towers—what was once a hotel next to it—into apartments they rent out. But underneath the airport is where the Mason brothers play.

The Kings and I make our way downstairs to the underground tunnels. The existing, functional airport had a bomb shelter back in the seventies.

They have safe rooms that the Masons use as prison cells. They have their own law enforcement at the Airport. Like the Kings, they don't put up with shit. They even hung four guys once for trying to steal from them. Made them an example. I can appreciate a man who takes action. Words are meaningless in our businesses.

We make our way down through the brightly lit tunnels and take a right at the end. Turner stands there dressed in a three-piece suit in front of a black metal door. "Kings."

"You have something for us?" Bones asks, getting to the point. He hates them but understands they can be useful at times. Now is one of them.

"The Masons always deliver," he states before unlocking the door and pushing it open. The joints creak so loud it makes my teeth hurt.

We step inside, where cages line either side of a single aisle. It smells like rotten eggs and sour milk. The first two jail cells are empty on either side but the third on the right has a man in it. He's lying on the concrete floor, naked and shivering in the fetal position with his back to us.

We pass a few more empty ones and come to another door at the end. Turner pulls a key out of his pocket and unlocks the padlock, pushing it open.

We step inside a large room. It's not lit up like the cell block was. It's darker with a musty smell. Inside the room is a much bigger cell than the others we passed to get here.

Solitude! Some just don't play well with others, even while in a cage.

A man is standing in the middle of it with his back to us.

236

At the sound of us entering, he turns around. "The Kings." He gives an evil smile, making his face look like the Grinch. If he grew a full beard and hadn't washed in a month.

We say nothing.

He walks over to the door to his cage and sticks his hands through the bars so he can grip them. "What do I owe this pleasure?"

"Kale, it's been a while," Bones states.

He snorts. "Last time I saw you, you were still sucking on your mother's tit. Can't say I blame you; she had a nice rack."

Grave goes to step forward, but Bones stops him with a hand on his chest.

Kale laughs. "Grave, still so sensitive."

His chest heaves with deep breaths. It's taking everything he has not to kill him right here, right now.

"Cross." His dark eyes turn to me. "I never thought you'd have the balls to kill that son of a bitch father of yours. But good for you. That paid me five grand, ya know?"

Kale Freeman was a friend of our father's. He wanted to be a Wisemen, but there was no place for a fourth. Our fathers pissed him off, so he went out on his own. Diamonds were his niche. Rare, expensive diamonds. I have to give it to him; he's made himself known in Sin City and is worth billions of dollars. Too bad he fucked over the wrong people.

"And Titan—"

"I don't need to go down memory lane," Titan interrupts him. "I'm very well aware what I've done in my life."

"I bet you enjoy fucking that wife of yours." He licks his lips, ignoring him.

Titan fists his hands, taking in a deep breath.

"Let's talk about you." I smile, knowing that going to the Mason brothers was the best thing to do. I knew they'd bring him to us. He's been hiding. Knowing the connection we have with our client. But running will get you nowhere. "You've been fucking over some very important clients."

He snorts. "I haven't fucked over anyone. It was a misunderstanding."

"Ten million dollars is more than a misunderstanding," Bones adds.

"What are you going to do, Bones?" He arches a brow. "Make me apologize?" Throwing his head back, he laughs at himself. I think he's forgetting he's the one in the cage.

"The only thing our client wants to hear is you choking on your own blood as it spills from your throat," I state.

His eyes narrow on me as he straightens in his cell. For a man with limited mobility, he seems to think he's God. "He could never touch me!" he hisses. "I have men who would destroy him."

"You don't own an army, Kale," Grave tells him. "You have puppets that do as you tell them. Anyone can take control of those strings at any time."

"Is that why you're here?" He starts yanking on the bars. "Huh? To take what's mine?" He bares his teeth like a rabid dog.

He knows he's fucked.

"My men will destroy you and everyone you fucking love if anything happens to me," Kale warns. "Fucking bury you with all those other bodies you hide out in the desert."

"That's a chance we're willing to take," Bones informs him. "Turner."

He pulls a new set of keys from his pocket and walks over to the cell. He unlocks it, pulling the door open wide.

Kale steps farther into his cell until his back is hitting the concrete wall. "I had a deal ... I'll get him the diamonds. If he goes back on it ..."

"We made a better one," I say, stepping into the cell. "We get half the shipment just for killing you."

"No ..."

"We already gutted one of your men. He had six." We returned those to the client. We won't be keeping the other half—our payment. That's what we owe the Mason brothers. They held up their end, so we'll hold up ours. That's how business works. We don't need the rest of the shipment promised to us by our client. We'll kill this sick bastard for free.

"That's not how this works!" he snaps.

"The game can change at any time," Bones tells him, coming to stand beside me. Reaching into his pocket, he pulls out his knife and flips it open. "I have a feeling you've swallowed something you shouldn't have."

He goes to run past us, but I grab the back of his shirt and yank him off his feet, slamming him down to the concrete floor. Bending down, I press my knee into his neck while Grave holds his hands above his head. Titan straddles his legs, and just like the last guy, Bones rips his shirt open.

"Open up," I say.

He screams, trying to fight us, and Bones places the blade into his mouth just as Kale closes it. The blade cutting him. Blood instantly fills his mouth, and he starts to choke on it.

"Boy, Bianchi would love to see this." Bones sighs, as if he's sad our client isn't here to see what he paid us to do.

"Oh, he is," Turner adds, and we look up at him. He casually leans up against the inside of the cell. This is a typical day for him. He points at a black dome in the middle of the room.

Mr. Bianchi—Luca's dad—made a deal with this sorry son of a bitch. It would have been a great partnership if Kale hadn't fucked him over. Now we'll own it. Just one more way for us to own this city.

Bones pulls the knife out, and the rest of us let Kale go. He rolls onto his stomach getting up onto his hands and knees, blood pouring from his mouth.

"Cough 'em up." Grave kicks his back.

We don't really think he swallowed them. No, he sold them. He really thought John Bianchi, who is a Don—the ringleader of the Italian-American Mafia—wouldn't give two shits that he fucked him over. Kale deserves to die a slow death just for that thought alone.

Titan was right when he told Turner he's seen men killed for less. Why he thought he was untouchable is beyond me.

Kale falls to his side. His hands come up to his neck, and he holds it as if that will stop the bleeding on the inside.

Bones leans down next to him, pointing the tip of the blade at his chest. "I always thought you were a gutless bastard." He smiles to himself. "Let's see if I'm right." Bones shoves the blade into Kale's chest and rips it downward, cutting him wide open.

TWENTY-SEVEN
ALEXA

I THROW BACK my sixth shot since Cross left me here with the girls what feels like hours ago. My temperature's rising due to the alcohol and the fact he's still lying to me. *Something is going on.*

I think I've proven to him that I can handle whatever he's doing. I know, I've probably only seen a small part, but I'm not a fragile flower. No, I'm a bomb that will blow out the side of a mountain. But I think a part of him wants me to be in the dark. I haven't gotten to ask Emilee or April just how much they know about their Kings. Maybe he's just doing what he thinks is right.

A guy who looks to be around our age squeezes his way up to the bar, pushing Jasmine out of his way. "Excuse you?" she snaps, turning to face him.

"Sorry." He looks at her, then to the bar, his head snapping to the right, getting a better look at her. "Hey, sexy." His smile widens.

She rolls her eyes.

"Are you interested in twelve monthly payments for eighteen years?" he asks.

April and I laugh out loud as Jasmine shoves him back into the crowd.

"I don't get it." Emilee frowns. "What's so funny?" She throws back a shot.

"Twelve monthly payments for eighteen years ..." I say slowly, hoping she'll get it, but she shakes her head at me after a long moment. "It means child support. He wanted to fuck her and knock her up."

"Oh." Emilee's brows pull together. "That was a horrible pickup line."

"Right!?" I signal to the bartender for another round. He acknowledges it with a head nod because we haven't moved from our spot since the guys left us. We're drinking like we're fucking fish.

"April?" We hear her name being called out.

We turn around to see Ethan coming toward us.

"Hey!" She holds her arms out for him to hug her.

Instead, he comes to a stop and looks her up and down, pulling his lip back at the short dress she's wearing. "Is Grave here with you?"

"Yep." She nods her head quickly.

"Fuck!" He runs his hands through his shaggy dark hair.

"What are you doing here?" She narrows her eyes on him. "You've been avoiding my calls and texts."

"I've been busy," he growls, his eyes searching the crowd. His eyes land on mine, and he asks, "Is Derek here?"

His question makes me pause. I don't know where Derek has gone. At what point did he walk away? He didn't go with the Kings, did he? Wherever they went.

"Ethan." She places her hand on his chest, trying to get his attention. "You need to come home."

"No," he snaps, taking a step back from her. "We don't live together anymore."

"But you could," she offers, stepping into him again. "Come live with Grave and me. Go to meetings ..."

"Fuck no!" He shoves her back from him, causing her to dump the entire whiskey sour she was holding all over her dress.

She gasps.

"What the fuck!" Jasmine shoves at his chest, making him fall back into another guy. "Get away from her!" she shouts.

April looks down at her white sweater dress and sighs.

"Let's go the bathroom," I offer. "Get you cleaned up. We'll all go," I say, grabbing her hand. I know Cross said to stay here, but I also remember what he and Grave said to Jasmine and me that first night here about it not being safe. I'm not sending her to the bathroom alone.

The four of us make our way through the crowd and down the hall. I push open the door and almost hit someone in the face. "I'm ..." I trail off as I look at the woman. It's Rachel. She stands there with her hands on her hips and a constipated look on her face.

"Oh, it's you." Emilee crosses her arms over her chest, popping a hip out. "You should have just hit her."

Rachel smiles at me, ignoring Emilee. "It must suck to be as insecure as you are."

"Excuse me?" I step into the restroom, getting closer to her. "I'm not ..."

"Having Cross fire me because you were afraid he wouldn't be able to keep his hands off me." She runs her pierced tongue across her teeth. "How does it feel to know I've fucked both your boyfriend and fiancé?" she asks. Walking by me, she adds, "He'll come back to me. They always do. You can't satisfy either one of them."

Come back? So, she's still fucking Mitch. That's exactly what she means, which I couldn't care less about. But Cross? I'd set this bitch on fire using his Zippo if she were to so much as touch his arm.

"Don't get so attached to this one," she adds, trying to push past me, but I grab the back of her hair and yank her farther into the bathroom. The girls enter, letting the door close shut.

"Get off me," she screams, and I shove her face into the wall by the door.

She turns around and charges me, shoving my back into a bathroom stall. The door flies open, and we fall to the floor. Normally, just the thought of being on a public bathroom floor would make me vomit, but right now, that's the last thing on my mind.

I pull my fist back and punch her in the face so hard it rips her nose ring out. She is screaming at me while I sit on top of her.

Her hands are flying, and one hits me on the cheek. I go to hit her again, but I'm ripped off her with an arm around my waist.

"What in the fuck are you doing?" I'm shoved into a wall, and Cross stands in front of me, pinning me to it.

I don't answer. Instead, I'm trying to catch my breath. It's been a couple of years since I've been in a fight. Forgot how exhausting it is. The moment the adrenaline wears off, I'm going to want to crash.

A quick look around him shows Titan yanking Rachel up, and he escorts her out with the girls on his ass.

"Alexa?" Cross snaps, gripping my chin and forcing me to look up at him. "I asked you a question."

"She ... she pissed me off." I manage to get out.

"Pissed you off?" he questions with a huff, clearly unhappy with my answer. I try to rip my face free, but he just holds on to it tighter. "I told you to stay at the bar."

"And I told you not to lie to me!" I shout back.

"Fine." He takes a step back from me, releasing my chin, and holds his arms out wide.

My eyes drop to his black combat boots and run up over his jeans and T-shirt. I blink, wondering just how much I actually had to drink. "Cross ..." He's covered in blood. "What happened?"

"You want the truth, Alexa? Here it is." He takes a few steps back and walks over to the sinks. Turning on the water, he starts to wash his hands and forearms. Blood covers the porcelain sink, splashing up on the countertop.

"Where did you go?" I ask, trying to rack my brain about how long he left me at the bar for. I can only count the drinks I've had but even that number may be off by a few.

"I had business to handle," he clips. His green eyes stay on mine in the mirror while he washes away any evidence of what he did. Or who he hurt.

I swallow, running a hand through my hair, pushing it from my face.

Once his hands are dried, he turns to face me once again. "You wanted to see the real me. This is it." He arches a dark brow. He's challenging me.

I know I should be terrified. There are a thousand questions I should be asking or just running from him. But I'm not. He's right; I wanted to see the real him. Cross—the Dark King. Here he is in the flesh, covered in someone else's blood.

I'm hot. Like physically burning up hot from my fight. My limbs heavy from the alcohol and my body tingling from the way he pinned me up against the wall after he pulled me off Rachel.

We haven't spoken about her. Ever. I know he fired her, but I never asked him to do that. He told me he had fucked her the night before I ran into him here at the Airport. And although I hated that he slept with her, I never worried about him doing it since we've gotten together.

He takes a cautious step toward me. I stand my ground. Not retreating. I'm not afraid of this man. Or what he's capable of. I'm stronger than he gives me credit for. Rachel was wrong. I can be whatever he fucking needs. A Queen protects her King. She stands in front of him because she knows he's got her back.

Fuck her. She can have Mitch. But Cross? He's mine. I won't give up my King. She'll have to fight me for him. And I refuse to go down easily.

He takes another step toward me. "Alexa—"

I step forward, going to him, pressing my lips to his, cutting off whatever he was going to say. I'm not in the mood for talking or fighting. "Fuck me!" I growl into his mouth as I hear "Play with Fire" by Sam Tinnesz and Yacht Money play through the speakers.

He lets go of me and pulls back. I can see the hesitation in his eyes.

"I can handle the real you, Cross. Try to prove me wrong," I challenge him back.

Without hesitation, he leans over, locking the bathroom door. "With pleasure, gorgeous."

I yank my skirt up, and he reaches between my legs, shoving my thong to the side. He plays with my already wet pussy while I rip his bloody shirt up and over his head, tossing it to the floor, my hands exploring the familiar curves of his muscles as they flex. There's not even a scratch on him.

He nibbles on my lip. And I turn my head to the side to give him my neck while my hands go to his jeans. I undo his belt, button, and zipper, pulling his cock free, and he bites into my neck, making me gasp.

"Turn around," he orders, yanking away and shoving me to face the wall.

But I can't kiss him in this position. He's now standing behind me. "Cross ..."

His hand comes up and covers my mouth, silencing me while his shoes spread my high heels wide for him. Then I feel his free hand between my legs and his cock slides into me, stretching me to accommodate his large size.

I moan around his hand, mine fisting the wall. Once he's all the way in, his now free hand drops from his dick to grip my left thigh, and he lifts it, my heel coming off the floor, allowing him to get deeper.

He fucks me from behind up against the wall in a bathroom at the Airport with blood on his clothes that isn't his, and I couldn't be more turned on.

CROSS

I LOWER HER shaking leg and turn her around to face me. She is panting, her big tits bouncing with each breath. I cup her chin and kiss her parted lips. "Don't think this means we're not going to discuss what happened later."

She gives me a weak smile. "Oh, we've got a couple of things to talk about."

I groan, pulling away from her and shoving my cum-covered cock into my jeans. She manages to walk over to the stall I yanked her out of and use the restroom. Seconds later, she exits and washes her hands. "Come on." I unlock the door and yank it open to find a line of women booing us as I pull her down the hallway for occupying the restroom.

I told her to stay at the fucking bar, but of course she didn't listen. I wasn't surprised to return and find her missing. Thankfully, the women's restroom was the first place we looked.

We return to the bar where the rest of the Kings are. The women are all smiling while the guys are shaking their heads. They've managed to clean themselves as much as I have.

"God, that was awesome. She's such a bitch," Emilee states, referring to Rachel. "Our girl needs a drink."

Titan already has one lined up and places it on the bar in front of her, and she throws it back.

I take the empty glass and slide it across the bar. "We need to go."

"What?" The girls whine.

I don't even give her a chance to argue with me. Taking her hand, I start dragging her out of this place. The Kings and I are bloody; we all need showers. People don't even look at us twice here. Shit like this happens at the Airport all the time. I just need to get her home before I end up killing someone else tonight. Thankfully, Turner offered to take care of the body we left in one of their cells. Otherwise, we'd be heading out to the desert to bury it.

"My brother spilled my drink all over me." I hear April telling Grave as he drags her along too.

"I'll take care of it," he assures her.

"He was mad we were here," she goes on, sounding sad.

"I'm sure he was," he tells her through gritted teeth.

We make it to our cars. The girls hug goodbye, and we put them in our cars before I turn to the Kings.

"Any word on where Ethan went?"

"No," Grave growls. "But that fucker is dead. I'm tired of this shit …" His voice trails off as he looks over at Bones. Grave's eyes are full of remorse. For once, he finally realizes what he's put his brother through all those years. The worrying, the unknown. Granted, he never put his brother's life in danger like Ethan has April, but it's not much different.

Bones slaps his brother on the shoulder. "We'll find him."

We look over as we hear someone approaching, and it's Derek. His wide eyes look each of us over, seeing the blood that still remains on our clothes. Bones is by far the filthiest. "You guys okay?" he asks, swallowing.

"Where the fuck did you go?" I bark, ignoring his question. He left them. Just like I told him not to.

He shoves his hands in the pockets of his jeans. "I saw Mitch and went over to talk to him to keep him away from Alexa. He was acting strange, avoided me, and came up with some lame excuse that he had to go. Then I decided to order a drink before I returned to the girls. As I was ordering, I looked over in time to see Ethan spill April's drink and Jasmine shoved him away... then they stormed off to the bathroom. What was I supposed to do?"

I can't be mad that he went over to talk to Mitch because he did the right thing. "You walk into the women's bathroom like you fucking belong there!"

He snorts as if that's absurd. But it's not, not here. I've done it to protect the girls. Other men do it with bad intentions.

"I'm out," Titan tells us, giving us Kings handshake hugs. "I wouldn't be surprised if my wife is puking in my car right now." He chuckles.

"See you in the morning," I call out as he climbs into his Maserati.

"Are you drunk?" Bones asks Derek.

"No. I only had one drink. Didn't get to finish the second one I ordered."

"Here, Jasmine's in her passenger seat. Drive her home." He goes to hand him the keys but then pulls them back. "Drive her home and then you go home. Got it?"

"Got it," Derek agrees.

With that, Bones drops the keys in his hand, and gets into his car.

"Hey, I'm sorry, Cross." Derek sighs heavily. "I didn't think—"

"It's fine," I interrupt him. "It all worked out. This time."

With that, I give him my back and get into my driver's seat. Alexa stays silent in the passenger seat, but I can feel the heat radiating off her body. She's pissed. I can't say I blame her.

Taking a quick look over at her, I ask, "Going to tell me what happened back there?"

"I don't see the point."

I snort. "You're joking, right?"

She stays silent.

"I found you on top of another woman in the bathroom. That's the point."

She's got her head leaning back against the headrest. Opening her eyes, she tilts her head to the side so she can look at me. "I hate Rachel."

"Why? Because I fucked her? Alexa ... she meant absolutely nothing to me."

"I can't help who you fucked before me. Just like you can't help who I've been with."

I tighten my hand on the steering wheel at that thought. Fucking Mitch. I can understand how she feels about Rachel because I want to fuck him up for ever touching her.

"She fucked Mitch."

So she does know that he's sleeping with her? I didn't think she'd care. Obviously, I was wrong. "What?" I growl. "Why the hell do you care that she fucked your ex?"

"I don't now ... I did when I found her in my bed with him ... and we were engaged at the time."

I did my research on her. Social media told me that she was once engaged, but he cheated on her? With Rachel? Knowing both of their track records, I'm honestly not that surprised. "I'm sorry," I say.

"Are you?" she questions, licking her lips.

There's no telling how much she had to drink while the Kings and I were down in the basement. It took longer than I expected it to. "Of course ..."

"Because if he hadn't cheated on me, I wouldn't be here with you right now."

"Good point. No. I'm not sorry. I lied. I take it back."

She laughs softly. "Rachel told me that you fired her because I'm insecure. I never once asked you to do that."

"It needed to be done," I say.

"Because of me?"

"Yes and no. I was with you. I only wanted to be with you, and she wanted something that I refused to give her." I reach over and grab her hand and bring it to my lips, kissing her knuckles. "I didn't want any additional problems in my way to getting to you."

"She said that you'd go back to her just like Mitch did."

I sigh, lowering her hand to my lap but keep ahold of it with mine. "She was feeding you lies, and you ate them up like you were starving."

"No. I wasn't." She snorts. "I was a little drunk and a lot pissed. I couldn't care less about Mitch, but you ... I care about you." She lowers her voice. "I love you, Cross."

"I love you too, gorgeous." My thumb gently rubs over her knuckles while resting on my thigh.

"I'm so tired." She yawns.

"And also drunk," I add with a laugh.

We pull up to the private back entrance of Kingdom and exit the car. Making our way up the stairs and into the double doors.

She leans into me, her head rolling across my shoulder. I reach down and slide my arm behind her knees and pick her up, carrying her into the elevator.

Once I get her up to the Royal Suite, I help get her undressed and into my bed. She opens up her pretty green eyes. "Get some rest." I lean down and kiss her head.

I go to walk away, but she reaches out, gripping my shirt. Looking down at her, she blinks, her drunken stare trying to focus. "Did you kill whoever it was?" she asks, letting go of my shirt, running her fingers over the dried blood.

I expected to have this conversation tomorrow once she's sober and pieces together all of tonight's events. "Yeah. He's dead," I tell her.

"Why? Did he hurt you?" she asks through a yawn.

I kneel next to the bed, reaching up to push her bleach-blond hair back off the side of her cheek. "No." *He threatened to hurt those who I love.*

The road to being a King is paved with dead bodies. Eventually, our sins will catch up with us and demand a payment for all the carnage we leave behind. They can have my Kingdom, but they will never touch my Queen. I will set fire to the world and watch it all burn, me included, before I let her pay for my sins.

She closes her heavy eyes, and whispers, "I love you, Cross."

I kiss her forehead once again. "Love you too, Alexa."

Walking into my bathroom, I get undressed and start the shower, needing to wash off before I can lie down with her and finally crash.

TWENTY-EIGHT
ALEXA

"WHAT THE HELL happened last night?" April asks, holding her face in her hand while we sit at a booth in Empire.

"We got fucked up." Jasmine laughs, cramming pancakes into her mouth. "Derek had to drive me home."

"My brother?" I wonder.

She nods. "Yeah, he came with me."

"But I thought he left us." I don't remember seeing him after Cross and the Kings disappeared.

"Damn, you were fucked." She laughs. "How do you feel after the fight?"

"Like shit." But it's not from the fight. After I woke up alone in Cross's bed, I managed to crawl my way to a shower, where I then threw up in it. Thankfully I was already sitting down, and the drain washed it away.

"Grave was ... well, is so mad," April adds. "I guess my brother ditched his fight last night after he found out we were there. Now he owes the Mason brothers again." She knocks her fist on the table.

"Is she alive?" I ask, looking at Emilee. She has her arm fanned out across the table, her head resting on it, and her dark hair is covering her face.

"I'm resting my eyes," she says in a rough voice.

We laugh.

"I'm pretty sure she's still hammered. I'm not sure she ever went to sleep last night." Jasmine wiggles her eyebrows. "If you know what I mean."

"At least someone got some." April yawns. "Grave was too pissed, and I think I fell asleep on the way home. Not sure. I woke up at six this morning dying of thirst."

Emilee sits up, throwing her hair off her face, and takes in a deep breath. "I did get fucked. And no, I haven't gone to bed yet."

A silence falls over the table, and I think back to last night. I remember all of it. Ethan showing up and spilling April's drink on her. The fight in the bathroom. Cross being covered in blood ... the restroom fuck. Him carrying me upstairs. Our conversation. It was the first time I felt loved. Really loved. And I want to return that favor to him. Because I feel like he's never experienced it.

AFTER THE GIRLS AND I FINISH BREAKFAST, I MAKE MY WAY down to Tit for Tat.

"Good morning, Alexa." Rachel's replacement smiles at me.

"Hello, Evelyn." I really like her. She's super nice and hasn't tried to fuck Cross, so that's a bonus. "Is he in?" I ask, pointing at the hallway.

"He just stepped out for a second. But you can go on back there." She picks up the phone on her desk that starts ringing.

I make my way down the hall and back to his room. Stepping in, I close it behind me. I know he doesn't have an appointment until later today because I heard him talking to Bones on his phone yesterday while on our way to the Airport last night.

Spotting his Zippo on the counter, I pick it up and run my finger over the engraved words. And they make me feel even better about my decision. To prove to him what it's like to be loved.

"Hey, gorgeous." I hear him enter behind me.

I turn to face him. "Hi."

He's dressed in a black Kingdom shirt that pulls tight against his chest, shoulders and tatted arms. Light wash jeans and black sneakers. You would never know he killed someone last night. The blood gone, probably washed down a drain. He shows no sign of remorse. And I didn't expect him to. That's not who my King is.

"Busy?" I ask, biting my lower lip.

"Never too busy for you." He comes up to me, wraps his arms around my waist, and leans down, kissing me on the lips.

I open up for him, and he deepens the kiss. His large hand runs up my back to tangle in my hair. I moan into his mouth when he pulls on it.

He starts to walk me backward, and I pull away. "I didn't come for sex," I say quickly before I'm lying naked in his tattoo chair.

He sighs, reaching up and running his hand through his hair. "If this is about last night ..."

"It is," I tell him, but not in the way he thinks. Turning around, I pick up his Zippo.

"Alexa ..."

I face him once again, holding it up, and he trails off, staring at it in my hand. I flip it open and light it up. I watch the flame dance gently in my hand from my soft breath. It's beautiful. How something so deadly can also be harmless. That's Cross. He is what he needs to be when he needs to be it. To a man stuck out in the cold, fire is what will keep him alive. To a man trapped in a car, fire is his enemy.

I was that cold, lifeless body freezing to death, and Cross came along and lit my world on fire.

Closing the Zippo, I look down at it, and my thumb rubs over the engravement once again. *We all have a cross to bear.*

"We don't have to bear our crosses alone," I say, looking up at him through my lashes. "You know that, right?"

He looks away from me, and I watch his Adam's apple move as he swallows.

I set the Zippo back on the counter and walk over to him. Cupping his face, I force him to look down at me. "I love you. And whatever cross you bear, I will help you carry it."

CROSS

I LIE IN my bed of the Royal Suite, the TV on but the sound off. Alexa sleeps curled up next to me. Her arm draped over my bare chest.

I rub my hand up her arm to her hand and turn it over, looking at the tattoo I gave her earlier today when she came to visit me.

She showed up at Tit for Tat. I thought she was going to walk away from me. After what happened last night, I wouldn't blame her. I showed her who I really was at the Airport. She said she could take it, but I wasn't sure how she would feel once she woke up this morning.

The tattoo she wanted proved she was right.

A cross on the inside of her left wrist. It's burning bright like a fire. "A reminder you're not alone." She had told me. It's a much smaller version of the one on my back. I got mine when I hated the world and wanted to cover up my past. She wanted hers to prove love is real and we have a future. A brand to show the world we bear the same cross.

I've only ever had the Kings. And although I love them like brothers, Alexa is my world. The piece I didn't know I needed.

She's not my redemption. No, she's my reminder that you don't need to be saved in order to be loved.

I kiss her wrist and set it back down on my chest, closing my eyes, knowing that when I wake up, she'll still be here.

EPILOGUE

CROSS

"**Y**OU SURE?" I ask, leaning back in my chair in the conference room.

Jeffrey nods. "Positive." He tosses some papers across the table. They slide to a stop in front of me.

Sitting the front legs down, I pick the report up.

"What are you doing with this information?" Bones is the one who asks.

Jeffrey throws his hands up. "You're the only ones who know what I've found. I know you Kings prefer to handle your own shit."

"We do." Titan nods.

"Then ..." He pushes his chair back and stands. "I'll leave you to it and wait for your phone call." With that, he picks up his cell and the bag full of money off the table and turns, exiting the room.

I slap the papers down on the table and place my tatted forearms on the surface. "He went to the police. Gave a statement."

"Of course, he did. Mitch is a pussy." Titan scoffs.

Shuffling through the papers, I pick up the tattoo stencil. I've been collecting these since I was young. When I got my first tattoo. The skull with a tilted crown and crossbones—all the Kings have one.

"So, he wanted to kill her and frame you for it?" Grave growls.

"Looks like it." I run a hand down my face, feeling my stubble. "And I'm guessing he wanted Rachel to take the fall." Two birds, one stone. Kill Alexa, put me in jail for loving her, and frame Rachel for having a past with me.

"Rachel is just as guilty as him," Bones states. "Doesn't matter what the motives were, she still acted."

I can't disagree with that. She is the only one who could have gotten into my safe at Tit for Tat and grabbed the stencils. I had them in a case. One was found outside of Lucky's in the parking lot during Jeffrey's inspection. I know it wasn't Alexa. So, Rachel is the only option.

"But the fire was started with accelerant inside of the bar. Wouldn't they have known she wasn't there?" Titan adds.

"I don't know." I rub my temples, feeling that headache coming on again.

"Maybe once they got there, they realized there was no turning back. They burn down her bar. It gets blamed on Cross, and then she never speaks to him. Actually, that works out better for him because she's still alive, and he can slide in." Bones guesses.

"It doesn't matter," I mutter, lifting my head. "The why, the how. All that matters is they did it."

"What do you want to do?" Titan asks me.

I glance over at Derek who sits there silently next to Grave. He looks as pissed as I feel but hasn't said one word. I told him to be here this morning to witness our meeting with Jeffrey. He's going to see how we handle shit and get a chance to redeem himself with the Kings. He will be my brother-in-law one day, and I'd hate to have to kill him. "What we always do," I answer.

"DID YOU SEND THE TEXT?" I ask DEREK WHILE STANDING AT the bar inside of the Airport. I've been here way too much in the past couple of months.

"Yeah." He nods, double-checking his phone. "Should be soon."

For someone who once hated us, he's more than willing to help us out now. Derek is the only connection we have to Mitch that Mitch won't see coming. And since he saw the report and understands what Mitch and Rachel tried to do—and the fact that Alexa's life is still in danger—he's out for blood. We'll make a King of him yet.

I tip back my rum and Coke, looking over at Titan. He stands at the other end of the bar and nods, acknowledging me. I can't see Grave or Bones right now, but I know they're here. We split up to cover more ground. This place is too big for one person, and we don't want to miss anything.

"They're here!" Derek shouts, holding his phone up to me. "In the basement playing blackjack."

"Let's go," I order before throwing what's left of my drink back and signaling to Titan. He steps away from the bar. "Respond," I tell Derek, but he's already typing away.

We push away from the bar and make our way through the crowd to the elevator. The basement spans the entire airport underneath. The west wing is where their jail is; the east wing is their casino. It's nothing like Kingdom—it's illegal and off the books. They don't even check IDs. Anyone of any age can come down here and try their hand.

We exit the elevator, and I fall back, allowing Derek to get ahead of me. I watch him make his way through the crowd and over to a table. He slaps Mitch on the back and starts up a conversation with him. Sitting beside him is Rachel, sipping on a margarita. They have no idea what is about to hit them.

Derek leans down, whispering something in his ear. Mitch nods a few times, then turns to say something to Rachel before he gets up and walks away with Derek.

They start to walk past me, and I turn my back to them, ducking my head. Once they are out of sight, I turn and make my way over to the table. Rachel sits there playing blackjack. Removing my wallet from my back pocket, I pull out a hundred-dollar bill and toss it down while taking the seat beside her—the one Mitch was just sitting at.

"That was fast ..." She trails off, looking over at me. "Cross?" She swallows nervously.

"Rachel."

Her breathing picks up, and she looks at the dealer wide-eyed, expecting him to help her out. He won't. They don't get paid for this kind of shit. That's what makes this place so dangerous for women like her and Alexa. They will turn a blind eye and walk away.

I reach out and pick up her drink. She has over half left. "Here." I hold it out to her.

She takes it with a shaky hand. "I don't know ..."

"Shh," I tell her, pushing her hair behind her ear, and a shiver runs through her. Leaning in, I whisper in her ear, "Drink up. You're going to need the liquid courage."

The ice rattles in her cup from her shaking hand holding it, but she does as I say and brings it to her lips. She takes a sip and goes to pull it away, but I put my hand under it, keeping it tilted to her lips. She can't swallow fast enough, and it drips onto her exposed chest and shirt. "Good girl," I praise her, and she chokes on it as I pull it away. "Let's go for a walk." I grab her arm and yank her from the table.

"Cross ... please," she begs, her heels trying to keep up with me. "I didn't start that fight. Alexa attacked me."

I laugh at her. She really has no idea what this is about. Good for her sticking to being innocent. She stays silent as I pull her down the tunnels and to the other wing of the basement. We come to the cells, and Turner stands there.

"What is this?" she asks nervously when she spots him.

"Rachel." He nods at her. "Cross, the Kings are waiting for you." Then he opens the door.

She goes to spin out of my hold and run away, but I grab her hair, yanking her to me. She screams out as I bend and throw her over my shoulder. She kicks her legs, and her fists pound my back the best she can, but she's weak.

I pass the row of cells and come to the next open door. Stepping in, I see Bones, Titan, Grave, and Derek in the larger solitary cell with Mitch kneeling in the center. He has his hands zip-tied behind his back, and he has two more around his neck, but it's not pulled tight enough to cut off his air. Not yet anyway.

I drop her in the middle, and she falls to the floor next to him. She quickly jumps to her feet, but Bones grips her hair, forcing her to her knees. "Cross ..." She cries like I'm going to save her.

"I know what you did," I tell her, not wanting to waste time. Alexa is over at Emilee and Titan's right now with the rest of the girls. They are having a girls' night—whatever that consists of—and I plan on crashing it and taking her home.

"What the fuck, man?" Mitch snaps, still pretending he has no fucking clue.

"No. No. I didn't do anything," Rachel rushes out. "It was Mitch ..."

"You bitch!" He goes to throw his body into hers, but Derek grabs him by the zip ties around his neck, pulling on it, choking him.

"Look familiar?" I drop a stencil from Tit for Tat in front of her.

She begins to cry. "It wasn't my idea."

"You wanted her dead!" Mitch manages to get out, still fighting Derek's grip. "You told me ... I have proof of that."

He does. I saw the photos in the report of their text messages. He did his part to throw her under the bus and was very careful with how he worded things. I'm sure, in person, he fed her full of shit. Got her wound up by promising her the world with me once Alexa was out of it.

"It may not have been your idea, but I have footage of you inside Tit for Tat removing those from my safe." I pulled the footage an hour ago, and sure enough, it was her. Thirty minutes before I got the call about Lucky's being on fire.

Bones shoves her forward, letting go of her hair, and she buries her face in her hands, now sobbing.

"Did he tell you that you could have me if Alexa was out of the picture?" I ask.

She nods at my question.

I kneel in front of her. Reaching up, I push some hair from her tear-streaked face, and she flinches from my touch. "I was done with you before Alexa came into my life," I tell her.

Her red-rimmed eyes widen at my words, and I stand to my full height.

"I'm sorry," she sobs.

"Too late," I say. Pulling out my Zippo, I flip it open and strike it across my jeans.

"Wait! No!" Mitch chokes out. "I have something ... diamonds ..."

I flip it closed, putting out the flame. "You what?" Bones is the one who asks.

He swallows and licks his lips. "I know where the diamonds that you're looking for are."

I hear Turner step into the cell behind me.

"He's bluffing," Derek hisses, yanking on his zip ties and forcing Mitch to look up at the ceiling.

"What is it that you know?" I ask him, nodding to Derek that it's okay for him to let up.

He lets go, and Mitch takes in a deep breath. "I have them."

The cell falls silent, and I reach up, scratching my chin. "You?" I question. He's clearly lying to buy himself some time to try and figure out how he'll get past us. But how would he even know we're looking for them?

Bones snorts, clearly also not believing him.

"I swear," he rushes out. "I was here to meet up with Kale weeks ago ..." He side-eyes Rachel for a quick second. "He gave them to me to hold just in case Turner was setting him up."

"Bullshit." Turner laughs at the mention of his name.

We never did find the other six—the ones we owe the Mason

brothers per our deal. Like we had expected, they weren't inside of Kale. We hadn't given up looking for them, but that was put on hold after finding out who was involved in the burning of Lucky's.

"I've worked for Kale for the past couple of months. He approached me here at the Airport and asked me to move product for him." He licks his lips. "I was going to tell him no, but he had seen me talking to Alexa and promised me I would have her."

I punch him in the face for even saying her name. I go to do it again, but Turner pulls me back and Mitch spits blood onto the concrete floor.

"You're lying!" I shout.

He shakes his head. "He knew her. Said he was friends with Lucky, who gave her the bar. That's where I first met him last year. I was up there seeing her, and he sat next to me at the bar." Blood drips down his chin. "He knew how much I hated you all. He asked me to work for him, then ..."

Grave snorts.

"It's true." Mitch goes on. "How do you think Derek knows so much about you guys?"

We all look over at Derek. He nods, not even bothering to deny it. "Mitch told me everything I know."

"Kale told me how he was friends with the Three Wisemen and how they stiffed him out of Kingdom." He licks the blood from his busted lip. "He saw you with Alexa here at the Airport and came to me."

I start to pace the room, my right hand playing with my Zippo. It makes sense. It's fucking crazy, but it connects the dots we're missing.

"He then called me and said that plans had changed. You were hot on his trail, and he needed to get rid of you, and the best way was through Alexa. I never meant to kill her. I knew she wasn't at Lucky's. I just needed her to think you were after her," he admits.

Rachel sobs, knowing that whatever he had originally told her was bullshit. He set her up. It was about Mitch getting back with Alexa all along.

"But Derek showed up before it could burn."

No one says a word, letting everything he's confessing set it. Bones was right—he's telling on himself like the scared little bitch he is, thinking the truth will set him free.

"I swear," he continues when none of us say anything.

"Okay," I bite, coming to a stop. "Where are the diamonds?"

"I ..." He trails off, looking over at her again.

"Look at me," I demand, running out of patience. I have a girls' party to get to.

"I saw you here the other night with her at the bar, and I wasn't able to get ahold of Kale. I knew something was wrong when I saw you guys head to the basement," he states. "I panicked and swallowed them."

Bones eyes light up, and Titan gives a soft laugh at the change of events. Finally, luck is on our side.

"I can get them," he rushes out. "I just need ten minutes."

"That's not necessary," Bones state, flipping open his knife. "Derek," he orders.

Derek grabs the zip ties and yanks Mitch to his back on the concrete floor. Grave straddles his legs while Derek holds the side of his face down. Mitch tries to fight them as Rachel jumps to her feet and tries to run away. I grab her from behind, wrapping one arm around her stomach, pinning her arms to her side while the other comes up to cover her mouth and force her to watch.

Bones shoves the knife into his stomach and cuts downward—blood pours out and onto the floor around him. Bones reaches in and digs around for a few seconds and then pulls out a tiny bag. Bones holds up his hand as blood drips from it onto Mitch. He lies there, his body convulsing a couple of times, then stops completely—he's dead.

"I believe we had a deal," Bones announces, standing and tossing the bag to Turner, who catches it midair. Some blood splashing on his clothes.

He smiles. "Never doubt the Kings."

"Hold her." I shove Rachel into Grave's arms as he stands.

I kneel, flip the Zippo open, and light it once again on my jeans. Holding it to Mitch's pants leg, I wait for the flame to catch and light him on fire. Then I stand and turn to Grave.

"He said she'd be there." She sobs in his arms. "That leaving the stencil behind with the company name would frame you. But you'd get off because of your connections. She'd be dead ... and I'd have you." She rambles out everything we already knew. Mitch played her, but she would have killed Alexa to play me.

"You were willing to let her die for what you wanted," I growl, the burning body quickly heating up the cell.

She sniffs, her eyes full of fresh tears. "Cross ... please?" Her hands reach to me to get away from Grave.

He lets go of her, pushing her into my chest. "Now I must do the same." I shove her down to the floor onto Mitch. The fire catches on her clothes, and she screams as it attacks her like a wild animal needing to feed in order to survive.

The smell of burning flesh gets stronger. It's a smell you'll never forget. It lingers for hours. And we all stand around watching them burn, making sure nothing is left, knowing that my Queen is safe.

EPILOGUE TWO

CROSS

WE ALL SIT around the table at Grave and April's, having Sunday breakfast. It's our newest tradition as our family grows. The girls coming into our lives makes us more and more human. Less evil in our everyday life.

"Hey, Alexa," Grave starts.

"Hmm?" She looks at him, slowing her chewing.

"Do you mind staying on at Crown? That is, until Lucky's is back up and running, and I can find someone else to take over."

She looks at me confused and then back at him. She swallows her food. "I don't mind, but I don't want to take that away from you."

"You're not." He reaches over and takes April's hand, bringing it to his lips. He kisses her knuckles, making her blush at the intimate act. "I want to come home and be with my wife after a long day at Kingdom."

Alexa starts nodding. "Yes, sure, that's ..."

A silence falls over the room, and April starts laughing.

"No!" Jasmine breathes, her palms slapping the table. "You got married without us?" she asks in disbelief.

"No, but ..." April holds up her left hand and smiles brightly, showing off the massive diamond that's on her ring finger. "We have a wedding to plan."

The girls start jumping up from the table, screaming and hugging one another. The guys laugh. Bones walks over to his brother and slaps him on the shoulder. "I'm proud of you, brother," Bones tells him. Grave nods, smiling, but I can see him trying not to get choked up about marrying the love of his life.

A lot has happened over the past two weeks. We've started renovations on Lucky's. We dropped the investigation and had Jeffrey sign off on the accidental report. Then Jasmine, Alexa, and I got into a very heated discussion when I told them I was paying for all of it. I didn't want either one of them to worry about it. Jasmine had already put up so much for Kink, and Alexa only had enough set aside from selling the studio to do the small remodel. I told her to keep the insurance money, and I would handle it.

Ethan is in jail. Grave finally had enough and called in a favor. Ethan was picked up during a sting operation for distributing illegal narcotics to a minor. He'll be away for a while. We're just glad he didn't kill anyone or himself. April tries to visit him, and he refuses to see her. She hates herself for it, but even more, she hates that he doesn't want to be better.

"I love you."

I look over my shoulder to see Alexa come up to me. Bending over the back of my chair, I wrap her arms around my shoulders from behind. "I love you too, gorgeous."

Reaching up, I take her left hand and turn her palm over and kiss her tattoo on her inner wrist. I do it all the time out of habit. A reminder that no matter what, she's by my side.

She kisses my cheek and skips off to go talk to Jasmine across the room, who is already scrolling through wedding pictures online with Emilee.

April plops down in Alexa's vacant seat beside me. "Congratulations," I tell her.

"Thanks." She laughs excitedly, but stops suddenly, and her face turns serious. "I was wondering if you could help me out with something."

"Of course," I say, figuring it's a gift for Grave with his birthday coming up.

"Do you have any openings next week at Tit for Tat?"

I frown because that was not what I was expecting. "I can make time." Tit for Tat doesn't have to be open in order to give her a tattoo. Hell, I did Grave's in a hotel, practically sitting in the dark because he wanted to wallow in his pity.

She shifts in her seat. "I, uh, I love Alexa's tattoo and Grave's ..." Her smile returns. At the mention of his name, he comes up behind her.

She lifts her hips off the chair and digs into her back jean pocket. "I drew something ..." She trails off, holding the still folded piece of paper in her hand.

"It's beautiful," Grave tells her lovingly.

She licks her lips. "I ... *we* want to get matching tattoos, and we would love for you to do them."

"Of course," I say, shifting in my seat to face her. "Just let me know the time and day that's best for you. I'll make myself available."

"It's ..." She gets choked up, and Grave starts rubbing her shoulders. "It's for the baby."

My chest tightens. It's the first time I've seen her show any emotion about their loss around him. Other than when we were here, and she asked him if he was still using. It just shows how far they've come.

I reach out my hand, placing it over hers, and smile. "I'd be honored to."

She gives me a sad smile and leans forward, hugging me. "Thank you," she whispers. Pulling away, she wipes her cheeks and gets up, walking away while pocketing the piece of paper.

I stand and face Grave. "Congratulations." I hold out my right hand to shake his, but he pulls me in for a hug, slapping my back.

"Thanks, brother," he whispers, choking on the word, and I hug him tighter before pulling away.

"Hey, where are Haven and Luca?" I hear Emilee ask no one in particular.

"Probably fucking," Jasmine answers, making us all laugh. "Must be nice," she mutters.

Alexa comes bouncing back over to me. She throws her arms around my neck. "The girls want to go wedding dress shopping."

"Okay."

"I'll only be gone for a few hours. When I get back to Kingdom, we can lay in bed and take a nap."

I run my hands down over her ass. My fingers slide into her pockets, making my cock hard. "We'll be doing something, but it won't be sleeping." Then I kiss her, knowing she's safe and all mine. If anyone threatens that, I'll make them pay the only way I know how—by setting their world on fire.

THE END

THE END

Thank you for taking the time to read **Cross** Did you enjoy the Dark Kings? Read on for the prologue from **Bones...**

Want to know more about *The Dark Kingdom Series?*

BONES

THE DARK KINGDOM

USA TODAY & WALL STREET JOURNAL BESTSELLING AUTHOR

SHANTEL TESSIER

PROLOGUE

BONES

Twelve years old

"**D**ILLAN, LET ME tell you what will get you through this life." My father sits across from me at the table while I eat a snack. "Show me a man in love, and I'll show you his greatest weakness."

I frown. "I'm not sure what you mean."

"I mean, he will put her first before anything else, even himself." Picking up his glass of scotch, he throws it back. My father is always drinking. Doesn't matter if it's six o'clock in the morning or midnight. "You and your brother will have a lot of enemies, son. And every one of them will know this."

"Why would we have enemies?" I'm not dumb. I'm old enough to know that my father does some shady stuff with very powerful men who are as rich as they are evil.

He smirks as if what I said was funny. "Because you two will have what others want."

"Love?" I question.

"No." He snorts. "Kingdom."

I don't want it, but I keep that thought to myself. He already knows how I feel about the hotel and casino he owns with his two partners—the Three Wisemen. My father just doesn't care. None of them do. I, along with my little brother and two best friends, will have no choice but to take it over one day.

My father holds up the empty glass and stares at it while speaking to me. "Love makes a man weak. Because a man in love would rather save her than himself."

My eyes drop to the table, and I think about his words. "But you married Mom," I say, looking up at him. I would never consider my father to be weak.

The corners of his lips turn up into a sinister smirk. "I didn't say a man didn't need a woman. I said a man in love is a vulnerable one. Although, women are useful for few reasons." His eyes meet mine. "You'll figure those out later in life."

WANT TO DIVE INTO THE LORDS WORLD?

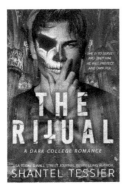

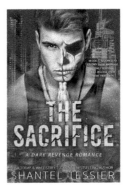

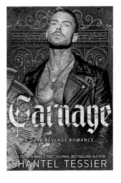

CONTACT ME

Facebook Reader Group: Shantel's Sinful Side

Goodreads: Shantel Tessier

Instagram: shantel_tessierauthor

Website: Shanteltessier.com

Facebook Page: Shantel Tessier Author

TikTok: shantel_tessier_author

Store: shanteltessierstore.com

Shantel Tessier's Spoiler Room. Please note that I have one spoiler room for all books, and you may come across spoilers from book(s) you have not had the chance to read yet. You must answer both questions in order to be approved.

9 798988 704980